CHAPTER 1

THE affair of the Glass House began quietly enough one
evening in late January, 1817. I passed the afternoon
drinking ale at The Rearing Pony, a tavern in Maiden Lane
near Covent Garden, in a common room that was noisy,
crowded, and overheated. Sweating men swapped stories
and laughter, and a barmaid called Anne Tolliver filled
glasses and winked at me as she passed.

The winter night outside was black and rain came
down. My rooms in Grimpen Lane would be dark and
lonely, and Bartholomew would not be there. Since Christmas, Bartholomew, the tall, blond, Teutonic-looking footman
to Lucius Grenville, had become my makeshift manservant, but tonight he had returned to Grenville's house to
help prepare for a soiree. That soiree would be one of the
finest of the Season, and everyone who was anyone would
be there.

I, too, had an invitation, and I would attend, though I
much preferred to visit Grenville when he was not playing
host. Grenville was the most sought-after gentleman in so-

ciety, being the foremost authority on art, music, horses, ladies, and every other entertainment prized by the London *ton*. He was also vastly wealthy and well connected, having plenty of peers and knights of the realm in his ancestry. His manners, his dress, his tastes were carefully copied. In public, he played his role of man-about-town to the hilt, employing cool sangfroid and a quizzing glass, a glance through which could humble the most impudent aristocrat.

I had come to know the man behind the façade, a gentleman of intelligence and good sense, who was well read and well traveled and possessed a lively curiosity that matched my own. People wondered why he'd shown interest in me, a half-pay cavalry officer who had passed his fortieth year. Though I had good lineage, I had no wealth, no connections, no prospects. I knew Grenville was kind to me because I interested him; I relieved the ennui into which he, one of the most wealthy men in England, often lapsed. He enjoyed hearing tales of my adventures, and he'd helped me investigate several murders and mysterious events in the past year.

I could not fault Grenville his generosity, but I could not repay it either. His charity often grated on my pride, but in the past year, I had come to regard him as a friend. If he wished me to attend the crush at his home, I would oblige him and go, although I would have to endure a night of rude stares at me and my regimentals.

Hence, I enjoyed myself sitting in this friendly, noisy tavern before I had to venture to Mayfair and face London's elite. The men here had come to accept me as a regular, and they passed good-natured greetings and banter with me. Pretty Anne Tolliver sent me smiles, but I knew she had a husband with beefy arms and a churlish disposition, and so I ignored them.

I first learned of anything amiss when I left the tavern to make my way home to prepare for the soiree. It was eight o'clock, the rain still fell, and the night had turned brutally cold. A hackney waited at a stand, white vapor

streaming from the horse's nostrils while the coachman warmed himself with a nip from a flask. I walked as quickly as I could on the slick cobbles, trying to retain the warmth of ale and fire until I made my rooms.

At least my lodgings had become something less than dismal since Bartholomew's arrival. He wanted training as a manservant, he told me, and begged me to take him on. A valet was the top of the servant class, and often had servants of their own to wait upon them. Grenville had lent him to me, paying for his keep, and now I had someone to mix my shaving soap, brush my suits, keep my boots polished, and talk to me while we chewed through the beefsteak and boiled potatoes he fetched from the nearby public house for our dinners.

I suspected Grenville's purpose in sending Bartholomew to me was twofold—first because Grenville felt sorry for me, and second because he wanted to keep an eye on me. With Bartholomew reporting to him, Grenville would be certain not to miss any intriguing situation into which I might land myself.

My rooms lay above a bakeshop in the tiny cul-de-sac of Grimpen Lane. The bakeshop was a jovial place of warm, yeasty breads, coffee, and banter. Mrs. Beltan let the rooms above it cheap, but I'd found her to be a fair landlady. The shop was closed now, Mrs. Beltan home with her sister, the windows dark and empty.

As I reached to unlock the outer door that led to the stairs, a voice boomed at me out of the darkness.

"Happily met, Captain."

I recognized the strident tones of Milton Pomeroy, once my sergeant, now one of the famous Bow Street Runners. The light from windows in the house opposite shone on his pale blond hair and battered hat, the dark suit on his broad shoulders, and his round and healthy face. In the 35th Light Dragoons during the Peninsular War, Pomeroy had been my sergeant. In civilian life, he'd retained his booming sergeant's voice, his brisk sergeant's attitude, and his utter ruthlessness in pursuit of the enemy. The enemy now

were not the French, but the pickpockets, housebreakers, murderers, prostitutes, and other denizens of working-class London.

"A piss of an evening," he said jovially. "Not like the Peninsula, eh?"

Weather in Iberia had been both hot and cold, but usually dry, and the summers could be fine indeed. Tonight especially, I longed for those summer days under the sweltering sun. "Indeed, Sergeant," I said.

"Well, I've not come to jaw about the weather. I've come to ask you about that little actress what lives upstairs from you."

I raised my brows. "Miss Simmons?"

Marianne Simmons, a blonde young woman with a deceptively childlike face and large blue eyes, eked out a living playing small parts at Drury Lane theatre. She lived in the rooms above mine, and stretched her meager income by helping herself to my candles, coal, snuff, and other commodities. I let her, knowing she might starve otherwise.

"Aye, that's the one. Seen her about?"

"Not for some weeks," I replied. Marianne often disappeared for long stretches at a time. I had once tried to inquire where she went on her sojourns, but she'd only fixed me with a cold stare and told me it was none of my business. I hoped she had not done anything foolish, like robbed a gentleman. Someone like Marianne, with no friends or connections, could so easily be hanged or transported for a crime as trivial as stealing a handkerchief.

"Well, then, sir," Pomeroy went on. "Can you come along with me and look at a corpse from the river? It might very well be hers."

I stopped, blood chilling. "Good God."

I had assumed Marianne's absence meant she'd found a protector, temporarily at least. In the past, she'd always returned before long, proclaiming her general disgust at men and asking whether she could share my supper.

"Pulled out of the Thames not half an hour ago by a

waterman," Pomeroy said, voice cheerful. "She looked
like your actress, so I thought I'd fetch you to make sure."

"There's nothing to tell you who she is?"

"Not a thing, so the Thames River gent says. She's not
been dead long. A few hours or more, I should say. Officer
of the Thames River patrol sent for the magistrate, who
sent for me."

So explaining, Pomeroy led me out of Grimpen Lane
and Russel Street and down to the Strand. My walking
stick rang on the cobbles as I strove to match Pomeroy's
long stride and tried to stem my rising worry. I doubted
Marianne would try to do away with herself; she had a
brisk attitude toward life, no matter that it had not dealt her
very high cards. She was not a brilliant actress, but the
gentlemen liked her bright hair, pointed face, and round
blue eyes. But accidents did happen, and people fell into
the river and drowned all too often.

I should not like to see harm come to Marianne. Though
the two of us had our differences, and she'd made it plain
that because I had no money she would never be interested
in me, I certainly would not wish so terrible a death on her.
I also wondered, if the dead woman proved to be Marianne, how I would break the news to Grenville.

We walked east on the Strand and entered Fleet Street
through one of the pedestrian arches of Temple Bar. The
road curved with the river that flowed a few streets away,
though the high buildings hid any aspect of it. This was the
haunt of barristers and journalists, the latter of which were
never my favorite sort of people. We fortunately saw none
of them tonight. I supposed they had retreated to pubs like
the one I'd just left, their day's work finished. Still I kept
a wary eye out for one starved-looking journalist called
Billings, who last summer had taken to roasting me in the
newspapers for my involvement in the affair of Colonel
Westin.

We walked all the way down the Fleet to New Bridge
Street, then to Blackfriar's Bridge and a slippery staircase
that led to the shore of the Thames. As we descended away

from the stone houses, the wind took on a new chill. The river lay cold and vast at the bottom of the steps, lapping softly at its banks and smelling of rotting cabbage. Lights roved the middle of the river, barges and small craft strolling upriver or back down to the ships moored at the Isle of Dogs or farther east in Blackwall and Gravesend.

A circle of lanterns huddled about ten yards from the staircase. "Saw her bobbing there," a thin voice was saying. "Told young John to help me fish her out. Dead as a toad and all bloated up."

As Pomeroy and I crunched over the shingle toward them, a man on the gravel bank turned. "Pomeroy."

"Thompson," Pomeroy boomed. "This is Captain Lacey, the chap I told you about. Captain, Peter Thompson of the Thames River patrol."

I shook hands with a tall man who had graying hair and a sunken face, long nose, and thin mouth. He was muffled in a greatcoat that hung on his bony frame, and his gloves were frayed. But though his features were cadaverous, his eyes were strong and clear.

The Thames River patrol skimmed up and down the river from the City to Greenwich, watching over the great merchant ships that docked along the waterway. Their watermen picked up flotsam from the river, either turning it in for reward or selling it. When they found bodies, they sent for the Thames River officers, although I suspected that some of the less scrupulous sold the poor drowned victims to resurrectionists, unsavory gentlemen who collected bodies to sell to surgeons and anatomists for dissection.

Thompson told me, "Pomeroy said the woman might be an acquaintance of yours."

"Perhaps." I disliked the possibility. "May I see her?"

"Over here." He pointed a finger in his shabby glove to the thin gathering of men and lanterns.

I stepped past the waterman who smelled of mud and unwashed clothes into the circle of light. They had laid the woman out on a strip of canvas. Her gown, a light pink muslin, was pasted to her limbs, the sodden cloth outlining

her thighs and curve of waist, her round breasts. Her face was gray, bloated with water. A wet fall of golden hair, coated with mud, covered the stones beside her.

She had been small and slim, with a girlish prettiness in her face. Her hands were tiny in shredded gloves, and her feet were still laced into beaded slippers. Although her coloring and build were similar, she was not Marianne Simmons.

I exhaled in some relief. "I do not know her."

"Hmph," Pomeroy said. "Thought it was her. Ah well."

Thompson said nothing, looking neither disappointed nor elated.

I went down on one knee, supporting my weight on my walking stick. "She had no reticule, or other bag?"

"Not a thing, Captain," Thompson replied. "Although a reticule might have been washed downriver. No cards, nothing on her clothes. I imagine she was just a courtesan."

I lifted the hem of her skirt and examined the fabric. "Fine work. This is a lady's dress."

"Might have stolen it," Pomeroy suggested.

"It fits her too well." I dropped the skirt and ran my gaze over the gown. "It was made for her."

"Or her lover sent her to a dressmaker," Thompson said.

I looked at her neck and wrists, which were bare. "No jewels. If she had a protector, she would wear the jewels he bought her."

"Someone stole them," Pomeroy continued his theme.

I touched the woman's throat. "There is no sign of bruising or force on her neck, nor on her arms. I do not believe she was wearing any jewels before she fell in. She was not robbed."

Thompson leaned down with me. "No," he said. "But she was murdered." He turned the woman's head to one side.

I recoiled, my hand tightening on my walking stick.

The entire back of the woman's head had been caved in, rendering her skull and hair a black and bloody mess.

CHAPTER 2

I looked down at the wound, an ugly gouge on the woman's otherwise pretty head. She'd not been much past five and twenty. A life snuffed out too soon.

"Do you know who did this?" I asked, my voice hard.

"That we don't, Captain," Thompson said. He looked at me sideways, his own eyes quiet, but in them I saw a spark of anger that perhaps matched my own. "Found the body, nothing else. She can't have been floating there long." He looked up at the waterman. "Maybe only thrown in this afternoon?"

The waterman nodded. He must have seen his share of bloaters, and Thompson must have, too. They'd know just by looking at the body how long she'd been in the water.

"How much had she drifted, do you think?" I asked. "Do you know where she went in?"

"She didn't go far," the waterman said in his reedy voice. "I found her fetched up under th' bridge."

He pointed. Blackfriar's Bridge lay just upstream of us.

I was night-blinded by the lanterns, but looked that way as though I could see the arches of the dark bridge.

"She'd been wedged there a few hours, I'd say."

Thompson got to his feet, swung his arms. The coat swung with him. "And she's only a few hours dead. That means she could have been pitched in near the Middle or Inner Temple. From the Temple Stairs, perhaps? About half past four this afternoon? What are the gentlemen of the King's Bench getting up to, I wonder?"

I saw in his eyes that he only half-joked. Why a pupil or barrister of the Temples would kill a young woman and toss her into the Thames I could not fathom, but someone there might have done so. Thompson thought so, too.

It would not be Thompson's task to investigate this crime. His jurisdiction lay on the river, and on the wharves and docks where thieves might break into the loaded merchantmen. Pomeroy and his foot patrollers would be the men combing the Temple Gardens to find someone who might have witnessed the crime. But I saw a gleam of professional curiosity in Thompson's eyes.

The same curiosity sparked in me, mixed with deep pity for the young woman. I, too, wanted to discover who had done this to so harmless a creature, perhaps spend a few minutes alone with the man when we found him.

As I made to rise, the woman's torn glove moved under my fingers. I felt something cool and metal. A ring had been hidden by the gloves, protected from the water. It was loose, even on her bloated finger, and slipped easily into my hand.

I rose. Thompson looked my way in curiosity, and I brushed off the mud and balanced the ring on my palm. Pomeroy crowded close, his heavy breath touching me.

The ring was a thick circlet of silver bedecked with a strip of diamonds. Even muddy, it glinted in the lantern light, smooth and whole and costly. It was the sort of ring a gentleman of fashion would purchase for himself, and perhaps bestow on his paramour as a keepsake.

"A gift from her lover?" Thompson asked, echoing my thoughts.

It made perfect sense to Pomeroy. "Must have been. Think he did her in?"

"No way of knowing," Thompson said. He picked up the ring, held it close to his eyes.

Pomeroy went on. "Here's what happened. The lady and her lover quarrel, he hits her or knocks her down. She falls, strikes her head, dies. He panics when he sees he's killed her, drags her down the steps at the Temple Gardens, drops her into the river."

"Possibly," I said slowly. "But if that were the case, why would the paramour not remove his ring and take it home with him?"

"Maybe he didn't know she had it on. She's wearing gloves."

Thompson turned the bright circlet in his fingers. "If the man were her lover, he'd have known she'd wear it, and look under the glove."

"Or, she was with a second lover," Pomeroy speculated. "A gent jealous of the gent what gave her the ring. They quarrel about the first gent, he kills her—accidentally or on purpose—but doesn't know she's wearing the ring."

"Could be," Thompson said. He did not sound interested in nebulous lovers. He was interested in the ring, a concrete link to a man, whoever he might be—husband, lover, father. No middle-class man had purchased that ring; it had a patina to it, was possibly part of a family collection. Jewelers served families for decades. If Thompson could identify who'd made the ring, he'd be closer to finding the man who owned it.

The waterman gazed silently at the ring, looking disappointed that he hadn't found it before he'd reported the body to Thompson. Thompson closed his hand. "We could put out a notice about the ring," he said. "That would likely only bring us a flood of people who want to take home a pretty gewgaw. The killer will probably be wise

enough to let the ring go. Or we could inquire at the jewelers."

He looked at Pomeroy, whose face fell. "Hate to think of walking up and down London calling at every jeweler from the river to Islington." Pomeroy preferred chasing known thieves and tackling them instead of slow, painstaking investigation. He eyed me speculatively. "The captain here knows most of the posh and upper classes. Maybe he could ask about who it belonged to."

Thompson also eyed me. He didn't know me and had no reason to trust me, but it was not unusual for a civilian to assist in crime solving. The magistrates' offices had nowhere near the resources they needed to patrol the London area, although the City of London itself had its own police. A citizen was expected to give chase and make an arrest when necessary, and to bring perpetrators to court and prosecute them.

Thompson would use me as a resource if he could, though I would get no monetary compensation. Runners received rewards if criminals were convicted, but a gentleman, like myself, did not get paid as a thief taker. If I helped with an arrest and prosecution, it would be Thompson or Pomeroy who would reap the reward.

Thompson watched me, drawing his finger and thumb down the sides of his mouth. "Do you think you could find out quickly?" he asked. "Every moment could take the murderer a step closer to the Continent."

"If he decides to run," Pomeroy muttered.

"I know a man who could possibly help," I said. "This is a prominent man's ring, and he knows prominent gentlemen's jewelers."

I could imagine Grenville's long nose almost quivering with interest when I presented the ring. Little exciting had happened since we'd concluded the regimental affair in the summer, and he had told me point blank last time we'd met that I needed to find him some new amusement.

Thompson nodded, dropped the ring into my hand.

"Ask your questions, Captain. Tell me the answers tomorrow."

I liked that the man spoke quickly and decisively; he was deferential, but not fawning. I gave him my word that I would keep him apprised of my success or lack of it, and he acknowledged it with the barest nod. But I had not mistaken the curiosity in the man's eyes. He, like me, did not like puzzles to remain unsolved. And I had the desire to find the person who had killed the pretty young woman on the shore. I could not imagine what harm a small woman like that could have caused anyone, and I was angry at whoever had hurt her.

I looked at her again, lying still, gray, her full lips slack, her fair hair limp. I slipped the ring into my pocket, took my leave of the men, and returned to the world above.

I reached Grosvenor Street in Mayfair at ten o'clock. The thoroughfare was packed with carriages, as I had expected it to be. No one who was anyone refused an invitation to one of Lucius Grenville's soirees, even on a cold January night.

I descended my very unfashionable hackney at the end of the line of carriages, paid over my shillings, and walked the rest of the way to Grenville's house.

The façade of Grenville's home was unostentatious, even plain. The simplicity of the outside, however, hid a magnificent interior, made even more magnificent tonight. Grenville's fortune was vast, his taste impeccable. Chandeliers glittered above a wide marble staircase that lifted to a landing arched like a Roman piazza. Hothouse flowers graced every niche of the staircase and expansive hall, their reds and blues and oranges vibrant against the white marble walls. The scent of the flowers mixed with that of the people—perfume, soap, pomade, fabric, perspiration.

I'd had the privilege of being shown over this house from top to bottom, of entering the rooms into which Grenville invited very few. Those private rooms revealed glimpses of the real man—intellectual, curious, fascinated

by the world; tonight, the public rooms showed only the lavishness that people expected from him.

I joined the throng entering the house, bowing politely to a matron and daughter and allowing them to enter before me. Both women glittered from head to foot with diamonds. The hall was loud with people talking, laughing, calling to friends they had not seen since the hunting season in autumn. Over this din the voice of an Italian tenor soared.

The purpose of a soiree was not only to enjoy drink, food, music, and the company, it was also to press one's way upstairs to greet the host. Grenville stood on the landing above, surrounded by a swarm of people eager for a few minutes' conversation with him. He bowed and talked and shook hands, the gracious host. Gentlemen lingered to look over his suit; ladies young and old smiled and flirted.

Tonight, he wore a fine suit of black in the very latest stare of fashion. A diamond stickpin rested like a chip of ice in his carefully tied cravat, and his hair glistened mahogany dark under the chandeliers. His black pantaloons encased tightly muscled legs, and his dancing pumps shone. He was not a handsome man, having a long nose, slightly pointed chin, and eyes that glittered like a ferret's; however, these defects did not bother the ladies of London, who viewed him with the same fervor as a gentleman might view an elusive fox. But Grenville had never married nor showed an inclination to do so. Instead, he squired about well-known actresses, opera singers, lady violinists, and the like with every evidence of enjoyment.

Quizzing glasses came out as I made my slow way up the stairs, gentlemen and dandies scanning me and my regimentals. The *ton* had grown used to me, but still wondered about me, especially since I'd had the bad taste to get my name in the newspapers, connected with murder and scandal. Usually, their rudeness annoyed me, but tonight I could not help wondering whether a gentleman here had given the young woman on the riverbank the ring, or had murdered her.

My situation was not unusual for the time—my family name was old and respected, but my father had run through what was left of the fortune, leaving me nothing. Many a long-standing family had lost money during the war or the years following it; gentlemen with fine education and family connections were forced to become tutors or secretaries in order to earn a living. They made little more than I did on my half-pay, although their employers no doubt gave them better accommodations than I could afford.

When I reached Grenville, his face lit with genuine pleasure. "Lacey," he said, gripping my hand. "I feared you would not come. The weather is foul."

"I was honored by the invitation."

It was what I was expected to say, what those around us wanted to hear. Grenville knew better than to take my words at face value. He leaned toward me, said in a low voice, "I need to speak to you, my friend. You can rest up in my sitting room if you prefer it to the crush. I'll join you when I can."

I raised my brows, but he could not explain further in the press of guests. I nodded, indicating that I'd accepted his offer, and let him relinquish his attention to the next guest.

I turned away, allowing a rather dithering old gentleman to seize Grenville's hand and monopolize his attention. I spied Bartholomew and his brother Matthias, clad in livery and dashing up and down the stairs with glasses of champagne, and motioned Bartholomew to me. "Evening, sir," he said, as I lifted a glass from his tray. He cast a critical eye over my regimentals, which he'd studiously brushed this morning, then hurried away again.

I took the champagne and slowly climbed the next flight of stairs to a quieter landing and Grenville's private rooms. I was grateful to his invitation to rest away from the crowds, because after seeing the corpse of the poor girl on the bank of the Thames, I was in no mood for polite conversation and false smiles. I had only a few true friends among the *ton*; one of them was Lady Aline Carrington, a

spinster of loud opinions and independent thought, but I could not expect her to give all her attention to me. The Brandons had also been invited, but they were not attending, Louisa had informed me in a letter, because Colonel Brandon did not much approve of Grenville.

The news disappointed me, because Louisa had been elusive of late, and I had hoped to speak with her. A few months ago, Louisa had helped me through a bad bout of melancholia. Her presence in my front room had been a bright beacon as I lay unmoving in my bed. When I showed signs of recovering, she left me to the care of my landlady and departed. In early December, she and her husband had gone north to visit one of Brandon's cronies in a hunting box. Since their return to town, I had not seen much of either of them, and I was not certain why.

I sipped the champagne as I opened the door to Grenville's sitting room. I looked forward to perusing Grenville's collections or dipping into one of his many fine books.

On the threshold I stopped. A slim lady in an ivory silk gown and a feathered headdress stood on the other side of the room, her back to me. Her attention was fixed on a row of tiny ivory figurines from the Orient that rested on a shelf near the window. She picked up one, turning it this way and that, admiring the cleverness of it.

If she had been any other lady, I would have believed that Grenville had given her leave to be here, to examine his collection. With this particular lady, I know he had not.

I cleared my throat. The lady turned. She saw me, looked me up and down, not in the least ashamed. "Captain Lacey. Good evening."

The dowager Lady Breckenridge was near to thirty, had a sharp face, deep brown hair, and inquisitive, dark blue eyes. I had met her the previous summer in Kent, while investigating the affair of Colonel Westin. She'd played billiards with me, blown cigarillo smoke in my face, and told me bluntly that I was a fool. I believe what had irritated me most was that she'd been right.

"Good evening," I returned.

She looked at me for a moment longer, then shrugged at the figurine in her hand. "I could not resist. I hear that Mr. Grenville's collections are the best in England, but he shows them to so very few."

I remained silent. I wondered whether she thought I would summon a footman to throw her out.

"They're very exotic, aren't they?" she continued when I said nothing. The figure in her hand was a ferocious-looking beast; only three inches long, it had two rows of teeth and a curving tail. She reached to return it to its place, but the sleek ivory slipped from her gloved hands and dropped to the floor. Fortunately, the figurine landed easily on the carpet and did not shatter.

Lady Breckenridge began to bend to retrieve it, but I crossed the room, bent down for her, and came up with the little creature in my hand.

"Always the gentleman," she said. She smiled at me. I was surprised and a bit pleased to see that it was without rancor.

I set the figurine back on its shelf. Last year Lady Breckenridge had, by letting me go through her husband's papers, helped me discover who had committed several murders, including that of her husband. She had never betrayed sorrow for her husband's death, and having met him, I could hardly blame her.

With any other lady, I would have had a stock of polite conversation ready to hand, and she would have a stock of polite responses. With Lady Breckenridge, however, such convention was useless. She would bat away any polite phrase with stinging wit and wait for more.

"I believe," she said, breaking the silence, "that you still owe me five guineas."

I had lost a wager at billiards to her the previous summer, but I had dutifully enclosed the note with a letter to her when I'd received my autumn pay packet. I'd made certain to pay that wager, not only because a man always

pays his debts of honor, but because I definitely did not want to be beholden to Lady Breckenridge.

She knew this. The glitter in her eyes told me. I bowed. "I beg your pardon. I will rectify the omission immediately."

Her smile deepened, as though she'd wagered with herself whether I would go along with her pretense or tell her to go to the devil.

We watched each other for a few minutes more, then she abruptly inclined her head and said, "Good evening, Captain," and sashayed her way to the door.

The musky scent of her perfume remained after she'd gone. I straightened the figurines on the shelf, wondering about Lady Breckenridge. Her blunt observations were every bit as pointed as those of Lady Aline Carrington, but Lady Breckenridge's eyes always held a spark of malice, while Lady Aline was kindness itself. I had learned, through Lady Aline, that Lady Breckenridge came from a very wealthy and powerful family; likely she'd married Viscount Breckenridge at her family's behest. There had certainly been no love between Lord and Lady Breckenridge; in the brief time I'd observed them, they had never even exchanged words.

I seated myself on the Turkish sofa to wait for Grenville, and pulled out a volume of the *Description de L'Egypte*. Grenville was the proud owner of these large folios of magnificent engravings and text put together by the scientific expedition to Egypt nearly eighteen years ago. Napoleon had been mad for Egypt, and had dragged artists, scientists, draftsmen, and architects with him to the Nile so that they might draw and measure everything in the country. We'd heard intriguing stories of the artists drawing while bullets rained down around them and of them using soldiers' backs as drafting boards.

The *Description* was immense, and few could afford it, but Grenville, of course, had procured the first volumes immediately on publication. He kept them in a specially

built cabinet, with shelves ready to receive the forthcoming volumes.

I amused myself flipping through the pages, admiring the artists' skills and astonished by the exotic temples and pyramids and statuary. Grenville had a passion for Egypt, had been there more than once. I wondered when he would disappear from foggy London to travel there again.

I was engrossed in drawings of colossal statues depicting seated men with hands on knees when Grenville finally entered.

I looked up in surprise. I had been sitting only an hour or so, and the soiree still raged below. I had not expected him until very late.

Grenville shut the door with an air of relief. "Quite a crush."

I closed the folio and returned it to its shelf while he moved to a side table and a decanter. "Claret? I've set aside the best."

He seemed in no hurry to tell me why he'd wanted to speak to me. He poured us both a glass of warm, red claret, sat on his favorite chair, crossed his legs, and drank deeply.

I supposed him working up his way to confide in me, but I was too impatient with my own task to wait. I removed the silver ring from my pocket and passed it to him.

Startled, he took it. "What is this?"

"Would you be able to tell me whom it belonged to?"

He set aside his claret, brought out his quizzing glass, and squinted through it at the ring. "A pretty bauble. Exquisitely made." He looked up, his eyes gleaming in sudden interest. "If one of my guests had dropped this, you would not make a point of showing it to me. Out with it. What is the story?"

I sat back and took a sip of the claret. "It was found on the finger of a dead woman earlier today."

CHAPTER 3

〜

I F I'd wanted to create a sensation, I would have suc-
ceeded admirably. Grenville's mouth opened. Astonished, he looked at the ring again. "Good Lord."

I quickly told him the tale. He studied the ring as I
spoke, turning it around in his hands, much as Thompson
had done.

When I finished, he was silent for a moment. "Interesting," he murmured, then he pocketed the quizzing glass
and his voice became brisk. "If she wore the ring under the
glove so it would not fall off her finger, that means that she
did not want to lose the ring, which indicates that she
probably cared for the paramour, whoever he is."

I rubbed my upper lip thoughtfully. "We are rather pre-
suming that the woman received this ring from a lover. She
might have stolen it herself. Although, in that case, she
would likely have tried to sell it, or given it to a lover of
her own. Or, the lover might have stolen it from the original owner."

Grenville peered at the band again. "Possibly, but it's

common for a gentleman to give his ring to his ladybird. Pity there is no inscription."

Indeed, a line reading "To my beloved Miss Smith from Mr. Worth," or some such would have been most helpful.

"However," Grenville squinted, "there is a jeweler's mark. Excellent. If it belongs to a jeweler in England, we will easily know for whom this ring was made."

"As easy as that?" I asked skeptically. "Pomeroy winced at the thought of looking in at every jeweler in the West End and Mayfair. I supposed we would have to."

Grenville's eyes twinkled. He was well and truly interested. "Nonsense. All I need do is ask my man Gautier. He knows every jeweler, boot maker, glove maker, hat maker, and tailor in London, not to mention the history of each business and the family who owns it. I wager he can tell us what this jeweler's mark is, in a trice."

He rose and tugged the bellpull, then he sent the answering footman for Gautier. Grenville liked to move quickly when something took his interest, which, in this case, pleased me. The sooner we could discover who the lady was, the more quickly I could lay my hand on her murderer.

GAUTIER, a fine-boned Frenchman who had, last summer, efficiently bandaged my hands after an impromptu boxing match, responded to Grenville's summons with perfect equanimity. He stared at the ring and the jeweler's mark inside for a long moment, then handed the ring back and announced it was the work of Mr. Neumann of Grafton Street. His glance told us he was surprised we'd had to ask.

"Excellent, Gautier, thank you," Grenville said. He flipped the ring in the air, caught it. "Tell Matthias to run and fetch Mr. Neumann here."

Gautier bowed and took this instruction in stride and glided from the room. I raised my brows. "It's a bit late, is it not?"

Grenville closed the ring in his fist. "I am certain your Mr. Thompson of the Thames patrol wishes you to be

quick," he countered. "Besides, the owner of this ring might be under my very roof right now. Best to find him and discover how much he knows right away, is it not?"

GRENVILLE'S surmise proved to be the case. While I knew Grenville's real motive was his curiosity, I was happy that he had enough power to drag a respectable jeweler out of his bed in the middle of a rainy night and bring him here to be quizzed.

The man, middle-aged with a handsome face running to fat, smoothly acquiesced to Grenville's request. He was a businessman, after all. Any connection with Grenville, no matter how small, could boost his custom. The quantity of brandy Grenville gave him, along with a large tip, doubtless did not hurt either.

Mr. Neumann studied the ring, gave us the name Lord Barbury, and departed to roll home in the luxury of Grenville's carriage.

Grenville's eyes sparkled black fire. Lord Barbury, he said, a baron, had indeed answered the invitation to the soiree, and was likely still in the house. He departed in search of the man, nearly bouncing in his polished leather shoes.

He returned not long after with Lord Barbury in tow. Lord Barbury was a tall man with deep brown eyes. Waves of thick, dark hair touched his shoulders and made his face look still longer. His chin was shadowed with beard, as though his whiskers sprouted as quickly as his valet scraped them off. He wore a black suit much like Grenville's, with an ivory-and-white-striped waistcoat. Heavy gold rings encircled his fingers and his cravat pin sported a large emerald. He was in his thirties, past his first blush of youth but not yet at middle age. A man about town, I assessed, living to go to his clubs, ride horses, gamble, and take a pretty mistress.

He frowned at me as Grenville briefly introduced us, then Grenville opened his hand and displayed the silver ring on his palm. Lord Barbury froze. "Where the devil did you get that?"

I said quietly, "A woman was pulled from the Thames earlier this evening. She was wearing it."

All the color drained from his face. "What do you mean?"

"This is your ring?" Grenville asked.

"Yes, it is my ring. I do not understand why you have it."

"Lacey?" Grenville prompted.

"The woman was small and pretty," I said. "She had blonde hair and wore a gown of light pink and beaded slippers. She wore the ring under her glove. She had been murdered, her head struck, before she was pushed into the river."

Lord Barbury gasped, as though the air had suddenly left his lungs. Grenville caught him as he sagged and got him quickly into a chair. I poured the man a glass of claret and handed it to him. Lord Barbury drank.

His hauteur and rage faded as he swallowed. "Please, gentlemen," he said, "tell me you are mistaken."

"I wish that I could," I answered. "She died at about half-past four this afternoon. Did you see her today?"

"No. I was to meet her later." He pressed his hand to his face. "I cannot believe this."

"Where were you, my lord," I asked, "at half-past four?"

He raised his head, eyes filling with rage. I held my ground. If he had killed the young woman, I would not care whether he were a baron or a boatman.

"At my club," he snapped. "How dare you think that I could do this, that I could harm my Peaches." His voice broke.

"I believe I saw you with her once," Grenville said. "A pretty young woman."

"Lovely and sweet as a peach," he said. "Which is why I call her—" He broke off. "Who did this to her?"

"That we do not know," Grenville replied. "An officer of the Thames River patrol and one of Bow Street are looking into it."

"Bow Street, bah." Lord Barbury waved them aside. "Trumped up watchmen who do nothing without a large reward dangling over their heads."

"You could offer the reward," Grenville suggested.

"Then they will simply scoop up anyone from the street and push through a conviction."

I watched him narrowly, not completely disagreeing with him. Pomeroy was diligent in seeking out his rewards, and he did enjoy arresting people, whether they had anything to do with the crime in question or not.

"Mr. Thompson of the Thames patrol struck me as being intelligent," I said. "He is interested in the truth."

Lord Barbury waved away Mr. Thompson, as well. "You do it, Lacey."

I raised my brows. "I beg your pardon?"

He faced me. His eyes held a mixture of grief and rage. "I have read how you run about finding lost girls and discovering murderers. Twitting magistrates is an admirable quality. Besides, at least you're a gentleman."

Lord Barbury had in no way convinced me that he had not himself murdered the woman called Peaches. He might have quarreled with her, he might have wanted to end the affair and she had resisted, she might have threatened him. His grief seemed genuine, but I had met men before who could portray grief and then turn around and laugh. It would be easy enough, however, to discover his whereabouts between four and five o'clock that afternoon, although a man of his standing could easily hire others to do his dirty deeds for him.

I said, "I will see what I can do."

"Please do," Barbury glared at me. His grief made him abrupt, but I sensed that even in the happiest of times, he was a man of impatience and one who brooked no fools. "I want to see whoever hurt Peaches, and I want to see him dance from the gallows."

Whatever I thought about Barbury, I shared his wish. No matter what Peaches had done in life, I vowed that the

man who had hurt that helpless and frail young woman would feel my wrath.

GRENVILLE and I learned as much as we could from Lord Barbury before he departed the house, sunk in grief, and the next day I visited Thompson to return the ring and tell him the story.

Peaches was in truth a lady called Mrs. Chapman, Lord Barbury had told us. She had a husband, a barrister, and significantly, his chambers were in Middle Temple.

Peaches, born Amelia Leary, had been an actress, rather like Marianne, moving from company to company, wherever she could find a role. However, her sweet charm had quickly and easily attracted Lord Barbury, and they had soon become lovers.

About five years ago, Peaches had disappeared from the theatre, and she and Lord Barbury had ceased to be a couple. Peaches, it seemed, had had ambition. She must have realized fairly soon that Lord Barbury would never marry beneath his station, so she'd turned her sights on another mark, a barrister called Chapman. I wondered why Chapman had taken a wife with Peaches' background, but perhaps he'd been flattered by her attention, perhaps the pretty Peaches had charmed him, perhaps he hadn't known much about what went on in the world of the theatre. In any case, she'd married him and dropped from sight.

A year ago, Lord Barbury, who himself had never married, had met Peaches again by chance. They'd discovered that their mutual attraction was still strong, and they'd begun another affair. They'd enjoyed a sweet reunion, Lord Barbury had said. They had generally met in two places: at the gatherings of a man called Inglethorpe, and at the Glass House.

Thompson's brows rose when I told him the latter name. We were sitting in his office on the Thames at Wapping, a bare room with desk and chair and a stool for guests. I had come alone, Grenville having had another appointment. He'd gone to look at a famous private collec-

tion of porcelain, an appointment he'd made weeks ago, but Grenville had looked rather disappointed that he couldn't traipse into the back lanes of the East End with me.

"The Glass House," Thompson mused. "A name that has no good attached to it. When magistrates or reformers try to close it, somehow their intentions are blocked. Have you ever been there, Captain?"

I shook my head. I'd heard of the Glass House, a name spoken by many an upper-class gentleman as a place to go for vice more exotic than that offered in the hells around St. James's. Grenville had never suggested taking me, and I hadn't had the inclination to enter such a place on my own.

"Nasty goings on there, I hear," Thompson continued. "I believe a man must be deep in pocket and long in pedigree to even cross the threshold."

That left me on the doorstep. Probably a barrister who lived on what people paid him to prosecute cases would be left on the doorstep, as well.

"Well, Captain, I will send for Mr. Chapman and tell him the disagreeable news," Thompson finished. "He will also have to identify the body."

"Do you mind if I am present when you question him?"

I fully intended to ask Chapman a few pointed questions myself. Chapman might well have discovered his wife's affair with Lord Barbury, met his wife in the Temple Gardens, quarreled with her, and killed her. I could not rule out Barbury, either, despite his impassioned plea to me to find Peaches' killer. He could very well have been angry and jealous; he was a large, strong man, and would be easily able to kill such a delicate young woman as Peaches.

Both men had strong connections to her; it was likely that she had been killed either by one of them or because of one of them.

Thompson nodded. "The magistrate, Sir Montague Harris, told me things about you," he said. "He's astute as they make them, and I've learned to trust him." He slanted

me a look that said he'd enjoy watching what I did, if not explicitly sharing Sir Montague's trust in me.

Sir Montague Harris had attended an inquest at which I'd given evidence the previous summer. I, too, had been impressed with the man's common sense and pointed questions, even if the magistrate in charge had found him irritating.

I left Thompson then, who told me he would send word when he fetched Chapman to identify the body, and I made my way back to Covent Garden.

GRENVILLE and I met later at the Rearing Pony to confer. I thought he'd prefer a more elegant meeting place, even our usual coffee house in Pall Mall, but Grenville professed himself happy to settle in here. He explained that here, at least, he would not be required by every passerby to render his opinion on a cravat, the cut of a coat, or the latest *on-dit,* as he had done all morning while viewing the porcelain.

I sensed that Grenville was growing weary of his role as most popular man in London. He betrayed a restlessness that had begun after our adventures last summer, and I wondered when he'd announce that he was returning to his world travels. I knew that when he finally went, I would miss him. Despite our differences in wealth and opinions, we had become friends. Perhaps it was because of our differences; he knew I would never toady to him, and I knew he accepted me as I was—one of the few people in my life to do so.

I repeated the conversation I'd had with Thompson and we debated what to do next.

The barmaid, Anne Tolliver, slid another tankard in front of me, giving me a warm smile. I returned it with a nod, and sipped my ale. "It would be helpful if we could piece together what Mrs. Chapman did yesterday. Where she went, who she met."

I stopped. Grenville was staring at me, a half-amused, half-exasperated look on his face. I frowned. "What is it?"

"How do you do it, Lacey?"

"I beg your pardon?" I grew annoyed. "If you mean Mrs. Tolliver, she has a wink for every gentleman in the room."

He studied me, his eyes sharp, then he gave a laugh and took a draught of ale. "Not *every* gentleman. But never mind." He traced a design on the damp table top. "We were speaking of Mrs. Chapman. We can quiz her servants, of course. Discover what friends she had, if she went to meet them, or if she told them what she meant to do that day."

"Lord Barbury mentioned a Mr. Inglethorpe."

Grenville looked slightly uncomfortable. "Yes, Simon Inglethorpe. He lives in Curzon Street."

The name meant nothing to me. "Who is he?"

"No one of particular importance," Grenville said. "He has much money and much leisure time. He enjoys social gatherings."

"So might many a man."

"Lately, he has taken to the new sort of gas that leaves one feeling euphoric. He invites ladies and gentlemen to partake of it in his upstairs rooms. Interesting that Lord Barbury decided to take Peaches there. I wonder why he did."

"Could she have gone there the day of her death?"

"That is possible. I could hope so. If she had had some of Inglethorpe's magic gas, she might not have felt the blow that took her life."

I did not understand how that could be, but I said nothing. "She might have made some acquaintance there," I said, "who could be able to help us discover her movements yesterday."

"I suppose it is worth a try," Grenville said.

It was a long shot, I knew, but I wanted to leave no stone unturned. The most likely person to have murdered Peaches was her husband—she'd been cuckolding him, and his chambers lay very close indeed to the place she'd died. Easy for him to slip away to meet his wife and kill her. He would know the ins and outs of the place, where

they would and would not be seen. Then again, she might have gone to this Inglethorpe's home and met someone there, gone away with them, and died by their hand, for reasons unknown. Perhaps Inglethorpe himself had killed her.

"Will you fix an appointment with Inglethorpe then?" I asked, lifting my glass of ale.

Grenville nodded. "He has gatherings Monday and Wednesday afternoons. I will send word asking him to admit you to the gathering, tomorrow."

My glass paused halfway to my lips. "You will not attend yourself?" That seemed unlike Grenville, who was usually adamant to be in the thick of things.

He flushed. "I keep my distance from Inglethorpe."

"May I ask why?"

"Oh, certainly you may ask." Grenville stopped, looked contrite. He lowered his voice. "If you must know, Inglethorpe propositioned me once. A few years ago. It was a bit embarrassing."

"I see." Such things had happened to Grenville before, to his chagrin. He was the object not only of women's aspirations, but of a few gentlemen's as well. "He is an unnatural, then?"

"I honestly do not believe Inglethorpe cares which way the wind blows. He seems to like sensual pleasure of any kind. He claims he does not hold my refusal against me, but I avoid him." He gave me a sharp look. "That goes no further than you, please, Lacey."

"I would never repeat your conversation to another," I said stiffly.

He sighed. "I beg your pardon. I have been put off by this poor woman's murder."

So had I. "Have you been able to discover, at all, if Lord Barbury was at his club yesterday afternoon, as he claims?"

Grenville nodded. "He was. At White's. I've met a few fellows who claimed he was there, though I'll poke about

a bit more and make certain. Though I do not like to think of him as a murderer."

"He might not have done it himself, but hired someone to kill her," I pointed out. "And made sure he was visible at his club."

"You are a cheerful chap, Lacey." He regarded his ale glumly. "But possibly correct. I like Barbury, you see. He is not fatuous or toadying. He says what he thinks, and I find that refreshing."

Grenville truly liked few people. I hoped for his sake that Lord Barbury did not turn out to be a murderer, but I could not dismiss him simply because Grenville approved of him.

He sipped his ale. "It is a bother that we don't know whether she was killed in the Temple Gardens or her body brought there afterward."

"True."

"At least in the Hanover Square affair, we knew where Horne was killed and more or less why." He made an expression of distaste, recalling the decadent Mr. Horne and his gruesome death. "This is different. This is the work of a brute."

I agreed. I wanted to look into the mystery for a more personal reason than Barbury's request and my own curiosity. When I had looked upon the childlike face of Mrs. Chapman, gray and dead in the light of the torches, fierce anger had touched me. Not only had the young woman resembled Marianne Simmons, she had also greatly put me in mind of my own estranged wife, Carlotta Lacey.

Of course, the dead girl could not have been Carlotta. The woman called Peaches had been in her twenties at most, and Carlotta would now be nearing forty. Carlotta lived in France, where and with whom, only one man in England knew, and he was the one man I would never ask.

The girl could also not, thank God, be my daughter. The child Carlotta had taken away from me when she'd fled so long ago would be about sixteen now, and Peaches had definitely been older.

But I hated to think of my own child lying dead somewhere, with no one to care. Barbury did not want Bow Street mucking about his affairs. Thompson investigated because it was his job and because of professional interest; Grenville helped in order to relieve his ennui. So far, I seemed to be the only one concerned for Peaches' sake, although I could be wronging Barbury with that assumption. Whatever Peaches had done, whatever choices she had made, she did not deserve what had happened to her.

I turned my glass of ale around on the table. "Another avenue of possibility is the Glass House. If Peaches and Barbury went there together, someone there might know her and know what she did yesterday."

Grenville made a face. "The Glass House. What do you know of it?"

"Little. It is a gaming hell that costs much to enter. It is in the East End, I believe."

"Number twelve, St. Charles Row, near Whitechapel," Grenville said. "I have been, and vowed never to go back. Every vice is available there, whether you have a penchant for gambling, or women, or men, or . . . well, anything you can think of." He watched me with his sharp, dark eyes. "I do mean every vice, Lacey. I wonder why Barbury went there with Peaches when he could easily have arranged a better place. Any connection Peaches formed there would have been a sordid one."

"Murder is sordid," I said.

He sighed. "You might be right. You usually are. I suppose you wish me to get you in."

"I do not like to presume," I began.

"You must presume, because you'll not gain entry on your own. I will take you, but I guarantee that you will not like it."

"I am not going for entertainment," I said.

"I know. But please, do not blame me if the place disgusts you. There. I have warned you."

I thanked him for his warning, and we finished our ale. We parted after that, Grenville returning to his luxuri-

ous carriage, me to my rooms in Grimpen Lane. Grenville promised to send word about when I should call on Inglethorpe. He was interested, at least. When Lucius Grenville became interested in something, he pursued it with a tenacity that Bonaparte would have envied. The murderer would be hard pressed to elude the both of us.

CHAPTER 4

❧

THAT evening, Thompson sent word to me that Chapman was due in Bow Street at five o'clock. It was a short walk from my rooms, though the weather cramped my injured knee, and I moved slowly. The magistrate's office, a tall edifice, encompassed numbers 3 and 4 Bow Street. Behind it, across a small yard, lay the strong rooms for the keeping of prisoners; the officers sometimes used the cellar of the tavern across the road for prisoners when the magistrate's house was full.

Church clocks were just striking the quarter hour when I entered and made my way to Pomeroy's room. Mr. Chapman was already there. In his early fifties, Mr. Chapman had a fringe of graying hair, small dark eyes, and an expression of one whose mind was always on his next task. He greeted Pomeroy and Thompson politely, although he looked in no way worried about why they'd brought him there. Apparently, he had not believed their story that his wife had been found dead, and seemed impatient for them to prove it. He was uninterested in who I was, and ex-

pressed a desire to get on with it, as he had important appointments.

Peaches' body had been placed in one of the buildings in the yard behind the house. Pomeroy led us there and unlocked the door. The stone room beyond was chilly and damp, a foul tomb for anyone.

Peaches, wrapped in a sheet, waited in silence on the table. Standing beside the shrouded body was Sir Montague Harris, the magistrate I had met the year before. I greeted him in surprise. He was magistrate at the Whitechapel house, I understood, far from here. The houses and officers often cooperated with each other, but if a magistrate from another part of the metropolis had not been asked to participate in an investigation, he had no need to. But Sir Montague looked very interested. He shook my hand, professing himself pleased to see me.

Chapman was introduced to him, but did not look impressed. "This must be a mistake, you know," he said, in a voice of one annoyed that the outside world had intruded on his workday. "My wife is in Sussex."

Thompson said nothing.

"That's as may be," Pomeroy spoke up. "But here we are."

He stepped forward, removed the wrapping from Peaches' face, and held his candle high. Silent and blue-gray in the circle of light, Peaches looked almost serene. Her ringlets had dried from her dousing in the Thames and lay on her shoulders, as silken and golden as a girl's.

Chapman stared at her a long time, his face unmoving.

"Well?" Pomeroy boomed. His candle wavered, and drop of hot wax splashed on Peaches' shrouded chest.

"That is my wife," Mr. Chapman said finally. "She was meant to be in Sussex." He sounded as though this breach of plans displeased him.

"I am very sorry, sir." Sir Montague's words were polite, but sincere. "From what Mr. Thompson tells me, she died quickly. Probably never knew what happened. Now then, sir, when did you last see your wife?"

Thompson quietly pulled the sheet over Peaches' face again. She was not a person any more, merely a figure under a sheet.

Chapman was saying, "I handed her into a hackney, bound for a coaching inn. She would take the mail to Sussex. That was three, no, four days ago."

"And where were you," Pomeroy broke in, "yesterday afternoon at half-past four?"

Chapman turned to him in mild shock. "Why is that important?"

"Because your wife was tipped into the river very near your chambers in Middle Temple at that time."

Chapman paled. "If you imply that I killed her, you are wrong. I dined that evening in the hall, with my pupil and fellow barristers. I never left it. I put my wife into a coach on Saturday, and have not set eyes on her from that time to this." He glanced at the shrouded body and flinched a little.

"Did you have any quarrel with your wife, sir?" Pomeroy went on.

A vein began pounding in Chapman's tight forehead. "What do you mean, asking me such a thing?"

"Did you know, for instance, that your wife was having an affair with a posh gent?"

Chapman's face suffused with color. He looked at the four of us, all silent, all waiting for his answer. I mused that although Chapman had not believed his wife to be dead, he very well believed she'd had a lover.

"You cast aspersions on my wife's reputation, gentlemen," he said at last.

"She'd been an actress, had she not?" Thompson asked. "Not many actresses have excellent reputations to begin with."

Chapman's jaw hardened. "That was years ago. She gave up the stage—everything—when she married me."

"An odd choice of a wife, wasn't it?" Thompson said. "For a respectable barrister?"

"That is really none of your business," Chapman said stiffly.

Sir Montague spoke, still polite, but his voice firm. "She was murdered, sir, which is a very serious crime. We will expect you at the inquest, day after tomorrow."

Chapman blinked at the word "inquest." "Surely, I will not be called to give evidence."

"A few things will be easier if you are there," Sir Montague said. He never lost his polite geniality. "You understand."

As a barrister, Mr. Chapman obviously did.

"Before you leave, just tell Mr. Pomeroy the names of the men you dined with, and your movements between four and five o'clock yesterday."

"Of course." Chapman's voice was lackluster.

We went back to the outside world, which was almost as dim as the stone room had been. Mr. Chapman did not shake hands with me or Thompson. He moved into the side room indicated to wait for Pomeroy.

"He must have done it," Pomeroy hissed, his round face wearing an annoyed expression. "Why are you letting him go?"

"So that you may watch him," Sir Montague returned smoothly. "If he is innocent, he will do nothing but grow enraged at the inefficiencies of the magistrates. If he is guilty, he will betray himself." Pomeroy looked thoughtful, gave him a nod.

"I would like to speak to you, Captain," Sir Montague said as Pomeroy went off to take a statement from Chapman.

Sir Montague led me and Thompson upstairs to the magistrate's rooms. The Bow Street magistrate was not there—he was even now presiding in the court below, where those arrested during the night would parade before him. He would hear the cases against the pickpockets, prostitutes, thieves, and thugs. He would then decide whether to let the culprits go free or to bind them over for trial. Mr. Chapman might very well appear at their trials at the Old Bailey, prosecuting for the accuser.

Thompson closed the door, and Sir Montague settled

his bulk on a wide bench. "I was pleased for the chance to meet you again, Captain" he said. "When Mr. Thompson told me Mr. Pomeroy had fetched you to view the body, I was interested. I remember how you tweaked the coroner's nose in Kent for not doing his job."

"No doubt I was impertinent," I answered.

"He was in a hurry and wanted his dinner. Your observations were apt and he ought to have paid attention. I would be pleased to hear your observations in this case."

He was watching me closely. As I had in Kent, I had the feeling that were I ever in the dock before him, he would peel me apart layer by layer.

"I agree with Mr. Thompson's idea that she was killed in the Temple Gardens, near the stairs," I said. "It would have been dark and few people would have been out in the rain. Also, as the wife of a barrister, she would see nothing wrong with answering a summons from her husband, or one purporting to be from her husband, to Middle Temple."

Thompson leaned against a plain wooden desk and folded his arms. "Why would her husband summon her there if he thought she were in Sussex?"

"We have only his word on that matter," Sir Montague said. "He and his servants will be questioned, of course."

"If she had returned to London to meet someone at the Temple Gardens," I put in, "she most likely hired a coach to let her down at Middle Temple Lane. Drivers can be questioned."

"Or the posh Lord Barbury hired a coach for her," Thompson put in. "I have an appointment to speak to him today; I will certainly ask him. I suggest she used the Sussex journey as a ruse to get away from her husband for a few days and meet her lover, Lord Barbury. Perhaps Chapman discovered the ruse and killed her in anger."

"Why would she answer a summons to Middle Temple if she were hiding from her husband?" I queried.

Thompson spread his hands. "Perhaps the other speculation is correct, that she met her end elsewhere and was

brought to the gardens. Her husband would know the gardens and know they would be empty at that time of day."

"Or it is the lover," Sir Montague broke in. "Perhaps she wanted to end the association and return to her husband's affections. In a crime like this, it is often one or the other, the husband or the lover. We only need discover which one."

"In this case," I pointed out, "both the lover and the husband claim to have been in places with plenty of witnesses at the time of the crime. Mr. Chapman in Middle Temple Hall, and Lord Barbury at White's."

"We will certainly ascertain that," Sir Montague said. "But we have yet to establish the involvement of a third party."

"What is your interest?" I asked Sir Montague. "Whitechapel is a long way from Bow Street, or even Blackfriar's Bridge."

His smile deepened. "I simply take an interest. And when I heard your name crop up, that interest increased." He exchanged a look with Thompson. "That and the fact that the Glass House might be involved."

"Which lays near Whitechapel," I said, repeating Grenville's words.

"It is a house I would like to shut down. Rumors of what goes on there are disquieting, but rumor is not evidence. Whoever owns the house is very powerful; whenever a magistrate moves to close it, he suddenly backs off very quietly."

His statement made me pause. I knew a man powerful enough to send magistrates scuttling away when he wished. He was a man named James Denis, and he had his finger in many a soiled pie. If Denis owned the Glass House, I could understand why Sir Montague wanted it closed and his difficulty in doing so.

"Only the very wealthy and important are let through the doors," Sir Montague went on. "It is not like a brothel or even a gambling den that my patrollers can infiltrate. Vice for the upper classes often stays hidden."

I knew the truth of that. "My friend, Mr. Grenville, tells me that places the fashionable frequent change rapidly. If you wait, interest will die, and the fashionable will go elsewhere."

Sir Montague's look was shrewd. "I do not want to wait that long. This house has fascinated for awhile now and shows no sign of abating. My men cannot go there, and neither can I. While my knighthood might get me through the door, I am too well known as a meddling magistrate." His eyes twinkled. Sir Montague was also hugely rotund, though his legs were thin, a profile that many would remember. "But you, Captain Lacey, have the correct social standing and connections."

I had suspected he'd get to that. Sir Montague could not enter the realm of the aristocrat, but Lucius Grenville could. And Lucius Grenville could take me with him, as he'd already offered to do.

I supposed that Sir Montague expected me to protest. Grenville had already offered to let me use his connection to enter, but I was not certain how happy he would be when he learned that I wanted to not only to investigate Peaches' murder, but to spy on Grenville's own cronies.

However, Sir Montague did not know how much I would welcome any opportunity to thwart James Denis. I despised the man and would happily get in the way of anything he did.

I regarded Sir Montague quietly. "What would you like me to do?" I asked.

"HAVE you ever thought of going into law, Bartholomew?" I asked the next morning. Bartholomew, towering over six feet tall, with golden blond hair and a youthful face for his nineteen years, stopped in the act of refilling my cup of coffee.

"Can't say I ever did, sir. I mean to be a valet." He paused, then poured more thick, black coffee into my cup. Steam rose from it, bathing my nose in the aroma of burnt beans. "Or a Runner. A chap needs learning to go to law."

"Then he apprentices," I said. I lifted the coffee to my lips. It burned my tongue, but I swallowed it down. "He apprentices to a barrister and learns the art of prosecuting in court." If I had stayed at Cambridge and finished, instead of following Colonel Brandon off to the 35th Light Dragoons, I likely would have found my way to one of the Temples or Lincoln's or Gray's Inn to learn to practice at the bar. My father had been pressing me that direction, as well as to marry a young lady for her fortune. Twenty years old and arrogant, I had told him to go to the devil.

My father had shouted at me for days, and I had shouted back. Grown man though I was, he had still been fond of beating me across the back with his stout cane whenever he could reach me. I had felt the brunt of that cane most of my life. I had witnessed many a flogging in my army life, but no soldier had ever beaten another with the vicious thoroughness of my father.

"I need an excuse to go poking about the Middle Temple," I continued. "You could put on a suit and pretend you are looking to apprentice to a barrister. You are about the right age."

Bartholomew grinned. He had very white teeth. "Any of that lot will peg me for a slavey right off, I open my mouth."

"Then keep it closed," I said. I chewed through another hunk of Mrs. Beltan's cheapest bread and downed the coffee. "Stay behind me and look shy. I'll be your uncle or some such, happy to be getting you off my hands."

His smile widened. "I'm your man, sir."

Bartholomew was as fascinated as Grenville by the fact that I investigated things. His last adventure with me had resulted in his receiving two bullets in his arm and leg, but that fact had not dimmed his interest. Bartholomew had recovered quickly and never sported a limp.

Unlike myself. I had received a nasty injury courtesy of French soldiers on the Peninsula, and had to lean on a walking stick. The stick sported a sharp sword within it,

which had come in handy more than once since my return to London and civilian life.

When Bartholomew was ready, we departed. As I closed my door, I was surprised by the sight of Marianne Simmons coming up the steps. She wore a bonnet of yellow straw tied with a green ribbon that made her girlish face more fetching than ever. She scowled at me, golden brows drawn over eyes of cornflower blue.

"Where have you been?" I asked, startled into rudeness. She'd been away longer than usual, and Peaches' death had worried me.

Her scowl deepened, as predicted. "None of your business, Lacey." She paused halfway to her floor to glower at me again. "None of *his* either."

She did not mean Bartholomew, who hovered behind me. She meant Grenville, who'd taken an interest in her and had twice given her money, asking for nothing in return.

I did not pursue it. She was correct, what she got up to when she was far from here was none of my business. I shut my door, but did not lock it. "There's half a loaf of bread on my table. Take it if you want it."

She gave me a freezing look. "I do not need your leavings."

I shrugged, but still did not lock the door. I followed Bartholomew down the stairs, hearing her ascend to her own rooms. I had no doubt that when I returned the bread would be gone.

Bartholomew and I set off along the Strand through Temple Bar to Fleet Street, then walked south, down Middle Temple Lane, which bisected the Middle and Inner Temples. The environs of the two Temples overlapped somewhat, with buildings belonging to Middle Temple straying into the areas of the Inner Temple.

I led Bartholomew past the courts and chambers and toward the hall and gardens.

Bartholomew wore a plain suit he usually put on to visit his mother, and he slowed his exuberant stride for my

slower one. His suit was cheap, though not shabby, but it did not matter. The middle-class men and young gentlemen who apprenticed here did not always come from families of wealth.

Pupils fluttered about the lanes and gardens like students anywhere—some with the frightened but determined look of young men resolute to prove they were good at something; some with the superior looks of those who already knew they were good at something; some with the devil-may-care looks of young men who lived for larks, and studies got done when they got done. At Cambridge, I had been, unfortunately, a member of the latter group.

The pupils spoke readily enough to us. I behaved like an uncle anxious to rid myself of a lad I was at wit's end what to do with. Bartholomew stayed quiet as instructed. The other lads looked at him either with awe at his size or with a spark of mischief as they debated how to make fun of him.

We received much jovial advice on which barristers to avoid, but no one mentioned Chapman. I had to inquire about him directly. I was directed to a tall, lanky young man who was taking a turn about the gardens. Mr. Gower was about twenty summers, very tall, very thin, with a crop of bright red hair. He had freckles all over his face and throat and the bony wrists that protruded from his gloves. He had a serious expression, but when I asked him about Mr. Chapman, he rolled his light blue eyes.

"Dull," he said.

I raised my brows, waiting for him to go on, but he closed his colorless lips. "Dull?" I repeated.

"Deadly. I was his pupil all Michaelmas term and now I've Hilary term to get through. I'm almost dead from yawning."

"Sounds the perfect man for the lad, here." I gestured with my thumb to Bartholomew.

Mr. Gower gave me a look that said he didn't think much of my senses. "Not what I'd wish on my nephew. Chapman passes up the most interesting cases and sticks

with what's safe and only needs two words to the judge to get a conviction. No style, no verve. But alas, one has to put up with it if one wants to become a barrister. *Someone* in my family must make a living."

"Mr. Chapman is married, I believe," I remarked. "Perhaps that makes him wish to choose cases that are safe."

Mr. Gower snorted. "You'd never think he was married. He never talks about his wife, never goes home. Just has me sifting through dull books all night. I hear she is a damned pretty woman. I'll not feel sorry for her, though, always being alone at home. It would be duller for her if he was there."

I found it interesting that Chapman seemed not to have told his pupil of his wife's death, of his journey to Bow Street to identify her. Doubtless Mr. Gower would be disheartened to learn he'd missed the only bit of excitement in Chapman's chambers all term.

"Do you dine with him?" I asked carefully.

"Every day in the hall." The lad gestured toward the square brick edifice behind us. "I sit with the students, of course. We debate a case most days. Thank God he doesn't choose them. He dines with the other barristers, but not the silks. Not that he don't want to." Mr. Gower winked.

A silk, as I understood it, denoted a King's Counsel member, a senior barrister—a most distinguished achievement.

"Did he dine Monday?" When young Gower looked a question, I added. "I called, but he was not in his chambers. I wondered if I had chosen a bad time."

"Oh, yes, he was there. Dozing over his pudding as usual. Saving up his waking hours to plague me with his dull books. I say." He brightened. "Would you like to slip away for a tankard? It's early, he won't miss me for awhile."

I resisted the urge to join him. Gower's easy manner was infectious, but I could not keep up the charade over a tall tankard of ale, nor could Bartholomew. I declined, thanking him for his time. He shrugged and departed,

walking away down the lane, back straight, arms swinging, whistling a tune.

I envied him. His young shoulders had borne no hardships; his only grief was nodding off over the pages of the tedious books Chapman assigned him to read.

Bartholomew and I strolled down to the Temple Gardens. The peaceful setting of green and trees was soothing, even in the winter cold. Young men in black gowns walked up and down the stairs, heads down, gowns flapping, like crows scuttling along the green. Older barristers hobbled in their wakes. All moved purposefully to and from the Inns and other buildings, seeming to ignore the gardens laid out for their pleasure.

A set of stairs led down from the gardens to the Thames. The steps to the water had existed since the time that these Inns had been the demesne of the Knights Templar; the stairs had led to barges when the Thames had been the most sensible route for traversing London.

"He couldn't have done her in, then," Bartholomew said as soon as we were out of earshot of the Temple walks. "If he were sitting at dinner, falling asleep."

"Not necessarily." It was an idyllic setting, with trees and green and the river below. It was here, if Thompson had been correct, that Peaches had met her death, or at least had had her body disposed of.

I walked halfway down the water steps and stared at the gray river flowing obliviously past us. "Middle Temple Hall opens onto the garden. He could easily have come out, met his wife, and gone back. It was nearly dark, and almost everyone in the Temples was dining. No doubt others in the hall nod off as well, and the students spend the time debating and arguing, not watching their elders."

"That's possible, sir," Bartholomew conceded.

"Anything is possible," I said crossly. "That is the trouble. What's more, it is probable. So is Lord Barbury bringing her here after she was killed to throw suspicion on her husband, who was dining so conveniently nearby." I shook my head. "I very much want to speak to someone who saw

Peaches alive that day. We know where she was to have gone, and where she should have gone, but not where she did go."

"'Tis puzzling, sir." Bartholomew dropped his deferential nephew pose and crossed his arms over his chest.

We prowled about then looking for signs that Peaches was killed here, although Thompson had told me the Bow Street foot patrol had searched the area, under Pomeroy's supervision. We found no stones with blood on them, nor did the murderer conveniently leave behind a bloody handkerchief with his embroidered initials, or other incriminating articles of clothing. Of course, anything could have been simply dropped into the Thames.

It began to rain again. It had poured rain on Monday, which likely had disguised any sign of violence. Bartholomew and I stayed until we were drenched, then gave up and returned home.

Once in Grimpen Lane, I retreated to my bedroom to change into dry clothes and told Bartholomew to do the same. When I emerged, my landlady, Mrs. Beltan, stood at the door.

"Your friend Mr. Grenville's been," she said. She handed me a folded square of paper. "Been and gone." Her plump mouth pursed. "He's taken Miss Simmons away with him."

CHAPTER 5

I stared at her. Rain still pattered outside, and the hall was cold and clammy. "Taken her where?" I asked, astonished.

"I couldn't say, sir. But she had her best bonnet on her head and a bundle under her arm. He fair dragged her away. He looked that angry."

I digested this. Grenville had seemed fascinated by Marianne from the day he'd met her, an interest he'd never denied. He'd given her a good handful of money, though it seemed to disappear with nothing to show for it. I wondered what she'd said or done to anger him, and where on earth he'd taken her.

"I will speak to him," I told Mrs. Beltan, who seemed to wait for an explanation. "If it's a question of the rent—"

"It's been paid to the end of the quarter. Your Mr. Grenville gave me a large note for it."

For that I could only wonder. I had known Grenville for a year or more now, but I could neither understand nor explain his actions.

The piece of paper he'd left instructed me to present myself at number 21, Curzon Street at four o'clock today. It was just going on twelve. I told the worried Mrs. Beltan I would look into the matter, fetched Bartholomew, and set off on my next errand.

I did not seriously think Marianne was in any danger from Grenville, but I had no idea where he would have taken her. Certainly not to his own house; at least, I did not believe so. A few lads in Russel Street told me they'd seen Grenville's carriage, but they told me nothing more helpful than it had gone toward Covent Garden and King Street.

I let it go. I doubted Grenville would appreciate me prying, and I was not quite certain who I was more worried for, Marianne or Grenville. However, I told Bartholomew to return to Mayfair and make sure all was well, then I took a hackney through the City to have a look at the infamous Glass House.

I rode in the rain through Fleet Street to Ludgate Hill, St. Paul's to Cheapside, Cornhill to Leadenhall Street. St. Charles Row proved to be just off Aldgate High Street, east of Houndsditch. The street looked respectable, if rundown. These houses, I surmised, accommodated the lesser clerks and bankers of the City not far away. None looked as though they would hold a fashionable hell.

Despite the chill, peddlers strolled up and down. Some carried boxes strapped about their necks from which they sold an assorted jumble of things, some toted baskets that held jeweled colors of fruit, some pushed carts that carried fragrant hot chestnuts. A knife grinder wandered about, calling his trade.

These peddlers, like most Londoners, dealt with the weather with a stoicism I admired. I had spent twenty years in warmer climes. In India, the hot ball of sun had blazed down upon us most of the time, and in Spain and Portugal, the summers had been roasting hot. I had often toyed with the idea of retiring to Spain when the war

ended, living in a sunny room over some quiet plaza. But circumstance had brought me back to London to shiver in the rain. My agreement with Colonel Brandon had forced me to give up many of my dreams.

The door of number 12, St. Charles Row looked no different from the doors of numbers 11 and 13. It had been painted dark green, but scratches here and there revealed that the original paint had been black. The knocker was tarnished and less than clean. Indeed, number 12, St. Charles Row did not seem a particularly prosperous address.

I lifted the knocker and listened to the hollow sound within. Almost immediately, the door was wrenched open, and a man peered out. He was not very tall, but stood straight and had a sharp nose and belligerent brown eyes. He said nothing. I held out my card.

He glanced at it once, but did not reach for it. "You were not invited," he said.

I remained standing with my card thrust at him a moment, then I unbent my arm and tucked the card back into my pocket.

"I took a chance," I said. "Mr. Grenville and I were curious."

For once, the magic name of Grenville made no difference.

"You were not invited," the man repeated, and slammed the door in my face. My hair stirred with the draft.

Knocking again produced no result. I turned away, more curious about the Glass House than ever.

"SHALL I lay out the black coat, sir?" Bartholomew asked me later that afternoon.

"Since it is the only one," I answered dryly, "I suppose you should."

Bartholomew took no notice of my sarcasm. He solemnly brought out my black frock coat, a fine thing that Grenville had persuaded me to purchase the previous year, and proceeded to brush it with an air of haughty concen-

tration. I had brushed it the day before, but forbore to say
so.

Bartholomew helped me into the coat, then proceeded
to flick it all over with another brush. He'd polished my
boots until they were supple and shiny, and had scraped
every bit of mud from the soles. I do not know why he
bothered, I would simply tramp through the mud in them
again.

As he worked, Bartholomew told me that Grenville had
not taken Marianne to his house, but his master had been
cross and touchy, and Bartholomew had not dared to ask
any questions. I thanked him and told him to take a brief
holiday that afternoon while I went to Inglethorpe's.

Another hackney got me to Curzon Street in Mayfair at
a few minutes past four.

Inglethorpe's door was much different than the one that
had nearly banged my nose in St. Charles Row. Its brass
knocker was bright and polished, the black-painted door
clean and free of scratches.

At the far end of this street, at number 45, lived James
Denis. During my last adventure, he'd given me information that I needed, and told me he'd expect me to attend
him whenever he whistled. I had retorted predictably. I had
heard nothing but silence from him since then.

Inglethorpe's door was opened by a tall, spindly footman with a blank expression. I handed him my card and
did not explain my errand. He looked at the card, ushered
me inside, and placed me in a small reception room.

All very correct. Mayfair reception rooms were designed to make the caller feel uncomfortable and wish to
depart as soon as possible. The furniture consisted of a
bench-like settee with gilded claw feet and one chair
whose cushion had been polished by a host of backsides. I
chose to stand and peer through lace curtains to the street.

After about a quarter of an hour, the footman reap-
peared and quietly bade me to follow him. He took me upstairs to the first floor and led me into a drawing room that
was rather crowded. The high ceiling was plastered with

white vines, and two chandeliers hung from plaster medallions, one in the rear of the room and one in the front.

Simon Inglethorpe came forward to greet me. He was middle-aged with black hair going to gray. His posture was straight, his shoulders back, but his abdomen was running to fat. Light blue eyes assessed me from under thick brows. "Captain Lacey." He shook my hand. "Sit down, please. We will begin momentarily."

I had already recognized, in a vague way, several gentlemen in the room from the clubs and social gatherings to which Grenville had taken me. But I definitely recognized the only two ladies present.

One was Lady Breckenridge. She was perched on an ivory-colored settee on one side of the long room, a cap of white lace making a fine contrast to her dark hair. Across from her, in a Louis XV chair, looking both eager and nervous, was a lady called Mrs. Danbury.

I had met Catherine Danbury several times before. She was a lovely, golden-haired widow and the niece of Sir Gideon Derwent. The kindly and unworldly Derwent family had befriended me last summer, professing to enjoy my tales of the Peninsular War. They had issued me a standing invitation to dine with them once a fortnight and regale them with such tales. Mrs. Danbury was not always present at these dinners, but I always looked forward to the occasions when she was. She was wiser than her innocent cousins, knowing a little more of life and the world than they, but she, too, was kind and friendly, with a refreshing air about her.

She smiled but was clearly surprised to see me. I gave her a polite nod in response, puzzled myself by her appearance here.

The only vacant seat was on the settee next to Lady Breckenridge. I bowed politely to her and sat down. She barely inclined her head, but a smile lifted the corners of her mouth.

Hands resting on my walking stick, I looked about the room. The gentlemen were Mayfair fodder, wealthy men

ranging in ages from twenty to sixty. They did not seem in
a hurry to speak, and neither did the ladies. Silence, it
seemed, was called for.

Inglethorpe returned to the room after conferring with
someone in the stairwell. He looked at each of us, and
beamed a smile. "Welcome, my friends. Now that we are
assembled, we will begin."

A liveried footman entered the room bearing a large silver tray. He set the tray and its contents on a table and departed.

I eyed the tray with growing curiosity. Three leather
bags lay there, blown up like water skins and fastened by
a stiff string. Inglethorpe lifted one and grinned. "Courtesy
of the Royal Society," he said. "I believe we shall have
ladies first."

He handed the skin to Catherine Danbury. She examined it as curiously as I did. Inglethorpe reached down and
carefully untied the string. "Hold it to your nose and
mouth," he instructed. She did so. He lifted the bag from
the bottom, then squeezed it gently. Mrs. Danbury jerked
back, murmuring a startled, "Oh!"

I started to her rescue, but Lady Breckenridge placed a
firm hand on my wrist.

Mrs. Danbury pressed a handkerchief to her mouth, and
sat back, blinking. Then a childlike smile spread itself
across her face. "My goodness," she said, and she laughed.

I relaxed. Inglethorpe turned to Lady Breckenridge and
offered the bag to her. She loosened the mouth of it and put
it to her nose, inhaling and squeezing the bag in a practiced
way.

Mrs. Danbury continued to titter, as though she could
not stop herself. Inglethorpe, grin wide, continued across
the room.

Lady Breckenridge closed her eyes and leaned back,
then opened her eyes again and smiled beatifically at me.
"Excellent for the humors," she said.

Mrs. Danbury found this incredibly amusing. The bag
passed to the gentlemen then, but emptied before it got to

me. Inglethorpe handed me the second bag and loosened the string for me. I lifted it to my nose and tried to duplicate what I'd seen the others do. A waft of air was forced into my nostrils, but it smelled in no way unpleasant, or, indeed, any different from the air in the rest of the room. I wondered if Inglethorpe was making fools of us.

As I passed the bag on, however, my lips and tongue began to tingle. It was a curious sensation. I touched my tongue to my lower lip and resisted the urge to tug it. Lady Breckenridge laughed quietly at me.

I turned from her and my injured knee collided with the gilded edge of the settee. I felt no pain. For a moment, the fact did not connect in my head, and then, in pure astonishment, I stared down at my leg.

I felt no pain. All day long my knee had throbbed in the damp, and now, it seemed just as it had been before I'd hurt it. For two years after the original injury, which had nearly shattered the bones, my knee and lower thigh had hurt continuously, some days more than others. Always the leg was stiff; every morning I had to walk about to loosen it up. If I used it too much during a day, I woke aching and cursing in the night. And now, I felt no pain.

Amazed, I stood, staring at the limb. Mrs. Danbury pressed her handkerchief to her mouth and laughed at me, her eyes shining. I grinned back at her.

"Do you like it, Captain?" Inglethorpe asked. He passed the second bag to Lady Breckenridge and picked up the third.

"Certainly," I answered.

I paced back and forth. I glanced at my walking stick, which I had left leaning against the settee. My bad leg moved where I wanted it to go without protest. I turned in a circle, resting my weight on my left leg. Nary a twinge. I laughed.

Inglethorpe handed the third bag to me. I took it and inhaled gladly, taking a long breath. I wondered what the concoction was. Grenville had called it a "magic" gas. But I felt awake and alert and rested. Brandy and gin left one

feeling heavy and sleepy, opium gave a false euphoria and a weightiness in the limbs, but this made me feel fine and fit. I wanted to leap about the room, and to my alarm, I found myself nearly starting to do so.

"Dance for us, Captain," Lady Breckenridge said. "Do, please."

Several of the gentlemen laughed. The others leaned back, idiotic grins on their faces. Inglethorpe, the only one who had not partaken, watched us all indulgently.

I crossed the carpet and held out my hand. "Do you waltz, Mrs. Danbury?"

She gazed at me in astonishment, and through the strange clarity I felt a twinge of embarrassment. Then she smiled, put her hand in mine, and rose to meet me.

I waltzed Mrs. Danbury up and down the long room and around Lady Breckenridge's settee to the windows. Lady Breckenridge turned to watch us.

I had learned to waltz in Spain, when the fashion first took. I had waltzed with Louisa, under her husband's glowering eye, and with the wives of other officers. My injury had, of course, put an end to this entertainment.

Never had I danced with a woman who simply wanted to dance with me. No pity for the lonely officer who had no wife to escort. No duty in attending the wives of superior officers. Just dancing for the pure joy of it.

Mrs. Danbury matched her steps to mine and rested her hand on my shoulder. I grasped her about the waist, my fingers fitting to the slim curve of her body.

I had not felt so well in a long, long while. I realized I wanted to kiss her. I wanted to lean down and touch her pale lips, to feel them open beneath mine.

She must have sensed my wish, for she whispered, "Everybody is watching."

I gave her a reassuring look and lowered my eyelid in a wink. I certainly would not cause a scandal, I tried to convey. She could trust me to be a gentleman.

Her smile broadened. We danced some more, moving

back down the room. I felt light on my feet and light in heart.

I lost track of time. I'd come here because Peaches and Lord Barbury had. I had planned to question Inglethorpe about Peaches, about who she talked to, what she and Lord Barbury did here, and whether she had come here Monday, either alone or with someone other than Lord Barbury. Inglethorpe had begun this entertainment at four o'clock; soon after four on Monday, Peaches had met her end.

Instead, I danced. Mrs. Danbury and I went around and around the room. She stared up at me, seemingly happy to be dancing with me. It had been so long since a lady had looked at me in such delight that I could not bear to break the spell.

The window darkened. Several of the gentlemen departed. Inglethorpe disappeared. Mrs. Danbury danced into me, a luxurious crush of female body. I at last let her sit down, out of breath, and I sat on a stool before her and looked at her in a way I had no business to.

She did not seem to mind. Her color was high, and her eyes sparkled. It was not like being drunk. I felt refreshed and aware and at last free of pain. Whatever the concoction was, I liked it.

A heavy wave of French perfume loomed over my right shoulder and Lady Breckenridge said into my ear, "If you want to know about Lord Barbury, Captain, you have only to ask me."

I looked up at her in astonishment. As usual, her dark blue eyes were enigmatic but held a knowing look.

She left the room without further word. The footman escorted her to the stairs before the door closed. She wanted me to rush after her. She wanted me to wonder what she meant and not rest until I found out.

Devil take the woman, that is exactly what I did. I rose hastily, made some excuse to the bewildered Mrs. Danbury, and hurried from the room.

Inglethorpe was on the landing. I hastened past him and down the stairs, barely acknowledging him. "Come again,

Captain," his congenial voice floated after me. "Perhaps next time you will persuade Mr. Grenville to accompany you."

I did not answer. I reached the ground floor hall, snatched my coat and hat from the footman, and plunged outside. The street had darkened and rain made it darker still. I did not see Lady Breckenridge at first, and balled my hands in frustration. Then another carriage moved out of the way and I spied her across the street, waiting near a closed landau. A footman, straight and prim, stood a few paces behind her.

She'd donned a jacket and hat, and she smiled at me as I made my way to her, her eyes glittering. "Shall you ride with me, Captain?"

I looked at the landau, rain streaking the black paint and leather top. An unrelated lady and gentleman riding in a closed carriage could be scandalous, although widowed women of the upper classes had some immunity. The rain decided it for me, as well as the fact that I'd made a fool of myself in Inglethorpe's sitting room and come away with no information.

I accepted.

CHAPTER 6

THE footman assisted his mistress inside first, then me. I found myself in a conveyance as opulent as Grenville's. The walls were fine parquetry, the upholstery, velvet. Boxes of coals warmed the air, and coach lanterns with candles lent a golden glow to the gloom of the darkening evening.

I sat down facing Lady Breckenridge, and the landau started with a jerk.

Her dark blue jacket was unbuttoned. Beneath it she wore a gown of light yellow and ivory stripes, cut modestly across the shoulders. It was made of finely woven cashmere, heavy against the chill of January, but silken enough to flow easily over her legs. Her dark hair was coiled in a heavy braid at the base of her neck, ringlets peeking from beneath the cap.

"Did you enjoy Mr. Inglethorpe's little entertainment?" she asked me.

I was still a bit breathless from all of it. "What was it? The concoction, I mean?"

She lifted her shoulders in a shrug. "Who knows? I am not a scientist. But you did not come for the magic air. You came to learn about Lord Barbury."

"I do not recall telling anyone so."

She gave me her usual stare. She was an intelligent woman, and no doubt had seen Grenville and I pull Lord Barbury aside at the soiree.

"I know that Mrs. Chapman was killed, and that poor Barbury is beside himself," she said. I must have looked astonished, because she smiled. "Servants gossip, Captain. They love to talk about us. My maid is always ready with the latest tidbit about my neighbors."

I should not have been surprised. Bartholomew was part of a vast network of Mayfair servants who gathered information better than any exploring officer ever did for Wellesley. He had connections below stairs in every house from Oxford Street to Piccadilly.

In addition, the newspapers this morning had printed an account of Mrs. Chapman's death, with a lurid description of the wound to her head and her sodden corpse, which they had probably gotten from the waterman who'd dragged her from the river in the first place. Her husband was mentioned, the hard-working barrister—was he a murderer? I imagined his pupil Mr. Gower had at last found something not dull about the man. Lord Barbury's name had not appeared.

"Barbury doted on the woman," Lady Breckenridge went on. "More than he should have, in my opinion. She was charming to him, but she was only an actress and not a very good one at that."

"Did you know her well?"

She gave me a disdainful look. "Hardly. She married above her station and had Lord Barbury quite on a string. At least Barbury had the sense not to marry her."

I wondered why Chapman *had* married her, and how she had persuaded him to do so. Peaches had been a lovely young woman; she might easily have convinced someone like me to take her to wife, someone with nothing to lose—

but a barrister who hoped one day to take silk? Lady Breckenridge and Thompson were correct; most actresses were considered to be common, and not respectable enough for marriage. It did happen, however, from time to time, and perhaps Peaches had made him believe she'd be a model wife.

"Did they go to Inglethorpe's often?" I asked. I assumed Lady Breckenridge had been there before. She had seemed familiar with the gas and how to take it. Mrs. Danbury, on the other hand, had not. She, like me, had been a novice.

"Good heavens, yes," Lady Breckenridge replied. "Anything novel or exciting, Peaches could not rest until she'd tried it. I believe she was not quite right in the head, if you ask me. She was always badgering Barbury to let her do things that were risky and dangerous. If he denied her, she would pout and fuss until he promised she could do as she pleased. Curricle races to Brighton, bloody fool things like that."

The information made me wonder how Peaches had fared with Mr. Chapman, a man described by his pupil as deadly dull. For a young lady who craved excitement, living with Chapman must have been misery. Of course, if Mr. Gower were correct, Peaches rarely saw her husband. She would have had plenty of opportunity for excitement without him.

I had been a bit wild and reckless, and frankly, stupid, in my youth, but I had always been able to stop when necessary and attend my duties. Some people could not, always had to have something interesting or, as Lady Breckenridge indicated, dangerous, in their lives, perhaps to remind themselves that they were alive. Their humors were unbalanced, I believed, as mine were toward melancholia, and they could not help themselves. I wondered if Peaches had been that sort of person.

"What is your interest, Captain?" Lady Breckenridge asked, her eyes bright. "You could not have been Mrs. Chapman's lover; she liked only men of wealth."

I let the insult pass, because it was the truth, even if rudely put.

I thought again of Peaches lying on the shore of the Thames, small, pretty, alone. She'd sought danger, and danger had found her. "She did not deserve what was done to her," I answered. "She was too young for that. Young and a bit helpless."

Lady Breckenridge snorted. "From what I knew of her, Captain, she was never helpless."

"She was certainly helpless against whoever killed her."

Lady Breckenridge lost her smile. "Perhaps."

"Did you attend the gathering at Inglethorpe's on Monday?" I asked.

"I did." She turned from the window, her features composed. "If you are going to ask me whether Peaches was there as well, the answer is yes, she was."

"With Lord Barbury?"

"Not in the least. She arrived alone and went away alone."

"Do you remember what time she left?"

"Not much past four. She seemed in a hurry."

So she must have gone straight from there to meet her killer. "Did she leave by hackney or private coach?"

"I am afraid I did not notice. I was not much interested in Mrs. Chapman. I was just pleased she'd departed."

"A bit early."

She shrugged. "She had her take of the gas, and off she went."

"Do Inglethorpe's gatherings always begin at four? No earlier?"

"Always. A man of regular habits, is Mr. Inglethorpe."

Regular habits and unnatural appetites, if he had tried to proposition Grenville. I wondered if Inglethorpe himself had played a part in Mrs. Chapman's death. She was a woman who liked danger, and he had provided it for her in the form of his magical gas.

We had been rolling through Mayfair as I asked ques-

tions and pondered her answers. I said now, "Your coachman can let me down anywhere. I did not mean to take advantage of you."

"Nonsense," she said, adjusting her jacket. "There is a
nasty rain. I will take you where you like."

"Grenville's then," I said. "In Grosvenor Street. It is
not far."

Lady Breckenridge tapped on the roof and gave the direction to her coachman. We rode the remainder of the
way in silence, she watching me with frank curiosity. We
did not exchange the small pleasantries that I might with
another woman, such as Mrs. Danbury. Lady Breckenridge had made it known the first time we'd met what she
thought of small pleasantries.

She did not speak until the landau was drawing to a
halt before Grenville's house. "I have a box at Covent
Garden," she said. "Quite a fine one."

I had no answer for that. She drew a silver card case
from her reticule, extracting a cream-colored card. "Giving this to a footman at the theatre door will allow you up
to it, any time you please."

I looked at the card resting between her slim, gloved
fingers. "I do not go much to the theatre," I said.

"But you might," she answered. "And you might want
to ask me another time about a murder."

She smiled, but the lines about her eyes were tense. I
realized, with a dart of surprise, that if I refused to take the
card, I would hurt her feelings.

I reached for it, glanced once at the name inscribed on
it, and tucked it into my pocket. Her expression did not
change.

I bade her good night and descended before Grenville's
plain-faced mansion. As the landau rolled away, I saw
Lady Breckenridge looking out of its window at me. She
caught my eye, looked languidly away, and the landau
moved on.

*   *   *

GRENVILLE was home, in his dressing room. Matthias let me in, but neither Grenville nor his man Gautier offered greeting while they went through the very important process of tying Grenville's cravat.

Matthias brought me a glass of brandy, and I seated myself and waited. Grenville's toilette was always elaborate and could take an hour or more if he were preparing for a sufficiently important occasion.

As I sipped the brandy, I felt strangely chilled. I rubbed my hands over my arms, and took another drink of brandy, feeling the beginnings of nausea. Another thing I felt was pain in my knee. The concoction was wearing off, and my leg began to throb with a vengeance. I gritted my teeth, drank deeply of brandy.

When Grenville finished, I rose to leave with him, and realized the height of my folly—I had left my walking stick behind at Inglethorpe's.

Matthias offered to run and fetch it for me. Grenville forestalled him, somewhat crossly, and bade him fetch one of his own. I accepted with neither protest nor thanks, uncertain of Grenville's mood.

Not until we were seated in his opulent coach, and we were alone, did I open a subject I sensed he did not want to discuss. "What have you done with Marianne?"

"She is well," he snapped. He flushed. "I have a house in Clarges Street. She is reclining there in the lap of luxury with plenty of sweetmeats to eat."

"She must be pleased," I said.

He gave me a rueful look. "Not really. She let me know what she thought of my high-handedness. But dear God, Lacey." His expression became troubled. "I found her in your rooms, eating the leavings of your breakfast."

"I told her she might have the last of the bread."

His cravat pin flashed as he turned his head. "She was shaking with hunger. If you had seen her . . . She was furious that I'd caught her eating like a starved mongrel. I cannot understand it. I've tried to help her, and yet, my charity seems to do no good."

"Marianne takes only what help she likes and disdains the rest," I said. "That is why I leave my door unlocked. She pretends to put one over on me."

He sighed. "Why the devil does she accept your charity and not mine?"

I shrugged, having no idea. "She has her own code of right and wrong."

"You are good to her, and good to worry about her. I have put her in a house where she might eat well and rest for a time, and she looked bloody indignant about it."

"It's rather like caging a feral dog," I suggested. "Taking care of it might be best for it, but it still bites."

He arched his brows. "Very apt. May we change the subject?"

I acquiesced, and he looked relieved. Grenville's motives were good, but I believed he'd met his match in Marianne. She liked luxury and money, but she also valued her freedom. I wondered how long she'd trade one for the other.

For the rest of the drive to Whitechapel, I told Grenville about Inglethorpe's gathering—who I had seen and what I had observed and what Lady Breckenridge had related to me about Peaches and Lord Barbury. I omitted that I had capered about with Mrs. Danbury like a fool.

I asked him about the gentlemen I had recognized there, and we discussed them until we reached the Glass House, although he could not tell me much. He knew them from his clubs, but not much deeper than that, though he agreed it was worth investigating whether they'd known Peaches and where they'd been when she'd died.

Rain still beat down as we drew up in St. Charles Row. The sun had long since descended, and early winter darkness had swallowed the street. We waited in the warm, dry carriage while Matthias hopped down and rapped on the door. The same man I had seen before peered out, but this time, the reception was different. Matthias told him something, and the door was opened, wide and inviting.

Grenville descended, and I followed more slowly. The

concoction had definitely worn off, leaving me slow and sore and more fatigued than before.

As I entered the house behind Grenville, the doorman gave me a measuring look. I pretended to ignore him, and stripped off my greatcoat and hat. Matthias took charge of them, not the doorman, who only watched in silence.

The front hall was paneled in dark walnut made darker still in the gloomy evening. A few candles in tarnished sconces lit the hall with a feeble light. The doorman led us up a staircase that twisted round on itself and led to a wide hall containing a large double door.

I heard laughter and voices from behind the door, talking, querying, pontificating, just as I would hear in any club or tavern. The doorman pushed the doors open, ushering us inside, and at last I understood why the ordinary-looking building was called the Glass House.

We stood in a well-furnished, softly carpeted room as dark as the hall below. The paneled walls were lined with drapes, brown velvet and heavy. One curtain stood open to reveal a window, but it looked into another room, not outside. The room behind it was dark, the glass reflecting the light of the front room. I assumed that the other curtains hid windows; the room was surrounded on three sides by them.

Men lounged on Turkish couches and chairs, legs folded or outstretched, talking, smoking, passing snuff boxes back and forth. Tables occupied one half of the room where the usual games of whist and piquet were played for high stakes.

A smattering of women roamed the crowd in silk gowns and carefully dressed hair. They were, to a body, beautiful of figure. They wore their expensive gowns with grace, and their jewels had been chosen with taste. They were nothing like the painted women of Covent Garden, or even actresses like Marianne. They were courtesans of the highest order, experienced, well bred, beautiful.

A few of the gentlemen looked familiar to me, including an infantry officer, but I did not really know them.

Several recognized Grenville. He glided among them languidly, fully in his man-of-fashion persona.

I did not see Lord Barbury among the card players. Perhaps he truly was beside himself with grief, as both Grenville and Lady Breckenridge had indicated, and stayed home.

As I looked about, I wondered why this house had such a reputation. I saw nothing that I would not see in any gaming hell in St. James's, although perhaps the ladies enticing gentlemen to play cards and dice were a bit cleaner. Gentlemen brought their mistresses to hells; the mistresses gambled just as avidly as the gentlemen.

"It seems rather ordinary to me," I remarked in a low voice. "Why would Peaches want to come here?"

"If she did like to come here, it does not say much for her character," Grenville said darkly. "Come, I will show you."

I followed Grenville to the first heavy curtain, which stood just behind the card players, who took no notice of us. Grenville took hold of the velvet drape and raised it enough so that we could peer behind it. A window looked into a small lighted room, cluttered with chairs and sofas and tables arranged in no pattern I could discern. Other than the furniture, it was empty.

"Nothing there," Grenville confirmed, and moved to the next window.

Behind that curtain we found gentlemen gathered around a hazard table while a lady dressed only in a corset, a knee-length skirt, and riding boots retrieved the thrown dice and handed them back to the caster. Her face dripped perspiration, and the muscles of her shoulders bunched as she reached for the dice.

Grenville dropped that curtain. "There is also a room for faro," he remarked, "and other more chancy games."

"So it is a gaming hell."

"Somewhat." Grenville raised the next curtain. "They also have opium, if you like, and of course, this."

He gestured to the window. The room beyond was

small, and only a chaise longue and a chair reposed in it. A lady lounged in a bored manner on the chaise, an open book on her lap. She wore a wig of bright red curls, and had a pointed but pretty face. "You choose your vice behind the glass," Grenville said, "then give the house master your bid. You may buy only one vice per night, so choose well."

I digested this. "Why not simply go to the usual gaming rooms? You can find hazard and willing ladies there."

"Not ladies such as these," Grenville said, indicating the reclining woman. "They are the courtesans who enticed Napoleon and the king of Prussia and the Austrian emperor. They are the highest of the high."

"And Peaches was a second-rate actress," I mused. "Why should she want to come here with such ladies present? Why should she want Lord Barbury here?"

Grenville shrugged. "Barbury told me that the proprietor provided them a private room. They never came down to the windowed room. And it is certainly a house her husband could never enter."

"Hmm," I answered, not satisfied. Surely Lord Barbury could have found a better place in which to meet his ladybird. But then, Peaches had craved excitement. Perhaps she'd not been satisfied with an ordinary nest. "It is too sordid for me," I remarked. If I had a pretty young lady with whom I kept company, I would prefer a cozy, private place, not a room in this rather seedy hell.

"The Glass House is a novelty," Grenville replied. "It will wane, as all novelties do. For now, it is a place to be seen. Because I have come tonight, they will no doubt experience a resurgence of popularity."

He spoke in a matter-of-fact voice, without a trace of pomposity. But he was correct. Any place Grenville visited instantly became the height of fashion.

He lifted the drape of the next window to find the blank back of another drape behind it. He released that curtain at once. When I looked a question, he said, "When a room has been taken by a patron, the curtains inside may be

closed. Or left open, as the buyer dictates. Some like to be watched."

I frowned my distaste. We moved down the walls and looked into other rooms. Grenville was correct, every vice was available. Some of the things I saw fueled my growing rage. I would be certain to mention this house to a reformer I knew; that is, if I did not begin breaking the windows myself.

"Have you found something to your liking, gentlemen?"

I turned. A small, plump man with a sharp nose and round brown eyes looked up at us, a salesman's smile on his face. His nose bore a scar from a long-gone boil, but his suit was fine and well tailored. Grenville regarded him with a look I'd come to recognize as true disdain. Grenville sometimes feigned the look for the benefit of his audience, but I sensed he genuinely disliked this man, whoever he was.

The man's dark eyes glittered with a cold light, even as he fawned. "My name is Kensington. Emile Kensington." He held out a hand.

I gave him my name and shook his hand. His palm was warm and dry, though his handshake was limp. "Room number five is quite intriguing," he went on.

I expected Grenville to say something, to go along with our pretense. Instead, Grenville stared at the man with cold annoyance. He was angry, as angry as I was, but I needed to keep to my purpose.

"I am interested in a woman called Peaches," I said.

The man jumped. I thought I saw his feet leave the ground. He pondered his answer for a moment, then fixed on a simple truth. "She is not here."

"I know that," I said. "She died two days ago."

The man's mouth dropped open. For a moment, pure astonishment crossed his features, then his glittering stare returned. "Died?"

"Found in the river," I said shortly. "She came here often, I am told. Was she here on Monday?"

His eyes narrowed, and he looked me over again. "Who are you, a Runner?"

"An acquaintance of Lord Barbury. He is, as you can imagine, deeply distressed."

I watched the thoughts dance behind his eyes. A woman who came here regularly, dead. Her lover, a powerful man. Trouble for the Glass House?

"I am sad to hear of his loss," Kensington said.

"Indeed," I said, not able to keep the chill from my voice. "Had she come here Monday?"

"I don't think so. I don't remember." He said the words in a rush.

"But she did used to come here?" Grenville put in. "I believe you provided her a private room?"

Kensington looked back and forth between us, wet his lips. "There was no harm in it. She wanted somewhere to meet Lord Barbury, safe from her husband."

"And they paid you well for it, I'd wager," I said.

He looked slightly offended. "Not at all. Peaches and I are old acquaintances. I knew her when she was a girl, just come to London to make her fortune. She wanted to bring Lord Barbury here, I was willing to oblige. They enjoyed it."

I wondered about that very much. If the house had been Peaches' choice, because she knew this Kensington, why had Barbury gone along with it?

Kensington's gaze shifted again, as though he'd argued with himself and at last reached a conclusion. "Ah, I remember now, gentlemen. Peaches did come here Monday. In the afternoon."

His memory was very convenient, I thought cynically. "Are you certain?"

"Yes. I had forgotten, what with one thing and another. She must have been at the laughing gas again, because she was in high spirits."

"What time was that?"

He thought. "Around four or so, I believe."

He was a little off; Lady Breckenridge put Peaches

leaving Inglethorpe's shortly after four, and she could not have reached here for another half hour.

"When did she leave?" I asked.

He shrugged. "As to that, I have no idea. I did not see her go. Never saw her again after she went up to the room."

"Which I would like to see," I said.

Kensington looked distressed. "No one goes above this floor, sir."

"Except Lord Barbury, and Peaches, and you," I answered, my voice hard. "And now I will."

Kensington opened his mouth to protest further, then closed it. I must have looked quite angry, and although Grenville's walking stick had no sword in it, it was made of ebony, hard and strong. Kensington could always call for the ruffians that every hell employed to keep order, but not before I could swing the stick.

Finally, he shrugged, produced a key, and led us to a narrow door behind one of the curtains.

That door led to a dark hall and a narrow flight of stairs. At the top of these stairs was another dark landing. Kensington unlocked a door, lifted a taper from one of the sconces on the landing, and ushered us into a cold bedchamber.

The neat plainness of this room contrasted sharply with the tawdry finery on the floor below. It held a bed hung with yellow brocade draperies, a dressing table, and two comfortable-looking chairs. It was dark now, and fireless, but I imagined it could be cheerful. Here, if Kensington spoke the truth, Peaches and Lord Barbury had carried on their liaison.

There was little personal about the room. I moved to the dressing table and began opening the drawers. Kensington looked a bit distressed, but he made no move to stop me.

As expected, I found nothing. Kensington would have had ample time to remove anything from this room he wanted no one else to see. Grenville looked over my

shoulder as I pulled from the dressing table a silver hair-brush, a handful of silk ribbon, and a reticule. I opened the reticule hopefully, but found little of interest. It contained a vinaigrette similar to the one Louisa Brandon carried, which a lady would open and apply to her nose when she felt faint, as well as a bit of lace, a comb, a tiny bottle of perfume.

Grenville lifted the bottle and worked the stopper open. The odor of sweet musk bathed my nostrils. "Expensive," he pronounced, then returned the stopper to the bottle. "A gift from Barbury?"

"Probably." I returned everything to the reticule.

We found nothing more in the drawers. Kensington stood just inside the doorway, watching us, looking more curious than alarmed.

"Why did she come here Monday?" I asked him as Grenville closed the dressing table.

Kensington shrugged. "Why shouldn't she? She was probably meeting her lordship."

"She'd made an appointment to meet him much later that night," I said. "Yet you say she was here after four in the afternoon. Why should she have come?"

Kensington hesitated. I watched him choose his words. "Captain, as I told you, I've known Peaches a very long time. She was a young woman who found life tedious, and it was no joy for her being married to a plodding husband like Chapman. She did not like to go home, and I sympathized. She'd retreat here when her husband grew too dull for her, and I was happy to let her. I believe she had told her husband some rigmarole about visiting a friend in the country, in any case, so she would not be expected at home. She had done such a thing before."

"Did she meet anyone else here that afternoon?" I asked pointedly. "Someone not Lord Barbury?"

"Now, as to that, I do not know. I told you, I saw her, but I did not see her after she came up here, and she was quite alone then. And I have no idea when she departed. You may, of course, ask the footman who opens the door."

I certainly would ask him.

"Now, gentlemen." Kensington rubbed his hands together. "I have been very good natured, letting you rummage through my rooms and ask about my friends. But this is a house of business."

Grenville gave him a look of undisguised disgust. He opened his mouth to denounce him, to tell him we would not stay another minute. I forestalled him with a look. Another woman of the house might have seen Peaches that day, might know who she had met. Peaches had died here, or very soon after leaving here, and I wanted to speak to anyone who had seen her.

"Please," I said. "Choose a room for us."

Kensington smiled. It was not a nice smile. "I have just the thing, Captain. Allow me to prepare." He gave a little bow, and glided away, leaving the door open behind him.

Once we'd heard him descend, Grenville turned to me. "Why on earth did you tell him that? I'd have thought you'd want nothing more to do with this place."

I explained, but he looked skeptical. "Such a lady may know nothing or be paid to know nothing."

"Perhaps, but it is worth a try. Now, while we have the chance, shall we see what else this room can tell us?"

"Kensington would not have left us alone if it could," Grenville pointed out, but he turned his hand to the task.

We went over the room again, looking under the bedcovers, through the dressing table, behind curtains, under the bed. I examined the tools at the fireplace, studied the heavy brass grating. I finished my search, empty-handed. The room was neat, well-dusted, impersonal.

I found nothing, and neither did Grenville, but I knew full well that Peaches could very likely have been killed in this room.

We found no evidence that she had been, of course. If she'd been killed here, then whoever had taken her from the room had tidied behind themselves very well. Or perhaps Peaches had gone with her killer willingly, and had

been killed somewhere between here and the Temple Gardens.

Kensington was waiting for us when we descended. He told me that he'd chosen Room Five for me, and he wanted three hundred guineas for the pleasure.

CHAPTER 7

◥◈◤

I felt my ire stir and nearly told Mr. Kensington what I thought of his three hundred guineas. Grenville, on the other hand, coolly handed it over. "I will wait for you," he said.

He returned to the front room, while Kensington remained with me, smiling.

I followed him, wondering what vice he'd decided a man like me would want. We did not return to the main room, but entered the front staircase hall. He produced another key from his pocket and took me to a small door a little way along the balcony that encircled the stairwell. He opened the door, gestured me inside, and closed and locked the door behind him.

We stood in a narrow corridor lined with doors on our left. I realized it ran behind the main room and the small rooms that encircled it. I wondered briefly what the builders brought in to alter the house had thought about the bizarre floor plan.

He took me to a door in the middle of this hall and pro-

duced another key. He had put the key in the lock and turned it, when I heard a cry. A child's cry.

It did not come from the room Kensington had led me to, but from the one next door. I turned to him, my countenance frozen. "Let me in there." I pointed to the blank door to the right.

His pleased smile sealed his fate. "It is taken."

"Nonetheless."

Kensington gave me a patient look. "The bid for that room was considerably higher, and has already been spoken for."

All the rage that had been building inside me since I'd seen pretty Peaches dead on the riverbank suddenly surged and focused on the small man with the oily smile.

I had Kensington against the wall in a trice, with the handle of Grenville's walking stick pressed hard against his throat. My leg was aching and throbbing, berating me for the punishment I'd given it that afternoon. It was likely that Peaches had either met her death here or met her killer here, and I believed Kensington knew that too, if he was not the murderer himself.

Kensington stared at me, eyes round but still holding a deep spark of confidence. "You do not know what you are doing, Captain."

"I believe I do."

He had mistaken me for a weak man. I was not. I pressed the handle of the walking stick harder into his throat, cutting short his air. I could kill him. I saw him realize that.

"If you insist," he said. His voice was still icy, if hoarse.

I eased the walking stick away. He gave me a long look, as though reassessing me, then he shrugged. Clearing his throat, he unlocked and opened the door of the second room.

What I saw within made my previous anger at Kensington seem like nothing. On the other side of the room, near the window, a girl who could have been no more than twelve stood pressed against the wall. Her cheeks and lips

were red with rouge; her hair was dyed a dull yellow. Girls like her prowled the environs of Covent Garden, the younger ones in the shadows of their older colleagues. I always grew angry when I saw them, and angry at the gentlemen who exploited them, thereby teaching them that they could earn money at so early an age. This girl was locked in, unable to leave, lacking even the feeble protection the street girls gave one another.

The infantryman I had seen in the outer room looked up in surprise when I banged in. He was in shirtsleeves and trousers, with his coat and accoutrements scattered about the room. He opened his mouth to protest, then closed it and rapidly backed away when I came at him.

The drapes to this room stood open, and two gentlemen peered in through the window. They enraged me even further. I lifted a chair and threw it at them. The glass in the window broke with a satisfying shatter, the casement splintering.

The infantryman swore. The girl watched silently. Kensington merely looked on, as though resigned to my tantrum. His lack of worry puzzled me, or would have puzzled me had I not been so furious. This place was vile, and knowing that it had played a part in Peaches' death infuriated me.

I grabbed the girl by the arm and dragged her out of there. She came silently, her eyes round with fear, but she did not fight me. Neither did Kensington. He simply watched me with that knowing look and stood aside to let me pass.

I took the girl to the main staircase, down, and out of the house. The doorman tried to stop me, but I slammed the walking stick into his midriff, and he fell away, clutching his stomach.

Outside, the night had turned bitterly cold and was still wet. Matthias blinked when he saw me coming with the wretched girl in tow, but he opened the carriage door and quickly shoveled us in.

Grenville ran from the house and sprang into the car-

riage himself, shouting at his coachman to go. We moved out into the street, and Matthias slammed the door before jumping onto his perch behind.

"Good Lord, Lacey," Grenville said, breathless, then he chortled. "You ought to have seen their faces when that chair came flying through the window. It was most gratifying." He switched his gaze to the girl.

She stared back at him, her kohl-rimmed eyes wide with fear. I wondered what to do with her now that I'd rescued her. I had taken a Covent Garden girl to Louisa Brandon last spring, though Black Nancy had been a few years older than this mite in grown-up clothes. I did not like to continue inflicting Louisa with my rescued strays, though I certainly could not take the girl home with me, nor could Grenville.

Then I remembered that I knew a family who would be both sympathetic to the girl's plight and able and eager to help her. Sir Gideon Derwent was a philanthropist and a reformer, and though I hesitated to impose on him, I could think of no other solution. I asked Grenville to take us to Grosvenor Square, and he gave the direction to his coachman.

"I had a chance to speak to the doorman while you went off on your adventure," Grenville said as the carriage joined a main thoroughfare. "He told me that Peaches did indeed arrive near to four o'clock on Monday. But he never saw her leave."

"He is certain?"

"He said he was at the door all that day. She came in but did not go out."

I sat back, easing my abused leg. "Well, that tells us much, then."

"She went out the back," the girl said.

Both Grenville and I started, swiveling our gazes to her. She was looking back at us with no less fear, but with some curiosity. Her voice was low, with an East End lilt.

"You saw her?" I asked abruptly, unable to gentle my voice.

She nodded, her artificial blonde curls bobbing. "Down the back stairs, through the scullery. Didn't stop to say ta."

"Was she alone?"

The girl looked taken aback at my tone, as though she regretted speaking. I tried to soften my questions. "It is important. Did she leave with someone?"

The girl shook her head. "Not that I saw." She glanced from me to Grenville. "Are you going to arrest her?"

"No." I stopped. "I am afraid she died."

The girl's mouth became a round O. "Peaches died?" She fell silent for a moment. "She was nice to me."

"Did she come often to the Glass House?" I pressed.

The girl shrugged her too-thin shoulders. "Sometimes. She didn't speak to anyone much."

"But she was nice to you."

"Let me stay in her room sometimes. Would tell me stories about when she was on the stage. Asked if I wanted to go on the stage."

"And do you?" Grenville asked. I heard the pity in his voice, though his expression remained neutral.

"Naw. Like as not, I'll marry a bloke."

Not if she were dead from disease or brutality long before she reached marriageable age. Kensington and his Glass House were doomed. If Sir Montague Harris needed evidence of sordid goings on in that house, this girl was it. If we could enlist Sir Gideon Derwent's help, public outcry would defeat the Glass House. Kensington hadn't seemed worried by my interference. He must believe that the guiding power behind the house—likely James Denis—would prevent me from doing harm. I was determined to prove him wrong.

I turned the topic back to Peaches. "Did she ever come to the Glass House with anyone?"

"A lord," the girl answered promptly. "She thought he was handsome. She was in love with him."

"Anyone else?" I prompted.

"No." The girl seemed more relaxed, more childlike

every moment. "Just him. She would go on and on about him."

Peaches and Barbury. Filled with affection for each other. "Did she speak to anyone else regularly? Besides you?"

She shook her head. "Peaches kept herself to herself. She'd natter with Kensington, because she knew him before. But no one else I ever saw."

"After Peaches left on Monday, do you remember seeing Mr. Kensington still there?"

"I think so." Her small brow puckered. "I don't remember."

I was disappointed, but let it go. Kensington could easily have followed Peaches out, killed her. She knew him, he could have gotten behind her, struck out—

"Are you taking me to a magistrate?" the girl asked.

I banished the horrible picture of Peaches falling to the pavement, her head a bloody mess.

"To a friend, who will look after you," I said.

Her fearful look returned. "I don't want to be looked after."

"Yes, you do," Grenville informed her.

Her apprehensive look grew. The girls in Covent Garden had nothing kind to say about the reformers that sometimes scooped them up—cheating them out of a decent day's wages, they said.

What men like Kensington had done to this girl was vile, and her innocent acceptance was still more vile. I knew houses existed all over London where such things went on, and that shutting down one would not eliminate them all. I had also seen girls like her while in the army, daughters of camp followers, or orphaned girls who decided that laying with soldiers was better than starving.

I could not prevent everything. But I could at least help Sir Montague Harris close the Glass House, and perhaps I could spell the end for one very powerful underworld gentleman. The thought buoyed me through my haze of anger and pain.

We reached Grosvenor Square, the most opulent in Mayfair, and stopped before the Derwents' tall house.

The Derwents were surprised to see us but behaved predictably. The entire family turned out to welcome me—Lady Derwent, thin and frail, with a bright smile for me and Grenville; the daughter, Melissa, her usual shyness melting in sympathy for the girl, who at last relayed that her name was Jean; Sir Gideon, robust and righteously angry at my tale. The only one missing was Leland, the son of the household, who was visiting his club with his cronies from school.

Likewise, I did not see Mrs. Danbury, which relieved me. I'd made a great fool of myself at Inglethorpe's and wanted to apologize to her for my behavior, but I was not yet ready to face her.

We left young Jean looking bewildered, surrounded by well-meaning Derwents, and returned to Grosvenor Street. Grenville, as usual, invited me in for brandy, but I declined. I was exhausted, annoyed, in pain, and not in the mood for pleasantries. Tomorrow was the inquest for Peaches, and I wanted to rest.

I took a hackney home. Grenville would have offered his coach, but he'd indicated that he would look in at his club, and I did not want to rob him of his conveyance. He conceded, saw me into the hackney, and said good night. Bartholomew would be awaiting me in Grimpen Lane, with the fire high and my bed aired.

I discovered halfway across London that I had only enough shillings to take me to Haymarket. I descended there and leaned heavily on Grenville's walking stick as I tramped toward home. The air was cold, my breath steaming, the rain like tiny needles on my face. I severely disliked cold. Perhaps if Grenville did decide to return to Egypt, I'd ask to go with him, as an assistant or secretary or some such in order to earn my way. The baking sun would no doubt be good for my leg as well as for the rest of me.

I longed to roll up my sleeves against the heat, letting

my skin tan, living a bit like a barbarian again. My young
wife had hated the sun, complained of it ruining her com-
plexion. She'd wilted in the heat, and God help me, I'd
been impatient with her. I'd snapped at her to be more like
Louisa Brandon, who had been a bit more robust and enjoyed the warm weather. I'd always been a bloody fool
where Carlotta was concerned.

A carriage rolled to a halt right in front of me. Annoyed,
I turned my steps to hobble around it, but the footman
jumped down and approached me.

I saw Lady Breckenridge silhouetted against the window,
watching her footman offer to take me home in the comfort
of her warm carriage. I was not particularly in the mood for
that lady, but the agony in my muscles made the decision
for me. I allowed the footman to help me into the carriage
and found myself opposite Lady Breckenridge for the second time that day.

"You look in a bad way, Captain," she said.

I expected her to mock me and my capering at Inglethorpe's, but her brows were puckered, and she did not
smile.

She'd obviously been to the opera; she wore a pale
pink, high-waisted gown beneath her heavy velvet mantle,
and her dark hair was curled fantastically and crowned
with feathers. She was a pretty woman, without possessing
the fragile, ethereal beauty so in fashion these days.

"My butler has a remedy for sore limbs and joints," she
was saying. "He wraps hot towels bathed in herbs about
them. Swears by it."

The thought of a scalding towel about my knee was a
pleasing one. "I thank you for your concern," I said.

"I see you did not quite understand Mr. Inglethorpe's
magic gas, Captain. It gives euphoria and removes pain,
but the pain returns and the joy fades. It is a pity, but there
it is."

A pity, indeed. When I'd breathed the gas, I'd felt normal again, a whole man, not one dragging himself, liter-

ally, through his life. I'd enjoyed simply being a man dancing with a woman, a pleasure too long denied me.

"Still," Lady Breckenridge was saying, "it gives us an
afternoon free of life's little pains and troubles."

"Is that why you attend?" I asked.

She smiled, as though pleased I thought her troubled. "I
go for the amusement of it."

Well, I had certainly amused her. I knew I ought to have
stayed with Grenville, dulled some of the pain with his
brandy, but I'd known that if I'd sat in one of his comfortable chairs, I'd be unable to rise again until morning. Lady
Breckenridge's coach, lit by warm candles in lanterns and
scented with her spicy perfume, was having much the
same effect on me. I leaned back in the seat and stifled a
groan.

"It distresses me to see you so," she said, frowning.
"Let Barnstable have a go, anyway."

It was then I became aware we were driving back
through Mayfair, slowly passing the houses of Piccadilly.
"I have laudanum at home," I said, "and a footman to give
it to me. You can simply take me there."

"You are stubborn, Lacey."

"Yes," I said tersely. "As you are, my lady."

Her smile returned. "Tit for tat, is that it? I find you refreshing, Captain, with your rudeness. You have perfect
manners when necessary, but when needled, your com-
ments are clearheaded and most apt."

"I would be flattered were I not in so much pain."

"Let Barnstable help you, then. He is a wonder."

"He certainly will be," I said, "if he can stop this." I had
not hurt so much since the original injury. And I only had
myself to blame.

She watched me with her dark, intelligent eyes. "You
shunned me in Kent last summer, Captain. Do you remember?"

"In Kent, you mistook my character." She'd been
predatory then, backing off in coldness when I'd rejected
her advances.

"I did, I admit. I thought you a hanger-on of Grenville, eager to rub elbows with the peerage, of which my husband was so fine a representative. I never dreamed you'd come there to investigate the Badajoz murder."

Over our billiards game, she had given me a warning against the wife of the man I was investigating, and she, unfortunately, had been right. I'd been angry with her, but I had been angrier, later, with myself.

"I'd be pleased to call a truce with you, Lacey. To be friends."

I only half-heard her through a haze of pain. "If you'd like," I believe I said.

We pulled to a stop before the Breckenridge house, now held in trust for Lady Breckenridge's five-year-old son, on South Audley Street. The façade was tasteful with fanlights on doors and windows, the door black and cleanly painted. I'd briefly visited this house the year before when investigating Lord Breckenridge. The hall was almost painfully modern—the floor inlaid with crosshatching reminiscent of a Turkish screen, alcoves filled with alabaster statuary, and black and gold Egyptian-style chairs with green upholstery lining the walls.

Lady Breckenridge's footman helped me from the carriage and into the house. I leaned heavily on my borrowed walking stick as he half-carried me up to a little first-floor parlor where a fire had been stirred high.

I welcomed the warmth, but I was in a bad way. Spasms of pain spread through my muscles and nearly made me ill. The footman lowered me to a sofa, and I gripped my leg and tried not to rock in pain.

Lady Breckenridge leaned down to me. Her breath smelled of mint and lemonade. "I will leave you in Barnstable's hands, Captain. You will be better, I promise." She patted my shoulder then glided out of the room.

The butler, summoned, bustled in with all his accoutrements. Barnstable was a man of about forty, with jet black hair that he slicked with pomade. He set out a wooden rack before the fire, then lifted steaming towels

from a metal box and laid them across the rack. Calmly, he removed my boots for me, then told me to take off my trousers.

I unbuttoned them and slid them over my hips and to the floor. Wiry black hair twisted and curled down my shins. My left leg looked little different from my right except for the cross-hatch of scars that puckered my knee. The innocent-looking leg was certainly causing me devilish pain.

The butler draped the first towel around my knee and pulled it tight. I sucked in a breath. He piled on several more towels, holding each with tongs. The heat began to seep into my muscles. I closed my eyes.

"Let those work for a time," the butler said. "Then I'll rub in some of my liniment. Loosen you right up, sir."

Already the warmth had eased some of the tension. The smell of mint on the steam reminded me of my nursery, of days I'd taken cold as a child. My nurse had used similar herbs in boiling water to clear my congestion.

"You are a fine man, Barnstable," I said without opening my eyes.

"My wife had the rheumatics something terrible, sir. This always eased her."

Barnstable let me soak up the heat for a few more minutes, then, when the towels were beginning to cool, he removed them. He opened a glass jar and scooped out a rather watery, white concoction that smelled of oil of vitriol, and rubbed it hard all over my knee joint and the muscle behind it. After wiping his hands, he replaced the towels with a fresh set, hot from the fire.

He left me to steep, gliding away with the towels and liniment. I leaned back again. The throbbing had ceased, whether because of the liniment or the heat of the towels, I did not much care. I hoped Barnstable would share the recipe for his liniment so that I could use it myself the next time my knee seized up.

I found myself drifting in and out of sleep. In half-dreams I pictured Peaches lying on the bank of the

Thames, dead and quiet, her body ruined with water. I had never seen her in life, but I imagined what she must have looked like, her face round, hair bright gold, her smile that of someone intrigued by life.

She seemed to smile at me now. "Take care, Captain," she said. "You are most impetuous." I agreed. My impetuousness had led me to trouble many times before.

I came out of the dream, thinking of the real Peaches. She must have been a very charming young woman. She'd charmed Lord Barbury into loving her, had charmed the dour Mr. Chapman into marrying her, had charmed Kensington into letting her stay at the Glass House when she wanted peace from her husband. She'd charmed me, too, into wandering about London looking for the man who'd killed her. The small hand with its too-large ring, the slender feet in pretty shoes had touched my heart.

Lady Breckenridge had called her common. I recognized that Peaches was the sort of woman whom men liked and women did not. Peaches had liked men, and she'd been content to live in their world. But a man had betrayed her, had killed her. I doubted a woman had struck that blow; it had been vicious and thorough. Her husband, jealous of her lover? Her lover, jealous of someone else? Or Kensington, for some unknown reason?

I would find out.

I drifted back into sleep. I dreamed of Peaches again, but this time, it was Louisa Brandon's lifeless body on the bank of the Thames, and my heart was breaking. I knelt beside her, touched her cheek. I awoke to Barnstable shaking me, my face wet with tears.

BARNSTABLE took me to a tiny bedroom decorated in Wedgwood green and delicate plaster moldings. The bed with green and gold brocade hangings took up most of the room, with only small space left for a bedside table and a fantastic black and gold chair decorated in leopard skin with gilt claws for feet. A fire warmed the room. Barnstable helped me undress completely and put me to bed. I

found the bed cozy and drifted to sleep almost at once. When I awoke again, it was still dark, but I knew it was morning.

The door opened and Lady Breckenridge entered the bedroom. She wore a dressing gown and her hair hung over her shoulder in a long, thick braid. She regarded me from the threshold for a long moment, then closed the door, crossed the room and climbed into the bed with me.

"Friends, you said," I murmured.

"Yes, indeed." She laid next to me and slid her arm around my waist, resting her head on my shoulder. I liked it there. The touch of another human being soothed me; it had been a long while since I'd felt it.

"I ought to go home," I pointed out.

"It is raining." It had been raining all night.

We lay quietly for a moment, listening to the water on the window panes. "I see Barnstable has done well by you," she said softly.

"Excellently well."

She did not answer, but the hand that lay across the blankets smoothed my chest.

She lay beside me for a long time. She did nothing but rest her hand on my shoulder, and her hair, smelling of lavender, brushed my cheek. The situation was pleasant. It was what a man and wife might do, lay side by side in comfortable silence, listening to the rain and thinking separate thoughts. I could not guess what she meant by it or what she wanted, but I did not want to break the spell to ask.

I drifted into sleep again. When I awoke, she was gone.

Barnstable's cure had worked wonders. When I rose from the bed, my knee hurt only a little, and the usual morning stiffness had much diminished.

Barnstable shaved me and helped me dress, then took me downstairs and put me into a carriage. It was still dark, still raining, still cold. Lady Breckenridge did not appear. Barnstable, thankfully, gave me a jar of his liniment to take home with me, and it was to him that I said my good-byes.

*   *   *

THE inquest for Amelia Chapman was held that morning at ten o'clock in a public house near Blackfriar's Bridge. Because the death had apparently been by means of violence, the coroner had called a jury. The rather blank-looking gentlemen of this jury sat upright in their chairs near the middle of the room.

Chapman stood and testified that the dead woman had been his wife. The surgeon who had examined the body gave evidence that the deceased had met her death from a blow to the head sometime between four and five in the afternoon on Monday. Thompson put forth his theory that she had been thrown into the river from the Temple Gardens, near half-past four.

The coroner called Chapman again and asked him all about his wife, his relations with her, her movements on the day he'd last seen her, and his on the day she died. Chapman trembled a little, unused to being on this side of the questioning, but his voice was steady. He did produce a fellow barrister who could claim that Chapman had sat next to him in Middle Temple Hall all through dinner on Monday afternoon. Chapman's red-haired pupil also volunteered that he had seen the man in the hall between four and five.

Thompson had had no luck discovering how Peaches had gotten to Middle Temple or the Temple Gardens. He'd questioned hackney drivers, but none remembered picking up Mrs. Chapman or delivering her anywhere. He had discovered that Mrs. Chapman had boarded a coach bound for Sussex, but had left the coach at a coaching inn near Epsom and disappeared. How she'd gotten back to London was a mystery. No other public coach admitted to having had her as a passenger.

During Thompson's evidence, Mr. Chapman claimed to feel faint, and he was allowed to leave the room with Pomeroy to attend him. Thompson proceeded to tell how a ring had been found on Peaches' finger, discovered to belong to one Lord Barbury. Lord Barbury had admitted to being the lover of Mrs. Chapman. Thompson had ques-

tioned him thoroughly, and Barbury had been able to sat-
isfy Thompson that he had stayed at White's club the
whole of Monday afternoon. Lord Barbury had played a
game of whist with Lord Alvanley and two other prominent gentlemen, who each swore that Barbury never left
the table from three o'clock to six. Likewise, Barbury's
coachman had been carefully questioned, and he had not
gone to Middle Temple, nor had he been summoned to
drive Mrs. Chapman anywhere.

I had told Thompson when I arrived of my findings at
Inglethorpe's and that Peaches had last been seen at the
Glass House, and about Kensington, who deserved further
investigation. But when Thompson mentioned the name of
the Glass House, the coroner immediately cut off his
words and bade him sit down. I remembered Thompson
and Sir Montague implying that whoever owned the Glass
House had several magistrates in his pocket, and I wondered if that were the case here.

The coroner instructed the jury, who quickly brought
back the verdict of murder by person or persons unknown.
The inquest was at an end.

From the look in Thompson's eye, he considered things
far from over. He had no time to speak with me then, but
left for his house in Wapping and other cases.

I departed the public house to run my own errands, one
of which was close by, in the City. Thompson had seemed
satisfied with Lord Barbury's alibi at White's, but I wondered if he truly believed Lord Barbury's innocence to be
established. I thought perhaps that Thompson had ideas of
his own, and I was sorry he'd had to rush away. I'd also
wanted to discuss the little girl at the Glass House with him
to establish when I could introduce her to Sir Montague
Harris.

The other errand I wanted to run today was to retrieve
my walking stick from Inglethorpe. While I still used
Grenville's walking stick, and my leg felt relaxed and
warm from Barnstable's ministrations, I wanted my own
walking stick back. Not only had it cost me a quarter's pay,

but Louisa Brandon had assisted me in choosing it. We'd gone to a Spanish sword maker, who had made a beautiful sword then a cane to go around it, with a cunningly hidden latch to release the weapon. Last spring, the cane had been broken in one of my adventures, and Grenville had had a replacement made. The walking stick had become not simply a prop; it now represented the kindness of my friends.

My first errand, however, was with a moneylender.

This particular moneylender had dealt with the Lacey family for generations. When the Laceys had been high in the world, the coffers of London had been open to them. My grandfather and father had each drawn on that tradition and managed to borrow enough to live a life of relative ease while squandering their fortune. The long war against France had not been kind to either my father or the estate, and now all that was left was the ruin of a house and the tiny bit of land on which it sat. The rest of the farms had been sold long ago to pay my father's mountain of debts.

I was the last of the family, a gentleman of reduced means, and I had begun to tire of this existence. In the army, I had led a life of much activity, and sitting idly at home did not appeal to me. I had already begun keeping an ear open for circumstances in which a gentleman might earn his keep, as a secretary, perhaps, or an assistant, sort of a gentleman's aide-de-camp. I planned to recruit Bartholomew in this task, since the lad seemed to know everyone in London, just like his master.

The moneylender I spoke to remembered my grandfather well, was his contemporary, in fact. I looked into the lined face, eyes undimmed by time, and wondered if my own grandfather would have lived longer had he not succumbed to hedonistic pleasures. The man facing me had suppressed his own desires with years of strict discipline. Now, he was in a position to condescend to me. His fortune had increased while the Lacey fortune had faded.

He lent me three hundred guineas. The price was a percentage of the money, payable in increments. I was not

fond of usury, but I had no choice. I signed myself into debt and left his house with the money.

I visited my bank and paid it into my account. I returned to the outside world and settled my uneasiness by purchasing coffee from a vendor.

I took a hackney to Mayfair, heading for Inglethorpe's residence to retrieve my walking stick. I would then continue to Grosvenor Street and leave a draft for three hundred guineas for Grenville, to repay him that which he'd given to Kensington the night before.

I descended at Curzon Street at half-past three. Bartholomew left me there, jogging off to Grosvenor Street to visit his brother and wait for me at Grenville's. As I stepped up to the door, a gust of wind sent rain under my greatcoat, and water poured from my hat brim. I lifted the knocker.

The door opened before I could let the knocker fall, the polished brass ripped from my hand.

"Ah, Captain," Milton Pomeroy said. "I was about to send a lad to fetch you. Returned to the scene of the crime, eh?"

Icy droplets slid under my collar and down my back. "What crime?" I asked sharply.

Pomeroy's flat yellow hair was dark with rain. "The crime of murder, sir. Mr. Simon Inglethorpe, gentleman. Laid out flat in his own reception room, dead as stone. And curious thing, Captain. It's your sticker that has him pinned to the floor. It's in him all the way through to the carpet."

CHAPTER 8

INGLETHORPE lay spread-eagled on the gold and cream carpet of the reception room. This same small, uncomfortable room had housed me yesterday while I'd waited for the footman to admit me upstairs.

Inglethorpe's expression was one of astonishment. His face was chalk white, and a thick rivulet of dried blood creased his chin. He wore tight black pantaloons that buttoned at his ankles, silk stockings, and pumps, the garb of a gentleman prepared to receive guests at home. Above the waist, he wore nothing at all, his white skin stark against the carpet. His stomach showed that he had slightly gone to fat, and his chest muscles were limp.

The sword from my walking stick stuck straight out of his chest, the blade surrounded by a circle of dried blood. The brass handle, which doubled as a hilt, shone faintly in the candlelight.

I turned to Pomeroy, dumbfounded. "When did this happen?"

"Just an hour gone, sir, since he was found. I was sent

for right away and arrived not much before you did. Butler last saw him at two o'clock this afternoon, upstairs. At half-past, butler glances into this room, and sees that." He gestured to the corpse.

I looked into Pomeroy's ingenuous blue eyes. He liked to lay his hands on a culprit, and I had the feeling that he would not scruple to arrest even his former captain on the slim evidence of my sword in the wound.

"You were a friend of Mr. Inglethorpe?" he asked me.

"We were acquainted."

"Lent him your stick, did you?"

"I left it here yesterday," I said coldly. "I was returning to fetch it."

"Yesterday, while you were calling on Mr. Inglethorpe. He'd invited you?"

I eyed him narrowly. "Yes."

"Butler says, too, that you were here with a gathering of Mr. Inglethorpe's friends. Butler says he saw you come in with your walking stick, that very one that's stuck in his master."

"I did not stick it there, Sergeant."

Pomeroy shrugged. "Sometimes you get into a rare temper, sir. I have seen what you are like when you're enraged. Ready for murder, sir, you are."

"If I had been angry at Inglethorpe, I would have challenged him," I pointed out.

"Not necessarily. I've seen you draw a pistol on a cove you disagreed with, and I've seen you knock a chap down, easy as breathing. No mention of duels then. Dueling too good for them, you said."

I held on to my temper with effort. "I was not angry with Inglethorpe, and I was not here today. I barely knew the man."

"That's as may be, sir. But that is your sticker. You weren't his friend, but you looked him up yesterday. Struck with fellow feeling, were you, sir?"

"Do not question me, Pomeroy. I do not like it."

"Just following orders, sir, same as always. You came here yesterday. I would like to know why."

I looked about the room, trying to shut out Pomeroy's prying. The reception room appeared unchanged from when I'd paced in here the day before, except that a neatly folded pile of clothing reposed on the chair. I moved to it and lifted a frock coat, waistcoat, shirt, collar, and cravat. Fine materials, fine tailoring. The cravat smelled of lavender oil.

"The dead man's," Pomeroy said. "Or so the butler says. Neither of us can decide why he was standing about bare-breasted in his reception room."

"What do the servants say?" I asked.

"Very little, sir. Inglethorpe was right as rain all this morning, then he came in here and that was that."

"He must have entered this room for some reason. To greet a visitor, most likely."

"Servants didn't open the door to anyone all morning, they say."

That did not mean no one arrived. Gentlemen of Inglethorpe's wealth generally let their servants answer the front door, but that did not mean he could not have admitted someone himself. Perhaps he'd spied the person arriving and hadn't wanted to wait for his butler to open the door.

The removed clothing suggested a romantic liaison—I could think of no other reason for Inglethorpe to so tamely remove his coat and shirt. The caller, then, might have been a woman, although I remembered Grenville in the Rearing Pony, his mouth twisted in distaste, proclaiming, "I honestly do not believe Inglethorpe cares which way the wind blows." A woman or man, likely a man, from the strength of the blow.

I had left my walking stick in the sitting room upstairs. Had Inglethorpe found it and kept it? Brought it down here with him, where his killer had found it a convenient weapon? Or had the murderer been a member of yester-

day's gathering, taken my walking stick away with him, and returned with it this morning?

My heart chilled. Mrs. Danbury had been in the room when I'd gone off without my walking stick. I remembered her, flushed with the magic gas, staring at me in dismay as I hurried after Lady Breckenridge. Lady Breckenridge had not taken the stick away with her; I would have seen her. That left Mrs. Danbury and the few gentlemen remaining in the room with her. I could not remember through the haze of the laughing gas which gentlemen they had been, though I reasoned that Inglethorpe's servants would probably know.

I certainly did not want to think of Mrs. Danbury returning here this morning, speaking with Inglethorpe, then stabbing him in fear when he made advances upon her.

My common sense came to my rescue. Inglethorpe had removed and folded his clothes deliberately, not torn them off in a frenzy of passion. I doubted Mrs. Danbury would stand still and wait for him to undress before stabbing him in panic. Also, I could see no reason for Mrs. Danbury to return to Inglethorpe's at all. If she had taken the walking stick, she could have had it delivered to my rooms, or given it to Sir Gideon Derwent to return to me when I next visited him. Lady Breckenridge had said that Inglethorpe's gatherings were held only on Mondays and Wednesdays and that Inglethorpe was most regular in his habits, which meant he would not have had a gathering today.

Why Mrs. Danbury had attended Inglethorpe's party at all puzzled me. She had not known how to breathe the air in the bag, which indicated she had not done it before. Had she, like Peaches, come to Inglethorpe's in search of a new sensation and excitement? Or out of curiosity? Or was she Inglethorpe's friend, and he had invited her personally?

My heart chilled again. If she were a close friend of Inglethorpe's, that brought me back to the possibility of her murdering him. I could imagine Inglethorpe eagerly hurrying to open the door for the pretty Mrs. Danbury. I certainly would have. Nor would I have objected speaking

with her alone in the tiny reception room. I could not over-
look the possibility that she had deliberately stabbed him.

I dropped the clothes back on the chair, frustrated. Inglethorpe's death must be no coincidence—Peaches had
come here the afternoon before she'd died. Had she told
Inglethorpe something that the killer worried about? Had
she been on her way to the Glass House to meet someone?
And Inglethorpe had perhaps known who? I had planned
to question Inglethorpe about Peaches yesterday, and of
course had missed the opportunity through my own folly.

I hoped Mrs. Danbury had nothing to do with any of
this. I admired her in her own right, and her cousins were
my friends. It was likely she'd simply come yesterday out
of curiosity and had returned home, innocent. One of the
other gentlemen present might have known Peaches, might
have heard her imparting to Inglethorpe her plans for Monday afternoon, might have murdered her for his own reasons, and then returned today and murdered Inglethorpe.

"Has Sir Montague Harris been informed of this?" I
asked.

"Couldn't say, sir. I imagine he will be."

"Bloody hell, Sergeant." I walked out of the room with
Pomeroy following.

"It's a nasty thing, sir, people sticking each other."

I turned to him. He stood behind me, cheerful and confident. He'd never had a day of melancholia in his life. "I
did not kill this man, Pomeroy." I took up my hat, clapped
it back to my damp hair. "But I intend to find out who did."

"Probably in your best interest, sir."

"Thank you, Sergeant."

I strode out into the rain. Pomeroy said something
jovial behind me, but I did not stop to respond.

I continued walking to Grosvenor Street, angry and worried, wondering what Inglethorpe had known—and what I
had overlooked. I needed to know more about Inglethorpe's household and his friends, and I thought over
ways in which I might find out.

When I reached Grenville's house, Matthias admitted me, but told me his master was out. When I informed him and Bartholomew of the news, their blue eyes rounded, and their square jaws dropped. "Lord, sir," Bartholomew breathed. "With your sticker?"

"Yes. It's a bother, that." I went over the plan I'd formed as I'd walked between Inglethorpe's and here. "Bartholomew, I'd like you and your brother to poke around Inglethorpe's a bit, get the servants to confide in you. Find out who was in Inglethorpe's house yesterday and this morning. Discover if any one of the staff saw what became of my walking stick between the time I left it and the time it ended up in Inglethorpe's chest. I want to know any gossip about Mrs. Chapman—who she knew and what she did whenever she went to Inglethorpe's, how well she knew Inglethorpe, and what they talked about."

Bartholomew nodded, as did his brother. They'd both helped me last year in the affair of Colonel Westin, and looked eager to involve themselves in my adventures again.

Before I departed, I pulled out the bank draft I'd made to Grenville for three hundred guineas. "Give this to your master," I said to Matthias. "And do not let him tear it up or put it on the fire. He'll likely try."

Matthias raised his brows and took it, mystified, but he nodded.

I left them to return to Grimpen Lane, impatient and depressed. Thompson was busily investigating Peaches' murder, of course, but everything was moving too slowly for me. I preferred the army method of spotting the enemy and charging him, rather than the slow process of asking questions and piecing together what had happened while the killer had the opportunity to flee. Or strike again.

I had hoped to confer with Grenville, over hot coffee or brandy, about Inglethorpe's murder. Grenville had a quick and logical mind and could set things out clearly. I always found it helpful to discuss things with him, a man who rarely let emotions cloud his thinking. I tried myself to sit

still and write everything out, but I was too moody to concentrate.

Inglethorpe's death worried me greatly. Peaches' death had seemed almost simple; she had likely been killed by one of three men: her husband, Lord Barbury, or Kensington. Inglethorpe's death opened more possibilities. Any of the three men already mentioned might have stabbed him, or any of the gentlemen at the magic gas gathering might have, or Mrs. Danbury, or even Lady Breckenridge. While I had some difficulty picturing the ladylike Mrs. Danbury wielding a sword, I had less difficulty picturing Lady Breckenridge doing so. Lady Breckenridge was a woman of determination, who'd viewed the death of her husband with relief, who retained her independence of thought in a world in which a woman was not encouraged to do so.

I remembered her lying against me, her head on my shoulder, how comfortable that had been. Had her motive been comfort, or duplicity? She had been kind to me last evening, in her own way, but I still did not trust her.

I pushed away the feeble notes I'd begun when Mrs. Beltan brought up my post. I had a letter from the Derwents reminding me of my dinner with them Sunday next and assuring me that young Jean was doing well. She was an orphan, they said, and Lady Derwent was looking into employment for which she might be trained.

I was pleased that at least the little girl would do well out of the tragedy. The Derwents would be diligent in looking after Jean and making certain she came to no harm.

My second letter set my teeth on edge. It was from my former colonel and invited me to dine at his Brook Street home that very night. I tossed the paper away and sank into the armchair before the fire to fume.

Last summer, Colonel Brandon had gotten himself caught up in one of my adventures and had acquitted himself well, helping me catch a killer. After that, he'd pretended to thaw toward me. All through the autumn, he had invited me to his house to dine or for cards, and to talk of our campaigns in Spain and Portugal and India. He would

drink plenty of port and pretend that the uglier incidents between us had never happened.

As autumn waned, however, the air between us became more and more strained, and we returned to stiffness and veiled insults. By December, Brandon had had enough of me. After Louisa had helped me through my melancholia, he'd taken her with him to a shooting party in the north, never even saying his good-byes.

Now this invitation. I did not doubt it had something to do with the fact that I'd become involved with yet another Bow Street problem. Brandon still regarded me as his officer, the man he had made. No doubt he wanted to call me onto the carpet and berate me for my recent activities.

But I was no longer his man. I was on half-pay, semi-retired. I could perhaps get myself transferred to another regiment, if another captain were ready for half-pay or wanted a place in the 35th Light Dragoons. We could negotiate a trade. But the long war was over, I had little to offer another regiment, and there were plenty of half-pay captains wandering about at loose ends. Also, cavalry nowadays was used to put down riots, a practice I disliked. Firing at enemy soldiers doing their best to kill me was one thing, firing at women and children, no matter how unruly, was something else.

Additionally, the regimental commander of the 35th Light had made it plain to Brandon and me on that last day in Spain that we had better take our feud away from the army. I could have brought charges against Brandon for what he had done, but I had not wanted his wife to face that shame. Our commander had snarled at Brandon and me as though we were recalcitrant schoolboys and called us a disgrace to the regiment, a reprimand Brandon had taken hard.

So here we were in London, both of us fish out of water, unable to tell the truth of why we'd left the regiment. We were alternately painfully polite and furious with each other. Louisa bore the brunt of it, trying valiantly to heal

the breach, because she blamed herself for the breach in the first place.

I could have told her that the rift would have come anyway. Though I had much admired Brandon when I was young and impressionable, we no longer saw eye to eye on most matters. As we'd grown older and he'd moved up in rank to colonel, we had drifted apart. The break would have come sooner or later, but on the night when Brandon had made clear his intention to divorce Louisa, the break had come with a vengeance.

With all this in mind, I descended at the Brandons' Brook Street house at eight o'clock that night, on time. My breath fogged white in the January air, and the cobbles were slick.

Brandon was in full lecturing mode that evening. The death of Simon Inglethorpe, via my sword-stick, was already the talk of Mayfair. As the footman served the meal, Brandon related how he'd been accosted at his club today by men asking him what his captain had got up to now. Louisa listened, her golden head bent while she toyed with a thin bracelet on her wrist.

I explained the Inglethorpe business over the stuffed pheasant, onion soup, sole, and fricassee of mushrooms. Brandon did not seem impressed by my story, and glowered his disapproval when I talked of the magic gas and how it had relieved the pain in my leg for a time. He berated me for my carelessness when I'd described leaving the walking stick behind in my hurry, clearly blaming me for Inglethorpe's murder.

He'd dropped all pretense of civility and this autumn's strained politeness. His blue eyes glittered with suppressed anger, and after the footmen had cleared the last plates, he abruptly told Louisa he wished to speak to me alone.

Louisa, who had been uncharacteristically silent throughout the meal, rose obediently. But her eyes, too, sparkled with anger. I stood when she did, and she came to me and kissed my cheek. Brandon's sharp gaze remained

on me until Louisa said her quiet good nights and left the room.

He did not wait long to begin his outburst, the real reason he'd invited me here tonight.

"Good God, Lacey, I have been hearing the most sordid of stories about you."

His color was high, his eyes fiery. Brandon had always been a very handsome man, tall and broad-shouldered, with hair of crisp black, eyes of cold blue. His face, though lined now, was still square and strong. "It is damned embarrassing," he went on, "to be approached at my club every day with some new tale of your exploits."

"Stay home, then," I suggested, my own anger rising.

"The latest offense I cannot even mention before my wife. I have heard gossip that you disported yourself wildly in a bawdy house, broke the furniture, and ran off with one of the women. For God's sake, Gabriel, what were you thinking?"

"Gossip has it wrong," I said, my voice clipped.

"How can you deny you were there? People saw you. They told me that even Mr. Grenville was shocked at your behavior."

"I was at the Glass House, yes."

"The Glass House." Brandon spat the name. "That you were even in such a place speaks ill of you."

"Have you been there?"

He looked outraged. "Of course not."

I believed him. Brandon was stiffly moral. "It is a place in which fine gentlemen think nothing of raping a twelve-year-old girl," I answered coolly. "She was the lady with whom I fled into the night. I took her away from that place and to the Derwents to care for her. I am sorry I broke only one of the windows."

The tale of my heroics did soften him. "Why the devil did you go to such a place at all?"

"Because a woman might have died there," I said.

His eyes narrowed. "The woman from the river?"

"Yes."

He frowned. I could tell he did not like the brutal murder any more than I did, but he merely gave me another look of disapproval. "You involve yourself unnecessarily."

I knew that. I always did. Even in the army, a puzzle or incongruity could intrigue me, even if it were none of my business. Maybe if I'd been a happy man with a wife and children to take up my time, I'd have been less interfering.

"If you had seen her, you would understand," I said. "I want to find the man who did that to her."

"That is Bow Street's business," he snapped. "Let your sergeant investigate crime and keep your hands out of it."

"Had I kept my hands out of it, a twelve-year-old girl would be raped again tonight."

He gave me a dark look. "You are evading the question."

"I no longer need to report to you, sir. We are civilians now. What I do is not your business."

He clenched his jaw. "It is when your name and mine, not to mention the name of my wife, are spoken together. I do not blame gentlemen for cutting you. If not for Louisa, I would do the same."

I rose, my temper fragmenting. "Do not stand on ceremony. I would be most relieved not to have to sit through these tedious nights while we pretend to be friends."

He got to his feet as well. "Don't you dare turn on me, Lacey. I took you in when you were nothing. You would have had no career and no standing but for me, and you know it."

He was right, and I could not deny it. It angered me that he still had the ability to hurt me. "You are correct, sir. Had I not followed you, I would be buried in Norfolk, poor as dirt with a wife and a passel of children to support. Now I am poor as dirt in London, and all alone. I suppose I do have you to thank."

"Go to hell."

"Gladly, if there I do not have to watch you pretend to forgive me."

His eyes flashed. "I've done with forgiving you,

Gabriel. I have tried and tried and you've spit in my face every time. By rights I should have shot you for what you did."

"Instead, you sent me to die as David did Uriah."

It was a mean shot, but my accusation was true. Brandon had sent me off with false orders straight into a pocket of French resistance. I had survived afterward only by crawling away across country, alone. Half-alive, I had at last been found by a Spanish woman named Olietta, who'd eked out a living on her tiny farm after her husband had been killed in the war. I murdered the French deserter who had more or less held her hostage, and she nursed me through the worst of my nightmare pain. At last, at my insistence, she'd dragged me back to the 35th Light on a makeshift litter, with the help of her six- and eight-year-old sons.

Later I'd regretted the decision to return at all. I might have stayed with Olietta, hidden away in the woods, while Wellesley and the English army pushed on to France and left Spain and me behind. Brandon and Louisa and everyone else had thought me dead. Why should I not have simply remained so?

But I had been too damned anxious to return, too anxious to let everyone know I was alive. And when I'd got back, I'd learned that Brandon would have been quite happy to think me dead.

"Was I not justified?" he hissed.

This was the first time he'd ever admitted, out loud, his guilt in the matter.

We were fighting about Louisa, of course. When Brandon had declared he would divorce Louisa, she had come to me. On a wild and rainy night she had fled to my tent, and I had comforted her. Brandon had forgiven Louisa, but never me. No matter that he claimed he'd repeatedly offered forgiveness, he never truly had. He hated me, and all the pretense in the world would not change that.

"No," I stated. "You were not justified. I wake up every morning knowing that."

He rarely let his rage show naked in his eyes, but he did so now. I thought he was going to come for me, but suddenly Louisa was there, between us, having stormed into the room while Brandon and I were busy shouting at each other. I looked down at her, swallowing my anger and what I'd meant to say to Brandon. Olietta had been dark, with deep brown eyes and brown skin. Louisa's hair was as bright as the Spanish sun.

"Stop this," Louisa snapped. "Gabriel, go home."

I controlled my voice with effort. "Your husband is displeased with me yet again. It is a wonder he let me into the house."

Her eyes flashed. "Blast you, Gabriel, why can you not simply bow your head? Is your neck so stiff with pride?"

Her anger stung me. It was like a whiplash, to see that anger. Her husband could hurt me, but Louisa could hurt me ten times as much.

"I cannot," I said, "because his idiocy hurts you."

Brandon raged. "How dare you speak so in my own house! Do you try to turn my wife from me before my eyes?"

I balled my hands. I was tired of these rows with Brandon, tired of Louisa looking at me with hurt in her eyes. The three of us could not occupy the same room without the old accusations, old anger, old sorrow bubbling to the surface.

I held onto my temper, made a frosty bow. "I beg your pardon, Louisa. I will go. Thank you for the meal."

Louisa merely looked at me, angry, unhappy, unable to answer me. I walked out of the room, my heart sore.

At the door, I looked back. Brandon and Louisa watched me, like two statues frozen in anger. We had been bound to each for many years, but the love and friendship we had once shared had dwindled to this. We were forever hurting one another, forever regretting. We would continue to do so, I realized, until we learned to let go. And I knew that day would be long in coming.

CHAPTER 9

I left the Brandon house for the icy night, swearing under my breath. Brandon could wind me into anger faster than any man alive, and it always took me a good while to cool down. I knew bloody well that he would not be able to provoke me to such anger if I hadn't once loved him. He'd been good to me when I'd needed his help the most, he'd used his influence to benefit me many times.

I had not realized at the time that in return he'd wanted unconditional love and unquestioning obedience. And I had ever been one to ask questions.

A boy darted into the street, sweeping horse dung from the cobbles, clearing a path for me. I tossed him a penny for his trouble, then made my way across the slick street. I was not far from Grosvenor Square, and I walked there, making for the home of Sir Gideon Derwent. It would be rude of me to arrive without an appointment, without invitation, but I was restless and annoyed and very much wanted to ask Mrs. Danbury a few questions. After the row with Brandon, I could not tamely return home and brood;

I wanted to push on with the investigation, to *do* something.

I regretted my impulse, however, when I arrived at the Derwent house, because Lady Derwent had taken ill.

I was surprised that the footman let me into the house, but he took my hat and greatcoat and led me upstairs to the rather grand sitting room on the first floor. He assured me that Sir Gideon would want to see me, and ran away to fetch him.

In only a few minutes, Sir Gideon himself entered the room, followed by his son, Leland. Leland was in his early twenties and had fair hair and guileless gray eyes. His father was a portly version of the son, with similar coloring, only slightly faded. Both father and son looked out at the world in all innocence, seeing only what they wanted to see. They believed me to be a man who'd had all the exciting adventures that they had not and probably never would. They were endlessly interested in tales of my life in India and France and Spain.

Father and son advanced on me eagerly, but I saw the worry on both faces. Typically, Sir Gideon brushed aside his own fears and was anxious to learn why I'd come.

"To inquire about Jean," I answered, naming one reason.

"Poor child," Sir Gideon said, nodding his head. "You were right to take her out of that place."

I could imagine no greater contrast to the Glass House than this. The ceiling of the drawing room in which we sat rose nearly twenty feet and was decorated with intricately carved moldings. Landscapes and portraits of Derwents covered the yellow silk walls, and matching silk adorned the chairs and settees. It was elegant and tasteful and serene, everything the Glass House was not.

"Her story is a common one, I am afraid," Sir Gideon went on. "She came to London to try to find work in a factory, and was met at a coaching inn by a procuress." He shook his head. "We cannot find all these poor children,

alas, but I will discuss the Glass House with my colleagues. That at least will be finished with."

"Attempts have been made to shut it down before," I said.

Sir Gideon frowned. "Yes. Odd that. You would think the outcry would be great. But I am determined to change that." Leland nodded in fervent agreement.

We discussed ways in which to see that the Glass House was shut down, while I readied myself to ask Sir Gideon if I might speak with Mrs. Danbury. But before I could inquire about her, the lady herself entered the room.

She looked at me without surprise; presumably, a servant had told her I'd arrived. She was cool and composed, comfortably elegant in a dark blue gown encircled with a sash of light blue. Her hair, as fair as Leland's, was twisted into a knot, bound with a ribbon. She crossed the room and pressed a kiss to her uncle's forehead. "Captain Lacey," she greeted me.

I had risen from my chair at her entrance, as had Leland. I bowed over her hand politely, and her eyes met mine. She flushed slightly and moved back to Sir Gideon. "Aunt is asking for you," she told him. "And she sends her greetings to Captain Lacey."

Sir Gideon excused himself and hurried from the room, clearly worried about his wife. Leland stayed and pretended he wanted to chat, but I saw in his eyes that he, too, longed to dash upstairs to see how his mother fared. At last Mrs. Danbury told him to run along, saying cheerfully that she'd keep me company.

Leland departed, leaving the double doors open—me alone in a closed room with Mrs. Danbury would have been most improper. The room was so large, however, that if we spoke in low voices in the middle of it, no one passing would hear us.

As soon as Leland disappeared, I asked, "How is Lady Derwent?"

Mrs. Danbury let out her breath. "She will recover this, I think. But she grows weaker with every attack."

She knew, as well as I did, that the day would come soon when Lady Derwent would not recover. "Please give her my best wishes," I said.

Mrs. Danbury nodded, her eyes cast down, but I could see she was pleased that I cared.

"I suppose you heard about Inglethorpe," I ventured.

"Yes, I did. It is gruesome. Poor man."

"Did you know him well?" I asked.

She looked up at me, surprised. "No. Hardly at all. He was a friend of my husband's. My second husband, that is, Mickey Danbury."

I raised my brows. "He was your husband's friend, but you did not know him?" My wife had known all of my friends quite well, whether she liked them or not, and Louisa was well acquainted with Brandon's cronies.

Mrs. Danbury flushed. "I rarely saw my husband's acquaintances."

I was not certain I believed her, but I did not pursue it. I knew that in many marriages in the *ton,* the husband and wife lived entirely separate lives. I found the attitude strange; why marry at all in that case?

"I was surprised to see you at his gathering, yesterday," I said, watching her.

"He invited me. I chanced upon Mr. Inglethorpe the other day in Grafton Street, and he asked if I'd like to attend. I was interested; I did not see what harm it would do."

I drew my thumb along the handle of Grenville's walking stick. "I wonder why he invited you, if he did not know you well."

A spark of anger lit her eyes. "I haven't the faintest idea, Captain. He simply happened to, that is all."

I made a placating gesture. "And you attended out of curiosity. What did you think of it?"

She hesitated, staring at me, uncertain. "I found it most strange. I have never felt a sensation like that. Have you?"

"No. It made me forget myself." I smiled ruefully. "As you observed."

Her flush deepened. "And I as well. I was a bit ill after-ward."

"I must apologize for taking the liberty of waltzing with you," I said. "I cannot account for my lack of manners."

She eyed me curiously. "Why did you?"

"I beg your pardon?"

"Why did you waltz with me?"

I hesitated. I remembered hearing music in my head, a tune of a fine waltz, and looking down at her bright smile and curved waist. "I wanted to," I answered.

She looked the slightest bit pleased. "It was I who made a fool of myself," she said. "In front of Lady Breckenridge, too."

It surprised me that she should care for the opinion of Lady Breckenridge, but then, Lady Breckenridge was a rung higher on the social ladder than she. Mrs. Danbury might have prettier manners, but Lady Breckenridge wielded more power among the *ton*.

"I must also apologize for leaving you there when I dashed off," I continued. "My only excuse is that I wanted to ask Lady Breckenridge a question before she disappeared. But I ought to have seen that you reached your carriage safely, at least."

She seemed far more comfortable with my polite apolo-gies than with my questions. "Not at all, Captain. I left soon after that."

"Perhaps you can help me, then," I said. "Do you re-member what became of my walking stick, which I left be-hind far too carelessly?"

She stopped, thought. "No, I am afraid I did not. I—" She flushed. "I am afraid not."

Her small hesitation disquieted me. Was she lying? And why? To protect someone? "Are you certain? You must re-alize that the person who took it could very well have re-turned today and killed Inglethorpe."

She looked horrified. "Good Lord, why should they?"

"I do not know. That is what my friend Pomeroy is try-

ing to discover. Did you speak to Mr. Inglethorpe at all before you departed yesterday?"

She shook her head, the ribbon brushing her neck. "No. I took my leave quite quickly."

"Good."

She raised her brows. "Why good?"

"Because I found Inglethorpe unsavory. I am pleased that your connection was not strong."

She stared at me, nonplussed. I had no right, of course, to lecture her about her connections. But I told the truth, I was pleased that she had not known Inglethorpe well. He was not the sort of man I wanted nieces of my acquaintance to know.

"Do you remember which gentlemen remained when you departed?" I went on. "One of them could have taken the walking stick."

She frowned again. "I could not be certain. I do believe Mr. Yardley and Mr. Price-Davies were there, but I really do not remember."

"Do you know either of those gentlemen well?"

"Not well, no. I saw a bit of Mr. Yardley before I married Mr. Danbury, but I've spoken to him little since."

I twirled the borrowed walking stick between my fingers. "I am wondering if either of those men could have taken the stick. And returned with it the next day."

She looked at me in shock. "Good heavens, Captain. You cannot seriously believe that Mr. Yardley or Mr. Price-Davies would murder Inglethorpe. Why on earth should they?"

Her vehemence surprised me. "Someone did, Mrs. Danbury."

"Well, yes, but it was the work of a tramp, or a madman. Captain Lacey, gentlemen of Mayfair do not stab one another with sword-sticks."

"They fight duels," I pointed out.

"That is entirely different, and not all gentlemen condone duels."

She gave me an admonishing stare, as though I ought to

be above accusing other gentlemen of so sordid a crime as murder.

I realized another difference between her and Lady Breckenridge; Lady Breckenridge, with her outlook on life nearly as cynical as my own, would have agreed with me. Mrs. Danbury, connected with the unworldly Derwents, refused to believe it.

"I know it is unpleasant to think so," I said, "but it might have happened."

"I am sorry you believe so," she returned, angry. "But I can assure you, I saw neither gentleman take the walking stick, nor do I believe that either of them returned and killed Mr. Inglethorpe. It was a housebreaker, whom Mr. Inglethorpe surprised. It must have been."

She had been hesitant a few minutes ago; she was adamant now. If she were hiding something from me, she took refuge in her anger. Her voice rang with sincerity.

I decided to change the subject before she summoned the footman to throw me out. "I would like to speak to Jean, if I can," I said. "I am certain Sir Gideon told you where she came from. I would like to ask her a few more questions about it."

Mrs. Danbury's color remained high, but she seemed relieved that I'd stopped talking about Inglethorpe. "I suppose it would do no harm," she said. "She seems to be a resilient child, not hysterical. But please do not upset her."

I promised to not tire the girl, and Mrs. Danbury summoned the footman and bade him fetch Jean from below stairs.

Her gray eyes did not soften while we waited in awkward silence. She obviously considered me a boor for implying that men of quality could murder one another. Likely she'd thought my long career in the army had made me believe all men capable of violence. And she would have been right. I'd seen gentlemen kill with joy, or with grim purpose, or with reluctance, and with all three at once.

Jean was led into the room by the footman very soon

after that. Dressed in a sensible garment, and with the kohl and rouge washed from her face, she looked like what she was, a child.

She did not curtsey, but gave a little bow to me and Mrs. Danbury. She was a working-class girl, with stubby fingers and a child's flyaway hair barely contained by a ribbon.

When the footman had departed and Jean had been settled next to Mrs. Danbury, I began.

"I would like you to tell me again about Peaches," I said.

Jean regarded me warily, perhaps wondering whether I'd come to snatch her away again. She moved a bit closer to the safety of Mrs. Danbury's arm, then she shrugged. "Peaches let me sleep in her room sometimes. I could lock the door. Only she had the key."

I was surprised. "Mr. Kensington did not have one?"

"No. I don't know. He never came in there."

But he'd opened it readily for Grenville and me, with a key. "Her room on the first floor?" I asked.

Jean looked puzzled. "No, her room in the attics."

I stared. Bloody hell. No wonder the chamber Kensington had shown us had been impersonal. No wonder he'd not been worried when we'd searched it. There had been nothing there to find, and he'd known it. I chafed that I had so readily believed him, damn the man. Kensington must have laughed to himself about how easily he'd tricked us.

"What did you think of Mr. Kensington, Jean?" I continued, containing my temper. "Was he a friend to Peaches?"

"I didn't like him," the girl answered readily. That was fine; I hadn't liked him either. "He and Peaches weren't friends. They shouted at each other a great deal."

Kensington had implied he'd let Peaches take refuge at the Glass House out of sympathy and old friendship. "What would they shout about?"

"He would say that he knew her before she became high and mighty, and she would say she'd always been beyond his reach. She laughed at him."

"Did he ever try to hurt her, or threaten to?"

"No. He seemed almost afraid of her, sometimes."

I thought of Kensington's mean, dark eyes, his oily smile. It pleased me that he had not held Peaches in thrall.

"Can you remember anything that happened on Monday, anything at all before Peaches went away that might be a little out of the ordinary?"

Jean's brow furrowed, but she shook her head. "Peaches came in. I heard Mr. Kensington start to shout at her, then she went on upstairs and slammed the door. Later, I saw her go down through the kitchen. She was smiling."

"Mr. Kensington did not go with her?"

"I didn't see him."

So I was back to Peaches disappearing from the Glass House and turning up in the Thames.

"Did she speak to anyone else? Perhaps tell them where she was going?"

Jean thought, then shook her head. "I didn't see."

I hid a sigh. "Thank you," I said formally. "You have been very helpful."

"Yes, sir," she said.

"The Derwents will look after you."

"Yes, sir." She sounded doubtful.

I had nothing else to add. She would have to learn trust, though I knew it would be difficult for her.

Mrs. Danbury announced she'd take Jean up to bed, effectively cutting short the interview and indicating she wanted me to go. I issued my good nights to her and the little girl, and again expressed my best wishes for Lady Derwent.

Mrs. Danbury condescended to give me a half-smile as I departed. Perhaps my gentle treatment of and concern for Jean had redeemed me in her eyes, a little bit, at least.

I returned home and spent a restless night. Today I had enraged Louisa, upset Mrs. Danbury, discovered I'd been duped by Kensington, and nearly been accused of murder by Pomeroy. Not the best day of my life, by any means.

I woke with a headache and received word from Pomeroy

that the inquest for Inglethorpe would be held that morning, in Dover Street, at eleven o'clock.

Before I departed for it, I penned Louisa an apology for my behavior at her house the night before. I knew I should not have let Brandon provoke me. I seemed to forever cause pain to the one woman I least wished to. I sent the letter in care of Lady Aline Carrington, Louisa's dearest friend. I disliked delivering it in this roundabout fashion, but I did not want Brandon to put it on the fire the moment he recognized my handwriting. Louisa would at least do me the courtesy of reading it, even if she, too, burnt it afterward.

It was just eleven when I slid inside the dim public house on Dover Street and took a seat near the back wall. The murder had been committed in the parish of St. George's and so the inquest was held there as well. The coroner called the proceeding to order. Sir Montague Harris had chosen to attend, and the coroner had called in a doctor, rather unnecessarily, I thought, because Inglethorpe had obviously died of the stab wound, and the butler could fix the time of death within half an hour. But I supposed the coroner wanted to be thorough. The doctor, a thin, spidery man with pomaded black hair, confirmed that because of the warmth of the body and the stickiness of the blood when he'd been found, that Inglethorpe had died not more than thirty minutes before that. In other words, by half past two yesterday afternoon.

The coroner interviewed the butler who had discovered the body. The man was nervous, wetting his lips and darting his gaze about, but no more uncomfortable than any man being asked such questions would be. He'd seen his master at two o'clock, he said, when he'd served him a light meal upon Inglethorpe's rising from bed. He'd gone back to the servants' hall and attended to duties below stairs until he'd gone to the first floor at half-past two. He'd found the front door standing open. He'd closed it, annoyed that the footman had not noticed, then stepped into the reception room and found his master.

The butler's lips were gray when he finished, and he walked heavily to his seat.

Pomeroy rose and gave his evidence about being summoned to the crime by the Queen's Square magistrate and finding Inglethorpe there, dead, and recognizing the walking stick as belonging to me. When he finished, the coroner asked me to rise.

From where I stood before the coroner, I could view the entire room. I spotted Bartholomew sitting to the right of the jury and Grenville next to him, his curled beaver hat resting on his knee. Grenville caught my eye, but sent no acknowledgment. The room was warm and stuffy, the smell of steaming wool and damp hair pomade just covering the odor of stale cabbage. My sword-stick, still covered with dried blood, lay naked on a table before the coroner.

I identified the sword-stick and explained how I had left it behind on Wednesday, when I'd attended a gathering, at Inglethorpe's invitation. The coroner asked what kind of gathering, and I told him of the scientific gas that Inglethorpe had had in the bags, which produced an interesting, but temporary euphoria. The coroner nodded, as though he'd heard of such things before. I explained that I'd returned to Inglethorpe's yesterday—to look for the walking stick, which I could not afford to lose—and had found the Runner, Pomeroy, there, who had informed me of Inglethorpe's death.

The coroner seemed quite interested in me. He tried to make me tell him that I had arrived at Inglethorpe's unseen at quarter-past two, crept in, and stabbed the man to death, being obliging enough to leave my own sword behind. Fortunately, I could place myself at the moneylender's in the City during the hour of Inglethorpe's death.

The coroner questioned me about why I had not returned to Inglethorpe's as soon as I'd realized I'd left the stick behind the day before, and I explained that I'd borrowed another from a friend, since I'd had other engage-

ments. He at last seemed to take my word for it, and dismissed me.

Calling the butler back, the coroner asked what had become of the walking stick between the time I'd left it and the time I'd returned for it. The butler, still nervous, said that he'd found no walking stick left behind in the sitting room where Mr. Inglethorpe's guests had gathered; he'd never seen it. Neither had any of the other servants in the house.

The coroner nodded, made a tick on his paper, and moved on to his next note. He questioned the butler about who had been in the house when Inglethorpe had died, which had been the servants and no other guests, according to the butler. The coroner then asked about the gathering the day before—one of those attending could have taken the walking stick, then returned and killed Inglethorpe with it.

Each gentleman who'd been present, including Mr. Yardley and Mr. Price-Davies, who Mrs. Danbury had indicated had remained after I departed, stood up before the coroner and told his story. Each was quite similar.

They had attended the gathering at Inglethorpe's invitation to partake of his magical gas. They had met in the upstairs drawing room, where'd they'd breathed the air and sat in comfort. The first three gentlemen had departed the house before I had. Mr. Yardley said he thought he remembered seeing the walking stick left behind, but he'd not mentioned it to his host. Whyever should he? he demanded when the coroner asked him why not. Inglethorpe had servants to clean up the rooms and restore any lost property. That's what servants were for, weren't they? He hadn't thought anything more about it.

Mr. Price-Davies hadn't remembered one way or another about any walking stick. None of the gentlemen claimed to have returned to visit Mr. Inglethorpe the next day, and all could put themselves somewhere else, with witnesses at the time of his death.

After this, the coroner summoned the two ladies who

had attended Inglethorpe's on Wednesday from where they had been waiting in a private room. Lady Breckenridge sat tall and straight before the coroner and told him in clear tones that she had gone to Inglethorpe's on Wednesday, left at about half-past four, hadn't taken Captain Lacey's walking stick, and had not returned to Inglethorpe's the next day. Between two and three on Thursday, she had been at her toilette, being attended by her maids, who could attest to that fact.

She easily fielded any question the coroner sent her way. In her dark blue pelisse and widow's bonnet, she looked quiet and respectable and elegant, but her eyes were as sharp as ever. She stared haughtily down her nose at the coroner, and if she'd had a cigarillo in hand, she would have blown smoke into his face.

Mrs. Danbury, on the other hand, looked unhappy to be present. Sir Gideon Derwent had escorted her, I was pleased to see, and he stood beside her while the coroner questioned her. She told the same story as had Lady Breckenridge; she'd gone to the gathering at Inglethorpe's invitation, partaken of the strange gas, then gone home. No, she did not remember noticing any other gentleman going away with the walking stick. She had gone out yesterday afternoon to shop, though she could not remember precisely where she had been between two and three, but she certainly had not gone to stab Inglethorpe.

The coroner nodded and dismissed her, and Sir Gideon led her away. Her face was white and she leaned heavily on Sir Gideon's arm.

It occurred to me, and I wondered if it had occurred to the jury, that the butler himself had the best opportunity with which to dispatch his master. He would know that everyone in the house would be safely out of the way, he could divert Inglethorpe to the reception room, and he could have hidden my walking stick beforehand and professed to have no knowledge of it. The butler must have thought so, as well, because his nervousness increased as the inquest went on.

The coroner finished, and then the jury went away to confer. When they returned, they gave their verdict, death by person or persons unknown. The coroner instructed Pomeroy and his patrols to continue investigating to find the culprit. He then closed the inquest, and dismissed us.

CHAPTER 10

L ADY Breckenridge emerged from the public house behind me as we all filed out. I tipped my hat, and she
bowed neutrally in passing. "Good morning, Captain," she
said, without stopping. "Ghastly hour to be dragged from
one's home."

She continued to her landau, her bearing poised. Her
footman quickly set a padded step stool before her, which
she climbed upon to enter the carriage. A pair of splendid
ankles flashed beneath her hem before she reached the seat
inside, and the footman closed the door.

I saw Mrs. Danbury being taken to the Derwent coach
farther along. Sir Gideon led her, his arm about her shoulders, looking worried. She did not look around or see me.

As Sir Gideon's coach pulled away, Sir Montague
paused by my side. "A relieving verdict for the coroner,
was it not?" he said cheerfully. "Must have been tricky
when he learned that all those Mayfair gentlemen might
have been involved. Gentlemen with influence, gentlemen
upon which his position depends, perhaps. Presiding over

the case of a drowned prostitute or a dead vagrant is so much easier."

The coroner himself walked by us at this point, his lips thin. Unembarrassed, Sir Montague bowed to him.

"I noted that the coroner did not mention Inglethorpe's clothes," I said. "Or lack of them."

Sir Montague gave me a conspiratorial wink. "Why complicate things, eh? Most curious, though, is it not? I am interested in those clothes."

I thought again about Inglethorpe, lying on his back, feet apart, surprised and alone. Fine pantaloons had encased his legs, and his coat and shirt and waistcoat had been neatly folded on a chair. His shoes—I stopped, frowning.

"What are you thinking, Captain?" Sir Montague's eyes twinkled in the weak winter sunlight.

"He wore pumps," I said. "But their soles were muddy."

"Is that significant?"

"It is if you are a gentleman of his standing. Those shoes were not meant to be worn outside."

Sir Montague raised his brows. "No?"

"Grenville must have a dozen pairs of slippers he wears only inside his house. Inglethorpe's shoes were meant to be worn indoors with pantaloons. More to set off his feet than for function. Yet, they had mud on them. As though he'd run out onto the street for a few minutes."

Sir Montague rocked a little on his heels. "To meet someone, perhaps?"

"Or he saw something," I offered, "and it surprised him, so he went out to investigate. Or perhaps he went out to bring a person back inside with him."

"Hmm. And then took off half his clothes. A lover, perhaps?"

"Perhaps." The explanation did not quite ring true. If a man had a sudden assignation, did he carefully remove his clothing and fold it neatly on a chair? Or were the clothes hastily dropped on the floor, or not completely removed at all?

"There may be something in what you say," Sir Montague said. "By the way, Mr. Thompson told me of your doings in the Glass House the other night." He chuckled. "You must have put the wind up them."

I was not so certain. Kensington did not seem easily frightened; in fact, he'd been a bit overconfident, even when I'd broken the window. "Kensington is key to the business of the Glass House and Peaches' death," I said. "I am convinced."

"Being convinced is not proof," Sir Montague pointed out. "I want no holes in this case."

"I know. The girl I rescued could tell you an earful. I believe Kensington might work for a man called James Denis, although I have not confirmed that. But if you are looking for a man powerful enough to block the magistrates and reformers, it would be Denis."

Sir Montague nodded gravely. "I have heard of him, of course. Corruption is rife, unfortunately, and his name crops up when corruption does." He looked thoughtful. "I'll question Kensington myself. Don't frighten him too much, yet. I do not want him slipping away, or turning to Mr. Denis for protection."

"I have also put Sir Gideon Derwent on the scent," I said. "The child is staying with him. He is a powerful man, in his own way."

"Indeed." Sir Montague gave me another nod and smile. "You have done well over this. We will close the Glass House yet."

I felt pleased he thought so, but I wished I shared his optimism. James Denis was powerful, and did not let things go easily.

Sir Montague and I took leave of each other then, he promising to keep me informed of what he did regarding the Glass House. He tipped his hat and strolled away, his walking stick tapping the pavement in a cheerful staccato.

I turned, thinking to make for a hackney stand to return home, and found my path blocked by the huge Bartholomew. "Hullo, sir. Mr. Grenville says, will you

please join him for a meal at home. He wants you to hear my news." He winked. "And I have a lot of it, sir."

Indeed, the lad looked almost ready to burst. But he manfully held it in and took me to where Grenville's carriage awaited. Matthias opened the door, and Bartholomew more or less pushed me inside and closed it behind me. The carriage, warm and smelling of heated coal, rolled away even before I'd seated myself.

Grenville sat on the opposite seat. He gave me the barest nod, then rested his hands on his own walking stick and looked out the window, pretending interest in the sights of Mayfair, which he saw every day. The carriage bumped its slow way through the streets while the black forms of landaus and carriages and hackneys scraped by us.

He was displeased with me, and I had a good idea why. I merely said, "Thank you for the invitation to dine. It is kind of you."

Grenville at last turned to me. He looked me up and down, brows together, as though he had not heard me. "For God's sake, Lacey, why did you give me that bank draft?"

I regarded him quietly. I knew he would become high-handed about the three hundred guineas, and I was not about to let him. "Do not dare to try to return it to me."

He turned red. "Good God, you know I cannot accept it. I paid that money to assist with the investigation, because I was just as curious as you. And if it helped take that little girl out of the Glass House, it was worth it."

"Perhaps," I said evenly. "But I have no wish to take advantage of my friends. The debt has been paid; that is the end of the matter."

He started to speak again, then closed his mouth and glared at me. "You are bloody stubborn and too damned proud."

"I am well aware of my shortcomings."

We studied each other, he in his impeccably tailored suit not a week old, me in my worn clothing topped with a frock coat that had been his gift to me last September.

Grenville rather liked to own people, I'd come to know, and he used his forceful generosity to do so.

"I do not want to quarrel over this, Lacey," he said.

"Then accept the money, and have done."

He looked angry. He did not like to lose. "It was a damn fool thing to do."

"Perhaps."

We shared a look. At last Grenville gave a nod and changed the subject, though I knew he'd later try to open the argument again. "Mrs. Chapman's funeral is today," he said. "Lord Barbury sent me word."

I relaxed a bit, absorbed the soothing heat from the punched tin coal boxes on the floor. "The coroner has released her body, then. I would like to attend."

"As would I," Grenville said. "Do you mind if I accompany you?"

"Not at all. I will be interested to see who will appear."

Grenville also expressed that interest, and we fell silent again. Fortunately, the drive to Grosvenor Street was short, and we had no time to renew our stiff argument.

Matthias let us out before Grenville's house and Bartholomew ushered us inside. Not long after that, I was seated in Grenville's dining room, eating the fine light repast his chef, Anton, had created for us.

When we'd finished and the two footmen had cleared the table, Grenville bade them sit with us and share their findings. The two big lads served us port and then sat down to slurp glasses of bitter and rest their elbows on the table in a comfortable manner that was in no way impudent.

Bartholomew had done admirably. "Mr. Inglethorpe's cook is my aunt's husband's sister," he said. "And she is quite chatty. So was the footman."

I had suspected the servants below stairs at Inglethorpe's would be far more forthcoming to Bartholomew than they would have been to Pomeroy, or even myself. Bartholomew had connections to them, and no doubt they had been eager to gossip about the excitement that had happened in their house.

Bartholomew pulled a paper out of his pocket, with words written in careful capitals, and handed it to Grenville, who spread it open on the table.

"They were full of interesting information," Bartholomew went on. "And, I talked to some of the slaveys of the men who were at Inglethorpe's Wednesday afternoon."

"Excellent," Grenville said, smoothing the paper. "Let us begin with Robert Yardley, who said today he remembered the walking stick, but not whether anyone took it. Most helpful of him."

Bartholomew took a drink of ale. "Mr. Yardley is a bachelor, sir. Lives in Brook Street. Has only one footman, who is a country oaf in satin."

"Would Yardley be likely to stab Inglethorpe through the heart with a sword?" I asked.

Bartholomew rubbed his nose. "Wouldn't think so, sir. Not much wherewithal, I'd say. According to his footman, he likes a soft chair and a footstool and his cup and saucer handed to him even when it is on the table right next to him. Mr. Yardley was at home yesterday afternoon, so his footman says, at the time in question."

"Unless the footman is lying for him," Grenville commented. "Now, what about Mr. Archibald Price-Davies—who saw nothing, knows nothing? Another helpful gentleman."

"Friend of Mr. Yardley," Bartholomew said promptly. "Likes horses, doesn't talk of much else." He chuckled. "Got Mr. Grenville into a corner one afternoon and plagued him about nearly every horse in London, wanting his opinion and such."

Grenville grimaced. "I remember."

"So, a nuisance full of his own opinion," I said. "But a murderer?"

"Could not say, sir. Maybe if he and Mr. Inglethorpe disagreed about a horse."

"An unlikely motive for murder," I said. "Although any of them could have exchanged heated words with the man and killed him in a fit of rage."

"He was at Tattersall's, yesterday, all day," Matthias put in. "If you can believe his groom."

"Very convenient," Grenville said. "Next is Lord Clarence Dudley."

"Marquess of Ackerley's youngest brother," Bartholomew said. "Would not do anything to mar his manicure, I would say. And I hear he is an unnatural."

"A sodomite?" I asked.

Bartholomew nodded, and Grenville and I exchanged a glance. Inglethorpe was known to be interested in gentlemen himself. And Inglethorpe had undressed himself for someone. Grenville said, "At the inquest, Dudley claimed to have been at home still in bed at three."

"Certainly he was," Bartholomew answered, "his valet says with the next gent on your list."

Grenville raised his brows, consulted the paper. "Arthur Dunstan."

"Mr. Dunstan goes about everywhere with this Lord Clarence Dudley. If you see what I mean, sir."

"Hmm," Grenville said. "No wonder they both mumbled a bit about where they had been. If they'd been frank, they'd have ended up in the dock themselves."

In the dock and then in the pillory. A man could be hanged for sodomy, but only if penetration was witnessed. Those merely strongly suspected of it would stand in the pillory, made vulnerable to the mood of the crowds that passed them. A man could die in the stocks if the mob were enraged enough.

"The last man is Mr. Carleton Pauling, MP," Grenville went on. "I know him slightly. I have not the remotest idea if he would kill Inglethorpe or why."

"He is a radical, sir, at least that's what everyone says," Bartholomew reported. "I suppose a radical could be a murderer. Except he was in Parliament that afternoon. Plenty of people saw him."

"Yes, so he claimed," Grenville said.

A drop of ink had puddled on the *C* of Mr. Carleton Pauling. "They each have alibis," I remarked, "confirmed

by their servants. Unless one of them is lying and has convinced their servants to lie as well."

"So where does that leave us?" Bartholomew asked. He sipped at his ale.

"Nowhere," I answered. "At least not yet. Bartholomew, could you and Matthias prevail again upon your acquaintance with these gentlemen's slaveys and discover for certain whether or not they picked up the walking stick? And whether any of them were acquainted with Mrs. Chapman, or at least an actress known as Peaches?"

Bartholomew nodded. Matthias looked eager, too, ready to render me assistance. To them, it was adventure.

We looked over the list again, but there was not much more to discuss. We sent Bartholomew and Matthias off, and Grenville and I made our way to Peaches' funeral.

THE sky had clouded over by the time we reached the burial ground of a church near Cavendish Square, but at least it did not rain. The vicar, who looked uninterested in the whole proceeding, waited while the mourners approached the grave. There were not many. Mr. Chapman stood stiffly near the vicar, rigid and displeased at missing his appointments. A thin woman stood next to him, looking enough like him that I guessed she was Chapman's sister. A prim-looking gentleman waited next to her, likely the sister's husband.

I spied Lord Barbury, wearing unrelieved black, his hat pulled down to hide his eyes, standing near the railings that separated the churchyard from the street. Farther back, in the shadow of a tree, I saw, to my surprise, Mr. Kensington. He saw me and gave me a belligerent stare.

Grenville and I arranged ourselves not too near the grave, but close enough so that we might pay our respects. The vicar, conceding that no one else would appear, opened the Prayer Book and began.

He must have read this service a good many times, because he went through the lines in a hurried monotone, in the attitude of a man who wanted to get out of the cold as

quickly as possible. Chapman stared at the ground, his mouth shaping the responses, while his sister and husband spoke them loudly and clearly. "Lord have mercy upon us, Christ have mercy upon us."

The vicar concluded the service, said the blessing, shook Mr. Chapman's hand, and disappeared back to the church. The sextant began the task of filling in the grave.

We approached Chapman, who looked in no way pleased to see us. "My condolences, sir," I said.

"I have nothing more to say to Bow Street," he responded at once.

"I truly came here to pay my condolences. I am sorry for your loss. She was too young for such a fate."

He scowled. "Did you know my wife?"

"No. But I saw her when she was found."

Mr. Chapman eyed me in an unfriendly manner, but I saw a bleak light in his eyes behind his habitual stiffness. Despite the self-righteous looks his sister and her husband wore, he might actually mourn his wife.

Chapman's sister glanced once at the sextant, who was cheerfully plying his shovel to the rich, black earth. "Blood will tell, I always said. And it has."

Not the most tactful thing, I thought, to say to a man who had just buried his wife.

"A gentleman named Simon Inglethorpe died yesterday," I said to Chapman. "In Mayfair. You might have read of it."

"I have better things to do than read the newspapers."

"He was an acquaintance of your wife," I went on. "Did you know him?"

Chapman bathed me in a freezing glare. "She apparently had many acquaintances."

"I have an idea that the same man who killed Inglethorpe also killed your wife."

"That is the magistrate's business."

He started to walk away, but I stepped in front of him. "Your wife was murdered, sir. I would think you'd be interested in discovering the culprit."

He eyed me in dislike. "Of course I wish to discover the culprit. But I have been a barrister for many years. I know that murderers are foolish people who do foolish things to give themselves away. The Bow Street patrollers will find him soon, and then I will prosecute." He gave me and Grenville a cold bow. "Good day to you, sirs."

He took his sister's arm and stalked away. The sister's husband, silent, but radiating disapproval, followed.

We watched as Chapman passed first Lord Barbury, then Kensington. He made no sign that he recognized either of them.

Kensington had remained under his tree, staring toward the grave, as though lost in thought. Grenville and I held a low discussion, then I made my way to Kensington, while Grenville approached Lord Barbury.

Kensington watched me as I walked to him. His eyes flickered when I stopped before him, but he stood his ground.

"You lied to me," I said.

Kensington drew himself up. "Do not be self-righteous with me, Captain. You were the one breaking the windows and the furniture. You have crossed a person who does not like to be crossed. It will be costly to have the window replaced."

"I do not give a pig's ear about your window. I asked you to show me Peaches' chamber, and you took me to the wrong room."

"Correction, Captain. You asked me to show you where she and Lord Barbury met. And I did."

"I want to see the other chamber she kept there."

He looked smug. "You cannot. It is locked, and only she had the key."

My hand tightened on my borrowed walking stick. "I do not believe you cannot enter that room if you do not want to. Let us visit the Glass House and try right now, shall we?"

He bristled. "You cannot force me to do anything, and you know it."

"I can always summon a magistrate. Sir Montague Harris has wanted to look at the Glass House for a long time."

He stared, incredulous. "I cannot believe you, Captain. You do not know your danger."

"I have some idea of it," I said dryly. I'd had run-ins with James Denis before. "What did you and Mrs. Chapman argue about the day she died?"

He looked startled. "I have no idea what you mean."

"You shouted, she laughed. What was the row about?"

"I do not remember. Perhaps I did shout something at her. Peaches could be quite a bitch, if you must know."

"She is lying dead not twenty feet from here," I said evenly. "Keep your remarks respectful."

"That does not change what she was. I knew her since she was eighteen years old and first in awe of London. I know everything there is to know about her, never mind her husband or her lordship lover."

"I believe," I said quietly, "that you also do not know your danger."

He gave me a deprecating look. "Very well, Captain, I will show you the bloody attic room. I planned to burn all her things anyway. They are of no use to me."

I opened my mouth to say more, but he looked past me and flushed. I turned. Lord Barbury had stopped behind me, with Grenville. Moisture beaded on Barbury's dark lashes. One man, at least, mourned for Peaches.

Lord Barbury did not look well. He seemed to have aged since Peaches' death; his eyelids were waxen, his face pale, the bristles on his jaw dark against his white skin.

"What the devil are you doing here?" he snarled at Kensington.

"Saying good-bye to my lass," Kensington answered.

Barbury's eyes glowed with anger. "Captain Lacey, do not trust this man. He is a snake, and he made Peaches' life miserable."

"Gullible fool," Kensington sneered. "You should ask what she did to *my* life."

"You used her until she had nothing left," Barbury snapped. "Then when she made it clear she preferred me to you, you tried to buy her back."

"And she came running. What does that say for you, my fine lord?"

"Gentlemen," Grenville interrupted. "We are standing in a churchyard."

"Not for much longer," Kensington said angrily. "Are you coming, Captain?"

Grenville looked a question. As Kensington whirled about and marched away, I told Grenville that I was going with him to have another look at the Glass House, to see what Peaches had left behind there.

Barbury started. His eyes betrayed his deep grief, but I sympathized only so far. If he had truly loved her, he would have married her and cared for her, damn her origins.

"Would you like to come with me?" I asked him.

He hesitated a long moment, then his gloved fingers closed and he looked away. "No," he said at last. "No, I do not want to come."

"Tell us about it tonight," Grenville said. "I've invited Lord Barbury to dine with us at my house. We'll begin at eight."

I nodded. Barbury looked at me again, his agony evident. He very much wanted to see what Peaches had left behind, to touch what she had touched, but knew that his emotions might get the better of him. I sympathized. When my wife had left me, sorting through her things and those of my daughter had been purest torture. I had been lucky that Louisa had been there to help.

I touched my hat to Lord Barbury and Grenville, then hurried after the disappearing figure of Mr. Kensington.

CHAPTER 11

⁓⁓

THE Glass House by day was a depressing place. Silent and lit by gray daylight, it felt like a place holding its breath. The only inhabitant I saw was the doorman, who gave me a belligerent stare as he let us in.

Kensington took me up two flights of stairs, past the room he'd shown me before, and up into the attics. Two doors stood one on either side of the low-ceilinged stairwell. Kensington still claimed he did not have a key, but the door he pointed out was a bit flimsy. I applied my boot heel to the latch, and on the third kick, it gave way, the wood splintering a little. Kensington looked startled, as though he'd believed me feeble, despite having seen me throw a chair through a window.

The room beyond was a bedchamber, quite a cozy one at that. It had been made as comfortable as possible with a thick rug and bed hangings of deep blue brocade, and plenty of pillows on the bed. An odd jumble of furniture was strewn about, but each piece had been chosen for comfort—a deep wing chair, a low writing table with a

cushioned stool, a settee with a side table littered with novels. A fireplace held the ashes of a fire not many days cold, the brass fender shone brightly, and the coal bucket was full.

"She did like her little luxuries," Kensington said, voice scornful.

"Yes," I said. "Now, go away."

He gave me an incredulous look, then laughed, his pudgy belly moving. "I admire your cheek, Captain. Watching you fall will be most pleasurable."

Still chuckling, he left the room and descended the stairs, leaving me alone.

I looked about the room, which had obviously been inhabited by a woman—feminine touches were everywhere, from the lace on the cushions to the hair ribbons on the dressing table. And in that room, in the gray silence of this house, I found Peaches.

I found her in the clumsily embroidered pillows on the bed, in the silver pen tray engraved with her initials—probably gift from Lord Barbury—in the dresses in the wardrobe that were all silk, all daringly cut, all too lovely for a respectable barrister's wife.

In the drawers of the writing desk, I found torn-out pages of newspapers dated six years ago, each page containing an article about a play. In each, the name "Miss Leary" had been circled with a charcoal pencil. Peaches had been Amelia Leary until her marriage, I remembered. The articles gave the highest accolades to the principal actors. When they mentioned Peaches at all, it was at most one line. "Miss Leary gave a fine performance as Bianca," was the lengthiest notice she received.

Another drawer held Lord Barbury's letters to her. She had kept them from the time they'd first met, after a performance one evening in Drury Lane. He'd written many letters during their first year as lovers, stopping only at her marriage. He had left London seldom, but he had written her every day, whether they'd met or not.

I skimmed through them, feeling like a voyeur. When

Peaches had decided to marry, Lord Barbury's tone was resigned. "I wish only happiness for you, my darling, and if this is the kind of happiness you wish, I will not stand in its path. A woman wants to be her own mistress in her own household with her own children . . . Nights will be long without you, but I am grateful for what joy you've lent me over this twelvemonth, which has been the happiest of my life."

After they'd met again several years later, she must have written to him, because I found his response: "Seeing you was like sunshine breaking through the greatest of storms, my sweet Peaches. You ask if we can meet again, and I say, my darling, that a hundred times I have thought of contriving to meet, and only great strength of will has kept me at home. Name the place, name the time, and I will fly there with the greatest of joy, if only to touch your hand, to look upon you, to hear your voice once again."

They'd met, and his next letters had been euphoric. Later letters spoke of her unhappiness with Chapman, of Chapman's jealousy when she was not at home, of Peaches' sorrow when she realized that she would never have children. Most of all, Barbury's letters expressed his great happiness that he and Peaches were together again—monotonously so. Occasionally, he admonished her about her craving for excitement, which would get her into trouble some day, he warned. Sadly, he had been correct.

All the letters had been addressed there, to number 12, St. Charles Row. She had used this place as a home away from home, a place to which her lover could send letters, in which she could dress herself as Peaches the lovely actress and meet Lord Barbury. Her husband would likely never find this place, and she probably had paid Kensington handsomely for the privilege.

I pushed the letters away and sat lost in thought. If Chapman *had* discovered this place, and his wife's duplicity, would it have driven him to murder? He would certainly have had reason to be incensed. She and Barbury

had been conducting a most intense affair, and she had obviously been quite disappointed in her marriage to Chapman.

True, Chapman had produced a witness to swear he was dining during the hour that his wife met her death, but I could not cross Chapman off the list of suspects just yet. Of anyone, he had the greatest motive, and Peaches had been thrown into the river very close to Middle Temple Hall.

Likewise, I still could not dismiss Lord Barbury. Like Chapman, he'd had witnesses to his presence at White's at the time in question, but he could have hired someone to carry out the murder. When Peaches had given up Lord Barbury the first time, the tone of his letters had been sad, but understanding. However, other letters had shown me a fiery, passionate man—a man who very much desired a woman and was almost ill with despair when he could not see her. If Peaches had told him she wanted to end their relationship a second time, or worse, had wanted to take a different lover, could Lord Barbury have been provoked to murder? I thought it likely. Many murders were committed out of jealousy and anger; the newspapers were full of such stories.

I folded the letters again and stacked them together. When I opened the last drawer of the desk, I found there another letter, unfolded and unfinished, lying atop a neat stack of blank paper. This letter was in a different hand and addressed to "My dearest, funny, sweetest Barbury." Not the salutation of a woman to a man she planned to leave, I thought dryly.

"We will have two delicious weeks together," she wrote, "when we can pretend that we belong totally and completely to one another. Oh, my darling, my heart beats fast with thought of days and nights in your presence, where you may touch my hand or my cheek any time as though I were yours forever and ever. And nights—how I long to be with you in the dark all night long, without fearing the clock and the dawn."

She went on for a few paragraphs in this vein, excitement and desire pouring from her pen. She never mentioned Inglethorpe, or her husband, or her method for deceiving him. Why she'd never finished the letter nor sent it, I could not discern.

The clean papers beneath the page were smooth and free of indentation. I toyed for awhile with the idea that Kensington had come in and removed a second page of the letter, one that incriminated him of her murder, leaving only the top page for me to find. But if he had, he'd removed any blank sheets that might have been under it to catch the indentation. The letter stopped a good two inches above the end of the page. She likely had only written that much, then tucked the paper into the drawer to finish later.

I folded it over on itself, hiding the excited, happy words, and laid it with the rest of the letters.

I found nothing else in the writing desk and finished my search of the room. Then I seated myself on the upholstered bench at the foot of the bed, my hand on my walking stick, and looked about me.

Peaches had lived here, loved here. Had she died here? Again, I had seen nothing that had obviously pointed to her murder, but Kensington could easily have come in and removed any evidence. I did not much believe that he did not have a separate key.

I found it strange that the house had this one oasis of calm, where Peaches had found refuge, a room in which to be herself. I had expected the room to be a terrible place, a prison, but it felt more like a sanctuary. Peaches had had this one place of her own, in which she could lock out her husband, Kensington, and even her lover if she chose.

I stayed there for a time, listening to the faint sounds of traffic outside, then I rose and gathered up the letters. There was a fairly large bundle, but I took them all. I gave the room a last look, then descended to the ground floor

of the house and bade the doorman run and fetch a hackney coach for me.

He was ill disposed to help me at all, but Kensington appeared and told the man to do what I said.

Kensington eyed the bundle of letters while I waited. "Finished prying, Captain?"

"For now," I said. I eyed him coldly. "Tell me, what exactly were you to her, all those years ago, when she was a girl and just going on the stage?"

"A friend, I hope," Kensington answered smoothly.

"What did you do for her? And what did you make her do for you?"

"I resent your implication, Captain. I managed to introduce her to a company of players, get her a part on a stage, expose her to people with influence. That is all."

"She did not like you."

"She was young. With a head full of romantic notions. Ladies, you know."

"If I discover you murdered her," I said, my voice steady. "May God have mercy on you."

His eyes flickered the slightest bit and his bravado faltered. He was not exactly afraid of me, but he was uncertain. I liked that.

A hackney coach rolled to a stop in front of the door, and I departed with my treasures.

IT was a long, slow, cold ride back to Covent Garden. We wound through the City to Fleet Street, then through the Temple Bar and onto the Strand and so to Grimpen Lane. It was dark by the time I climbed the stairs to my rooms.

Bartholomew was there, tidying, brushing my regimentals for my evening meal with Grenville and Lord Barbury. I bade him find me a box for the letters, and he returned from the attics with a small one of rough wood, into which the letters just fit. I would return them to Lord Barbury, to do with what he liked.

When Bartholomew deemed the regimentals ready for me, he helped me into them. Before I'd finished fastening

the cords on my coat, someone knocked at the door. Bartholomew went to answer, then returned to tell me that Mrs. Beltan, my landlady, was asking for me.

"It's Mrs. Brandon, sir," Mrs. Beltan said when I reached the front room. "She's downstairs and would like a word."

I descended and entered the bakeshop in some disquiet. Louisa usually thought nothing of walking upstairs to my rooms, leaving her footman to gnaw bread and wait for her. That she'd chosen to send Mrs. Beltan upstairs for me worried me somewhat.

The shop was full of customers at this time of day, including Louisa's footman, who was chewing on a pastry. Mrs. Beltan led me to the little parlor behind the shop and closed the door behind me.

Louisa waited there, in a room that reminded me of Mrs. Beltan herself. Everything was plump and cozy and old fashioned. Cushions covered nearly every flat surface, cushions that were fat and tasseled, thin and embroidered, plump and plush. They were piled on the Turkish couch, the two chairs, the window sill, and the shelves of a cupboard.

Louisa sat on the Turkish couch and did not rise when I entered. Her eyes, which had blazed at me in anger a few nights ago, looked tired.

"Louisa, what is it?"

I went to her and raised her hands from her lap. She did not protest when I pressed a light kiss to each, but she kept her fingers loosely curled.

"I beg your pardon," she said, her voice weary. "I did not mean to worry you. I've only come to ask you for a favor."

"You know I would do anything for you."

"Good. Then I will ask you to please cease baiting my husband."

She looked up at me, and I stilled. In her eyes was something I had never seen before. She was not angry. She had gone beyond that.

"He is easy to bait, Louisa," I said lightly, trying to stem my rising alarm. "He has no imagination."

"I know. He is as stubborn as you are."

I released her hands. "Thank you very much."

"You can stop this, Gabriel. You simply will not."

I took a step back, gave a bitter laugh. "You would like me to pretend that things are well and mended, as we did all last autumn? That was not easy, as you must have known. I am pleased that we have returned to normal."

She rose in a rustle of cotton, her cheeks red. "I see. So you are happy to stand there and tell me how glad you are that you and Aloysius have returned to bickering like schoolboys? I am tired of it, Gabriel. Tired of your arguments and of being caught in the middle. I am tired of you."

Her words struck me like pistol balls. She rushed on. "Do you think I enjoy knowing what you fight one another about? You are dear to me, Gabriel, dearer than almost anyone in the world, you always have been. You have told me I am dear to you."

"You are," I said. I felt a dull pain in my chest.

"Then why do you force me to choose? I am loyal to my husband. I always will be. He deserves that."

My temper broke. "For God's sake, why? The man was ready to put you aside because you disappointed his selfish plans for fathering a dynasty. He deserves you spitting on him."

She shook her head. "I do not think he ever meant to divorce me. Not truly."

"No? He made a damn good pretense of it."

"I misread him. I know that now. He hurt me, and I wanted to hurt him back."

"So you came to me that night simply to hurt him?" I asked, tight-lipped.

She stared at me, anguished. "I do not know why I did what I did that night. I ran to you because I was afraid and confused, and so angry, Gabriel, you do not know how angry."

"I have some idea."

Her eyes were clear gray, like rain-washed skies. "No, you do not. He had wounded me at my weakest point, and I was furious at him for that. He had shattered my pride, and I wanted to strike back at him. You took me in and were so indignant on my behalf, and that pleased me."

"It pleased me, too," I said, remembering.

I had hated Aloysius Brandon that night. When Louisa's tears had ceased enough that she could tell me her story, I had been ready to murder Brandon on the spot. Louisa had several times tried to give him his hoped-for son, and had failed each time. The enlightened Colonel Brandon had blamed Louisa. I knew she secretly blamed herself, though she never voiced the thought.

I, on the other hand, put the blame squarely on Brandon. If he'd treasured Louisa as he ought, likely he would even now be surrounded by a horde of children.

"I believe what angered him most is that you took my side against him," she said.

I smiled wryly, hurt tainting my words. "Not finding you in my arms?"

Not in bed. I had held her close, letting her cry on my shoulder, while I had tumbled her hair and kissed her forehead. We'd been sitting on a camp chair, her cradled on my lap, the morning after she'd fled her husband, when Brandon had come looking for her. I never forgot the look on his face. For all his bluster that he wanted to give her up, he damn well never meant for me to have her.

"No," Louisa said now. "We'd both stood against him, and he could not bear that. He has always been much more worried about his pride than his love."

She was wrong. Brandon had wanted to kill me. He had certainly tried to kill me later.

"He is proud," I agreed. "His pride will be the death of him."

"I could say the same of you," she retorted.

I could not argue. I had asked her, this past summer, why she stayed with the irritating man. She had replied

that she remembered the man he was, the admirable, brave, and compelling captain who had lured me from my Norfolk home. She still saw that in him, she'd said. I could only see a man who'd let his achievements puff him up until he raged at minor disappointments. He'd wanted everything: the perfect wife, the perfect family, the perfect career, and perfect devotion from me, the man he had created. He'd almost had everything until his pride had destroyed it.

"I cannot help baiting him," I said, hiding my uneasiness behind a sardonic tone. "He needs reminding that he ruined me. He can wait as long as he likes for me to fall on my knees and beg his forgiveness. I enjoy reminding him that I've had done being his toady."

She glared at me, furious. "Do you think *I* enjoy it? Watching you at each other's throats, hurling abuse at one another? I left the room the other night, but I would have had to flee to the next county to avoid hearing you. The servants, too, were most embarrassed."

"I know you get caught in our cross fire," I said, chagrined. "I am sorry. You know I never mean to hurt you."

"But it does hurt me, and neither you nor my husband let that stop you. How many times will you apologize to me, how many times will I forgive you for friendship's sake? I am running out of forgiveness."

I looked at her in sudden apprehension. "You are the dearest friend I have in the world, Louisa. I try to keep my temper around your husband, but he is so damned provoking. I could chew through a spoon trying to hold in my anger when he begins pontificating. You must know by now that reconciliation is impossible."

"Well you ought to chew through the spoon, then. And I know you will not reconcile. Both of you refuse to unbend. My meetings with you enrage my husband, as you know they do. I believe you encourage visits between myself and you simply to annoy him. And so they must stop."

The floor seemed to tilt like the deck of a ship.

"Louisa, when I meet with you, it has nothing to do with your husband."

"You might think so, but in the back of your mind, you know you are rubbing salt in his wounds. And you delight in it." She sighed. "I, too, am not guiltless. I have kept up our friendship, meeting you and telling him of it, almost daring him to say there is anything untoward. But defiance grows wearying after a time. I want it to stop."

My world tilted further. "What are you saying? That we must sacrifice our friendship to soothe Aloysius Brandon's temper?"

"I am saying that this farce has gone on long enough. If you and my husband will not reconcile, then I will not take your side against him. He is my husband; I live with him day after day, and I do not want to be at war with him. I am too old for this. I am forty-three, Gabriel, rather long in the tooth for storms. I want peace."

"You will never find peace with Brandon," I said darkly. I knew I was behaving foolishly, but a great gap of fear had opened at my feet.

"You are wrong. When he is not reminded of you or confronted by you, we are a most tranquil couple."

She was wrong again, I thought desperately. Her so-called tranquility was not harmony; it was simply the avoidance of painful subjects.

She lifted her chin, as though daring me to contradict her. "I deserve that peace. I want it. And so I want you to stay away."

I felt sick. I wanted to reach out and hold onto something. "You are abandoning me?"

She looked at me a long time, her eyes sad, but tired. "Yes," she said quietly.

I tried to still my panic. She had no obligation to me, I told myself. We had been thrown together during our years in the regiment, she a commander's wife, me the cocksure officer who had risen on my own bravado. In times of fear, triumph, grief, and joy, I had always known Louisa would be there. She was the firm ground in the

quagmire of my life. Even when she was not physically present, the mere thought of her had been enough to bolster my spirits. I had gotten myself out of many a tight spot on a battlefield by swearing that I would make it back so I could tell Louisa the tale.

Now, in London, with our lives so dramatically changed, I needed her more than ever. I was lost here, but I was never lost with her.

She fingered her cloak. "You have forced me to choose, and I have chosen. I came here only to tell you."

My panic threatened to overwhelm me. "Damn it, Louisa, seeing you, our friendship, that is what makes me live from day to day."

Her eyes blazed anew, ingots in the cold room. "Do not dare blackmail me with guilt, Gabriel. And do not dare fall into melancholia to sway me back to you. Next time I will not come running."

It cost her to say those words. I saw that. But she had forced herself to say them. She was tired of me and my temper and my melancholia. She had finished with me.

And I could not bear it. "Louisa, for God's sake. I'll lick his boots if you want me to. I'll attend Sunday dinner and raise a dozen toasts to him. I will do what you want."

She regarded me sadly, the heat gone. "It is too late. Let it be done with."

"At least give me a chance to put things right, or at least make them better for you."

"No," she said. "This entire rift was my doing from the beginning. Mine. So I am putting it right. You and Aloysius will have to live with it." I must have looked as anguished as I felt, because her expression softened. "I do not mean I will cut you forever. We may speak when we meet. But nothing deeper than that. I cannot pretend any longer."

She turned away.

"What do you mean?" I said. My throat ached. "What do you mean you cannot pretend? Cannot pretend you care for me? Tell me plainly."

She was at the door, hand on the door handle. "Any words I tell you, you will twist. I will not let you."

She opened the door. The voices of Mrs. Beltan's customers came to us, riding on a scent of warm yeast and baking bread. I could not call after her. I could not beg her to stay. I could only stand there, my hands curling and uncurling, while the woman I cared for most in the world walked out of my life.

CHAPTER 12

I lost track of the time I sat in Mrs. Beltan's parlor after Louisa had gone. I'd sunk down onto the pillow-strewn couch where she had sat, unable to move, unable to think. Time seemed to forget about me, and I forgot about it.

I could not believe I had been such a fool about a woman I cared for—again. I had loved my wife, Carlotta, loved her to distraction. And yet, I'd been impatient with her, brushed her aside with brusque words or snapped rebukes. All the while I'd think that later I would make it up to her, that I loved her so much that I could explain and ask for forgiveness, and she would understand. I could not see that all that time I had hurt her, and hurt her deeply. And then, when later came, she had been gone.

I'd been furious with myself when I'd discovered she'd eloped with her lover, knowing I'd only had myself to blame. I'd sworn that if ever I had another chance at happiness, I would be the kindest, most patient man a woman could ever know. I had learned my lesson, I'd thought, a hard and painful one.

And what had I done? Louisa had stood beside me through every one of my troubles, when Carlotta left me, through everything in the army, and now in London when our lives were so different. I owed her my very life. And, so, to repay her, I'd hurt her, letting my feud with her husband blind me to the fact that I'd abused my friendship with her and profoundly distressed her.

I sat there, angry with myself, and also angry with her. Why had she not told me I'd upset her before this? Why had she not told me so that I might stop, might make amends before it was too late?

The answer, of course, was that she had told me. Since our return to London, Louisa had tried time and again to make me reconcile with Colonel Brandon, to put the past behind us. And time and again, I had refused.

I was a blind, bloody fool, and in that little parlor, warm from the baking ovens of Mrs. Beltan's shop, I faced that naked truth.

I was still there when Bartholomew came to fetch me for the supper with Grenville and Lord Barbury. He informed me worriedly that Grenville's carriage had called for me, and I'd be late if I did not leave. I did not much care. The appointment now seemed insignificant and unimportant. I nearly told Bartholomew to go to the devil and leave me alone.

The lad watched in bewildered concern. I imagined him scampering off to Grenville, telling him I'd fallen into one of my melancholic fits. I certainly did not want Grenville charging across London in the rain to check on me.

I sighed, got to my feet, and let Bartholomew lead me out. He handed me my greatcoat, and we walked to the waiting carriage. Part of me wanted to abscond with Grenville's carriage, fly after Louisa, and beg her to reconsider. I would never do so, of course. Her happiness was far more important to me than my pride, which was one area in which I excelled over Aloysius Brandon.

The world was still dripping and gray when I arrived in Mayfair at Grenville's. We supped again in his ostentatious

dining room at a table meant for a dozen. This evening, only three of us sat here, Grenville at the head of the table, I to his right, and his guest, Lord Barbury, to his left.

As I'd noted at the funeral, Barbury had aged since Grenville's soiree, his face thin and wan. He wore three rings, large and loose on his bony fingers.

As I pretended to eat, I grew annoyed again at Louisa for choosing this of all evenings to tell me to go to the devil. Grenville's French chef was the finest cook in the land, but I could barely taste the food. I sat slightly removed from the luxury I'd been invited to partake in, attempting to keep my mind on the conversation. Grenville was talking to Barbury about inconsequential things, and it was dashed hard to concentrate. Why could not Louisa have left the task for another day?

Grenville's footmen served us quietly and efficiently, not intruding on the conversation, but always there to fill a glass or hand in a new dish. I knew that Grenville valued good food, and would let no distractions interfere with the enjoyment of it. It was like art to him; he considered shoveling in beefsteak while bellowing to one's neighbor to be the height of barbarity.

I sipped from the heavy, cut-crystal glass and tried to pay attention. Grenville had tonight as a centerpiece a small, black stone obelisk, its base covered with Egyptian picture writing. I knew full well this had come straight from Egypt, not from a shop on the Strand that specialized in Egyptian-style objets d'art. Grenville's collection was magnificent. Sometimes he opened it to the gawping public of London, but usually only a privileged few were allowed to view it. I wondered why he'd decided to display the obelisk tonight.

I idly traced the hieroglyphs as he and Lord Barbury murmured about some scandal at White's. I wondered what the writing said. French and English scholars were busily working to translate it based on finds they had brought back from Napoleon's somewhat disastrous campaign in Egypt. They had already discovered that the little

pictures were representations of sounds rather than actual pictures, a writing like Greek or Chinese. I wondered if those scholars, with their heads down in their texts, had even noticed that the war was over.

I speculated again about how long it would be before Grenville's itchy feet took him off to exotic lands. A few weeks ago, when it had been icy cold, he had spoken wistfully of Alexandria and the Nile, the vast empty spaces under a baking sun. I knew in my heart that one day he'd become bored with London, and he'd simply go.

I would miss him. He was another friend I'd come to value, and I knew I had not been as gracious to him as I could have been.

I came out of my reverie to find the table being cleared of the final course, a chilled sorbet that I'd barely touched. Grenville turned to our purpose. I had given Lord Barbury his letters, plus the one that Peaches had begun to him, upon my arrival; he'd looked at them with great sadness.

Grenville bade me report on what I had found at the Glass House, and I roused myself enough to tell them of the attic room and my conversations with Kensington.

Barbury listened, alternately saddened and angered. When I finished, he declared, "Kensington is a brute. He always was."

"He claimed that he brought about Mrs. Chapman's start on the stage, when she was very young," I said. "Can we assume that he was more than just her mentor?"

Barbury shook his head. "She never explained about him fully. If you are going to ask whether he'd ever been her lover, I do not know. She never told me. I suppose he must have been."

"How did he react when she married Chapman?" I asked.

"He tried to stop her." Barbury studied his port. "God help me, so did I. I wanted to keep her to myself."

"You could have married her," I said bluntly.

He looked up, flushed. "I know that. I did not for many reasons, none of which seem important now. Yes, I realize

that if I had defied convention and married her, she would be alive today."

He closed his mouth with a snap. I was angry enough to be pleased he felt remorse. I had become irritated with Lord Barbury when I'd stood in the room Peaches had inhabited. He'd had a treasure and not realized it. He'd had a chance to have what I'd thrown away, and he'd carelessly tossed it aside.

"At the risk of being indelicate," Grenville said, "why did she continue to live with Kensington after she met you? Is it not usual to find a ladybird a house of her own?"

Barbury nodded, not looking offended. "I did find her a house. She told me she preferred living where she did. I cannot imagine why."

Because she had not wanted to be caged, I realized suddenly. Like Marianne, who would rather live in poverty in the cheap rooms above a bakeshop than in a gilded cage provided by Lucius Grenville. Peaches might have had a freedom to come and go at the Glass House that she knew she'd not have with Lord Barbury. That attic room had not felt like a prison to me; she had stayed there by choice, and she'd kept the key herself.

It made me wonder about the precise relationship between Peaches and Mr. Kensington and exactly who'd had a hold over whom.

"I read her letter to you," I told Lord Barbury. "She was excited about deceiving her husband into thinking she would be in Sussex, but she did not elaborate upon the deception. Did she tell you her plans?"

Barbury shook his head. "She sent me a message on Sunday, asking me to come to the Glass House. When I arrived, she told me that she'd tricked her husband into letting her leave for a fortnight. I was pleased. She begged for us to attend Inglethorpe's gathering the next day, but I said I could not." He took a sharp breath. "I'd already set an appointment to meet Alvanley at White's to talk about a horse I wanted to buy from him. And then I planned to attend Mr. Grenville's soiree. I told her I'd meet her again

after that. I thought—" He broke off, pressing his hand to his eyes. "I thought we'd have plenty of time."

Grenville tactfully sipped port, letting Barbury recover. After a time, I asked, "Did she speak of planning to meet anyone else for any reason? At the Glass House, or elsewhere?"

Barbury lifted his head. His eyes were moist. "No. She chattered on as usual, but of nothing significant. She did not mention anyone else."

I traced my finger over a hieroglyph that looked like a horned snake. "She wanted to go to Inglethorpe's, you say. Do you know why? Did she mention someone she wanted to speak to there?"

"No. I tell you, she said nothing. She simply enjoyed Inglethorpe's laughing gas, that is all."

I tried another tack. "Did she ever speak much to, or about, the other gentlemen who went there?" I named the five who had attended Inglethorpe's gathering the same day I had. "Or Lady Breckenridge?"

Barbury looked mystified. "We kept ourselves to ourselves. Peaches found Lady Breckenridge rude and a bit stuck up. But she liked Inglethorpe. She talked to him, and she talked to me, and that was all."

"So, you made an arrangement to meet at the Glass House after the soiree," I said, thinking it through. "She went to Inglethorpe's by herself, and then returned to the Glass House, alone, presumably to her attic room, at sometime after four o'clock that day. She was heard arguing with Kensington—or at least he was shouting at her—then she departed by the back door soon after, never to be seen again."

"Lacey," Grenville said quietly. Barbury's throat worked as he studied his port.

"I beg your pardon," I said. "I am only trying to decide what happened."

Lord Barbury looked up, a spark of anger in his eyes. "I know you must believe I might have killed her, Lacey. That I myself met her in my carriage near the Glass House

and took her to the Temple Gardens to murder her. But I swear to you I did not. I would never have hurt her, gentlemen, never. I loved her dearly. She was my life."

He bowed his head again. I wanted to question him further, but Grenville caught my eye, shook his head. I fell silent. In my mood tonight, I squarely blamed Lord Barbury for Peaches' death, whether or not he had struck the fatal blow. He had treated her carelessly, and she had suffered for it. I knew, watching him, pale and wretched, that he realized that truth as well.

WHEN Lord Barbury had departed, Grenville blew out his breath. "Poor devil," he said. "I am certain he did not do it, Lacey. Lord Alvanley and several others put him at White's between three and six o'clock that day. He certainly was nowhere near the Glass House or the Middle Temple."

"I agree that he was probably at White's," I answered. "But powerful men can hire others to do work that would soil their hands. Remember Mr. Horne of Hanover Square."

He grimaced. "Yes, he was sordid enough. I suppose your Thompson and Pomeroy are trying to discover whether he or Chapman hired a thug to kill her."

"Thompson is thoughtful and thorough. If there is such a connection, I imagine he will find it, eventually." I drank some port and pushed the glass aside. "There is one more person I would like to speak to, who might have known Peaches. An independent witness, if you like."

Grenville looked puzzled "I can think of no one. Whom do you mean?"

"Marianne Simmons," I said.

He stared at me a moment, then color suffused his face. "I see."

"Is she still in your house in Clarges Street?" I asked. "Or has she legged it?"

His flush deepened. "Oh, she is still there. At least, as

far as I know." He rotated his glass, catching candlelight in the red liquid.

"Marianne has been on the stage ten years at least," I explained. "She is bound to have known Peaches at one time or other. She might be able to tell me something about her past—who she knew, what her connections were. Something we might have overlooked."

"Yes, I understand," Grenville said, his voice strained. "Very well, let us visit her. We will go on the moment if you like."

I did like, and so we finished off our port and left the dining room.

I ought to have known, of course, that Lucius Grenville could not simply shrug on a greatcoat over his evening clothes and dash out to his carriage. His suit was meant for dining indoors, and he had to redress to go out into the rain.

I accompanied him upstairs, and he summoned his valet, Gautier, who began to dress him with exquisite care. As I watched Gautier help Grenville settle a frock coat onto his shoulders, Bartholomew came looking for me. He handed me a folded and sealed letter. "Fellow delivered this for you."

The paper was heavy, expensive, and had no writing on the outside. "Why was it brought it here?"

"Don't know, sir. The fellow scarpered before I could ask."

Grenville watched me in his cheval mirror, his arms stuck straight out while Gautier brushed off the coat. The mirror had one rectangular pane of glass that moved up and down with counterweights, depending on which part of himself Grenville wanted to view.

I broke the seal, unfolded the paper. Something fluttered to the floor. I leaned down and picked it up.

I stared at it, my fingers growing numb, then I dragged my gaze back to the letter. Only one line had been scratched across the page.

"Damn," I said fiercely. I crumpled both papers in my fists. "Damn it all to hell."

Grenville, Bartholomew, and Gautier stared at me in surprise. The paper that had fallen was my note of hand with the moneylender. It had been paid, all three hundred guineas of the debt cleared. On the other sheet had been written in careful script: "With the compliments of Mr. Denis."

GRENVILLE tried to stop me racing away to confront Denis on the moment, but I would not be swayed.

"Lacey," he said hurrying down the stairs after me. "You cannot burst into Denis' house and wave your fist under his nose."

I did not answer. James Denis had been playing a game with me for nearly a year now, devising tricks designed to draw me more and more under his obligation. He wanted to own me, he'd said, because he saw me as a threat to him. He had found Louisa when she'd gone missing, learned the whereabouts of my estranged wife, given me information that had helped me solve not one, but two murders, and now had paid my creditors.

Grenville at least persuaded me to let him accompany me, along with Bartholomew and Matthias. We rode in silence to number 45, Curzon Street and I descended before Denis' tall, elegant house.

I thought Denis' minions would stop me at the door, but I was admitted at once. Grenville and his footmen, on the other hand, were told to wait. Grenville began to argue. Bartholomew and Matthias bulked menacingly behind him. I left them to it and strode up the stairs after Denis' footman, who stood taller than Bartholomew and had a face like a pitted slab of granite.

The footman did not take me to the study in which I usually spoke to James Denis. He led me instead to a small, empty sitting room coldly furnished with blue and gold French chairs. The window was covered with heavy,

blue draperies that gave the room a somber air and cut out all noise from outside.

The footman informed me he'd tell Denis I'd arrived. He smiled, showing me that his canine teeth had been filed to points. He looked like a coachman turned pugilist, which was no doubt exactly what he was. He left me alone.

Although a small fire burned on the hearth, the room was chill. No paintings adorned the walls, which were covered in ivory silk fabric marked with fleur-de-lis. It was an elegant room in which no expense had been spared, but the effect was cold and unwelcoming.

James Denis kept me waiting there for the better part of an hour. I had no idea what had become of Grenville. He might have been thrown onto the pavement, for all I knew. The window in the little room in which I waited faced a bare and dark garden in the rear of the house, so I did not even have the privilege of looking to see if Grenville's coach still waited for me.

At long last, the large footman opened the door and told me to follow him. He led me not to Denis' study, but to, of all places, the dining room.

No meal had been laid here. The long Sheraton table was bare, and an unlit chandelier hung ponderously from the high ceiling. A few sconces had been lit between the long, green-draped windows, but again, the room gave the impression that a visitor was not to become too comfortable. I wondered what Denis' private rooms were like. Did he retain the cold elegance of the rest of the house or had he made them warm and personal?

James Denis was seated at the end of the table with the firelight behind him. He was a youngish man, of thirty perhaps, with dark hair and dark blue eyes. His face was not unattractive, though thin. He always dressed in well-cut clothing that was not too ostentatious, rather like Grenville, who kept a subdued wardrobe of obvious expense.

Outwardly, Denis looked little different from any other gentleman of Mayfair—young, wealthy, fashionable. His

eyes, however, told a different story. The cold in them ran deep, like a river beneath layers of ice. Whatever human warmth had ever dwelled in this man had long ago vanished.

"I see that you received my note," he said.

I stopped in front of him, ignoring his gesture for me to sit. "I have many things to do," I answered. "Tell me what you want, so that I can refuse and continue with my errands."

He steepled his fingers, unimpressed. "I have been informed that a few nights ago you entered the Glass House and went on a tear. Broke windows, destroyed furniture, frightened paying customers. Not very tactful of you."

I leaned my fists on the table. "I will not apologize for that."

"As a matter of fact, it is precisely about the Glass House that I wish to speak to you."

"I will close it," I said, my voice tight. "The wheels are already in motion. Once the reformers and the magistrates have enough public opinion on their side, it will fall."

He went on as though I'd not spoken. "The Glass House is managed by a man called Kensington. I do not like this man, but he usually does not worry me; most of what he turns his hand to fails. This time, however, he has done something a little more dangerous. He has paired himself with another, to whom he answers solely. That person is called Lady Jane, and she is a rival of mine."

I stopped, my curiosity overcoming my anger. "What are you talking about?"

"I am speaking about the Glass House. You seem opposed to it, and I am willing to help you shut it down. This time, we happen to be on the same side."

I stared at him, mystified. I ran through my assumptions and rearranged them in my head. "You are telling me that you do not own the Glass House?"

"No. It is a profitable venture, but one a bit too distasteful for me."

James Denis was not a man to be trusted, but I could not

help lending credence to his statement. He did not like sordid dealings, and had in the past punished those who had used his resources to do sordid things for their own gain. I ought to have remembered that, but in my anger, I'd blamed him without thought.

I straightened. "So, this Lady Jane owns it? Who is she?"

"I am not certain that she actually owns the property, but she is the intelligence behind the business," Denis said. "The name 'Lady Jane' is an affectation. She is French and no more high-born than that actress who lived upstairs from you. She was not a French émigré, but a republican and fond of Bonaparte. She came to England after the Bourbon king's restoration in 1815, refusing to live under the French monarchy again."

"Is she a procuress?" I asked.

"Is, or was. She started as a prostitute, I gather, a long time ago. I heard a tale that a French aristocrat bribed her to hide him during the Terror, and she bled him dry. In any event, she arrived on England's shores with a fortune, however she obtained it."

"And she is a rival to you? How?" I could not imagine such a thing.

"She is cunning and clever and has acquired a good deal of money. She has bought influence, and she has thwarted a few of my schemes or outright pulled my clients out from under me. She is bothersome and tricky, and I would like to see her brought down. Like you, I believe the Glass House to be a loathsome place, and I would enjoy seeing it closed."

"You have become a moralist, have you?" I snapped.

He leaned forward, eyes chill. "I confess I share your distaste for certain practices, Captain. I have no tolerance for a pederast. He is a man who cannot control his lusts with his finer feelings or indeed, with his common sense. In short, he is a fool." He gave me a wintery smile. "If you desire to return to the Glass House and break more windows, I will lend you all the assistance you want."

He sorely tempted me. I disliked James Denis and his power, but I thought that I possibly disliked the Glass House more. James Denis knew that. His cold smile confirmed it.

But I knew I played into his hands. He could have moved to close the Glass House at any time. But once he'd learned of my interest, he'd suddenly decided to seize upon an opportunity to dispose of his rival. Not only would closing the Glass House hurt Lady Jane, he would have done me yet another favor, pulling me further into his debt. His help, as always, came with a price.

His power, on the other hand, could ensure success, and girls like Jean would never have to fear the Glass House again.

I tapped my walking stick to my palm. "Very well," I said, containing my anger. "I will tell the magistrates about Lady Jane."

He looked pleased, or as pleased as he ever looked. "Excellent, Captain. I will, as you say, put more wheels in motion."

"Perhaps you can tell me something else, while you are doing me favors," I said. "What do you know about a woman named Amelia Chapman, called Peaches, who was connected to the Glass House? She died on Monday."

He raised a brow. "I know nothing of her, save what I read in the newspaper. A young woman, married to a barrister, found dead in the Thames. Murder, not suicide. If Kensington or Lady Jane killed her for their own reasons, the news did not reach me." He twined his fingers together. "If, however, I do hear anything of it, I will inform you."

He had given me a vital piece of information last summer in the Westin affair, which had certainly increased my debt to him. He only looked at me blandly now, not reminding me of the event.

I leaned to him again. "If you continue this," I said quietly. "You will make me angry enough to simply break your neck."

His returning look was cold. "I have told you what I

will do, and you know my price. We are finished, now, Captain. Good night."

I glared back. He held my gaze, but I saw a touch of un-easiness in his eyes. That satisfied me. It satisfied me very much.

CHAPTER 13

I met Grenville at the door, where he had been barred from further entrance to the house. Once in the carriage, I apprised him in clipped sentences of what had occurred between Denis and me upstairs.

"Good God," Grenville said. "So there exists a person who worries James Denis? That is a bit unsettling."

"He seems confident that we can depose her. However, I do not quite trust everything he told me."

"No, of course not. But he claims to know nothing of Peaches?"

"Nothing whatsoever. He seemed a bit surprised that I asked."

Grenville fell silent, his dark eyes troubled. I knew he believed I should tread more carefully where James Denis was concerned, but Denis infuriated me. He wielded power over too many, and no one seemed disposed to stop him.

We proceeded to Clarges Street, as planned, to inter-view Marianne. Grenville's house there, just round the cor-

ner from Piccadilly, looked much as I expected. Narrower than its fellows, the house was nonetheless one of the most elegant on the street. The façade was gray plaster with white pediments over the door and windows.

The interior exuded the same quiet elegance. A polished staircase spilled into a tiled hall, from which doors led to high-ceilinged, well-furnished rooms. The foyer smelled of beeswax and the pungent odor of linseed oil.

A maid in neat black and white bustled to meet us and curtseyed. Grenville divested himself of his greatcoat and hat and gave them to the stolid lad who had opened the door for us. "Where is Miss Simmons?" he asked.

The maid hesitated. She glanced at the footman. "We are not certain, sir."

"Not certain? What do you mean, not certain? Is she not in the house?"

"She has not gone out, sir, no. Dickon is positive about that. He has not moved from the front door since early this afternoon, and she had dinner in her room after that."

"She might have gone down through the kitchens," I offered.

"No, indeed, sir. She never came through that way. Cook has been down there all the day. We've been watching special."

"Well, she cannot have vanished," Grenville snapped. "She had dinner in her room, you say?"

"Yes, sir. At seven o'clock. I went to put her to bed not an hour ago, but I could not find her. She's not in her bed chamber, nor in any of the other rooms."

"Hell," Grenville began.

I cut him off. "Will you allow me to try?"

The boy and the maid stared at me. Grenville's eyes narrowed. "If you believe it will do any good. She has done this once before. Damned if I know where she disappeared to."

I was not listening. I moved past them to the stairs beyond, cupped my hands around my mouth and bellowed, "Marianne!"

My voice echoed through the banisters, up through the
intricate arches of the stairwell, and rang against the
painted ceiling, four stories above. After a moment's silence, a door slammed open somewhere near the top of the
house and we heard the sound of light footfalls. Soon after
that, Marianne looked over the railing on the top floor, her
golden curls tumbling forward like a girl's. "Is that you,
Lacey?"

Grenville glared at her. "What the devil are you doing
up there?"

Marianne ignored him. "What do you want, Lacey?
Have you come to take me home?"

"No, I came to ask you a question."

Marianne's hand tightened on the banister. Then she
nodded. "All right. Come up to my chamber."

Grenville started up the stairs. Marianne backed away
from the banister, poised to flee. "No. Captain Lacey
only."

"This is my house!"

"Lacey alone. Or you can search for me all you like."

I had never seen Grenville so enraged. He rarely let his
temper get the better of him, especially not in front of
his servants. His face was nearly purple, and the cords
of his throat pressed his cravat.

"Grenville," I said quickly. "Please allow me. I need her
help if she can give it."

Grenville's eyes sparkled with rage. At that moment, I
believe he hated me. But Grenville had spent a lifetime
mastering his emotions. His position as the top man of
fashion depended upon him keeping a cool head in every
situation. I watched him deliberately suppress his anger,
drawing on his sangfroid. His color faded, and the alarm-
ing throbbing in his neck subsided.

"Very well," he said stiffly. "As you wish."

He turned and stalked through double doors into the
grand drawing room. He even managed not to slam the
door.

I ascended the stairs as quickly as I could. Marianne

came down to me and we met on the second-floor landing, then she led me to the chamber in the back of the house.

The chamber was a boudoir. A sumptuous bed, Egyptian style, with a rolled head and foot and a lavish canopy, stood at one end of the room. Comfortable chairs in the same style stood about, and a bookcase with glass doors offered a fine selection of books. Landscapes of idyllic country scenes hung on the walls, and a dressing table piled with perfume bottles and brushes and combs stood near the warmth of the fire.

Marianne wore a silk peignoir, fastened in front with dark blue ribbons, a finer garment than any I'd ever seen her wear. But her face was white, and her hands shook.

"Lacey," she began, her voice low and fierce. "You must make him see reason."

"Why? What has he done?"

"He has made me his prisoner, that is what he has done! He will not let me go out unless Dickon or Alicia stays close by my side. They are dull company, I must say. And I may go only to places he allows me to go."

"Perhaps he does not want you running off to another protector," I suggested.

"Why the devil should I? There's not a gentleman in London who can give a girl a finer house and better dinner than Lucius Grenville, and everyone knows it."

"Then what is the matter?"

She pointed a rigid finger at the door. "What is the matter is *him*. He will not cease bombarding me with questions. He wants to know why I want to go out and where I want to go and why the devil I want to go alone. It is my business, I say."

"He has made a considerable investment in you, Marianne."

She ignored the observation. "Lacey, take me out of here. Ma Beltan's place is at least respectable, and a girl can feel like she owns her own soul."

The blue ribbons trembled. Her eyes were wide, pleading. I did not quite understand her fear. I said slowly, "I

would have thought you'd like living in luxury. This house is one of the finest I've ever seen, and it seems he's showered you with whatever you could want."

"He has." She looked angry to admit it. "He has given me plenty of gifts. But he dogs my footsteps. I cannot bear it."

"You puzzle me, Marianne. I had it in my mind that you liked Grenville's attentions."

A flush stole over her cheeks. "I do."

"Then why not stay and enjoy what he gives you? You have always encouraged me to get as much out of him as I could."

"Because I—" She stopped. I saw her rearrange her words. "I cannot be his prisoner. No matter how gilded the cage."

"Who is it you want to leave the house to visit?"

Her flush returned. "No one."

"Grenville deserves to know whether you have another lover. Or a husband."

She gave me a scornful look. "Do not be daft, Lacey. I would not let a husband live off me even if I had one. Or a lover."

"Then what did you do with Grenville's money?"

She chewed on her lower lip. The previous year, Grenville had made her spontaneous presents amounting to thirty guineas, a goodly sum. The money had instantly disappeared with no explanation.

"I told you before," she said. "I gave it to my sick granny."

"No, you said it was your sick mum. What happens to the money, Marianne?"

She glared at me. "Are you spying for him now?"

"No." I stopped before I lost my temper. "Anything you tell me, I will not impart to him, unless you give me leave."

"Oh, yes, I forgot, you pride yourself on your honor. But I will say again, it is none of your business. And none of his, either. The money was mine to do with what I liked,

so I did what I liked. I did not give it to another man. I am not that foolish."

I regarded her quietly for a moment. "What do you fear he will do if you tell him the truth?"

She shrugged, but her gaze was uneasy. "Who knows? Even you do not know what he can do, do you? As much as he is your friend, you do not really know him."

I had to concede this truth. Grenville was a powerful man, and if he chose to patronize me, or Marianne, he did so for his own reasons.

"I will speak to him," I said.

"Tell him he has no right to keep me here, locked away. That I —"

I held up my hand. "I said I would speak to him. You might try being kinder to him, Marianne. I know from experience that you are a trial to live with."

She made a face at me, but she relaxed somewhat. "I do not live with him; he barely comes to see me. He has never even asked for what a gent usually asks for. I do not understand why not."

I had no wish to involve myself in *that* particular problem. "What you mean is, you cannot tease him like you do the others. You cannot control him."

She lifted her chin. "Well, I will not allow him to control me."

"That, you will have to fight out between yourselves," I said with finality. "I will ask him to consider giving you a bit more freedom. I agree, you cannot give up your entire life for a few froufrous."

She smiled. "You are a true gentleman, Lacey. I have always said so."

"Yes, when you are not calling me other names. But enough, I did not come here to argue with you about Grenville. I came to ask you a question."

Her brow furrowed. "What sort of question?"

"I want to know if you ever knew an actress called Peaches."

Marianne laughed suddenly, then spun around and

plopped ungracefully on the chaise longue. "Even I have heard of you running about smashing windows at the Glass House. Be careful somebody does not bring suit against you, Lacey."

"They would get little from me in any case." I seated myself on a chair facing her and rested my hands on my borrowed walking stick.

She quirked a brow at me. "So you want to know all about poor dead Peaches, do you? I never liked her, but it's sad that she came to such an end."

"You did know her then."

"Oh, yes, a long time ago, when she first came to London, fresh from the country. She was certain she'd take the public by storm." Marianne settled back, warming to her tale. "So many girls are like that, you know, certain they'll become the next Sarah Siddons. Peaches was no different. She'd come from a family of strolling players. Her father and mother had died of fever a few years before, and she decided London was the place to make her fortune. Her idea—she told me this—was that she'd appear on the stage in London, be raved over, and attract the attention of a man of great fortune who would marry her." She shook her head. "The truth was, Peaches was a second-rate actress and the people of London didn't pay her much attention. Once her novelty wore off, she was more or less ignored."

I could imagine a very young Peaches watching, frustrated, as the premier roles and the accolades went to others, while she was lost in the crowd. I remembered the newspaper articles she'd saved. They had mentioned her in passing if at all—usually, her name was printed only as part of the supporting cast.

"But she met Lord Barbury," I pointed out.

"Yes, Barbury, the poor fool. She quite threw herself at him. She did have a sweet smile and a pretty face, but usually, gentlemen simply wanted a night with her. But she'd refuse them—saving herself for something better, she'd say. The result was that the gentlemen began to ignore her, as well."

"Except Lord Barbury."

She nodded. "He was besotted. She was certain he would marry her, but Peaches was always a bit blind. Barbury was in love with her, yes, but he had no intention of taking a nobody actress to wife. He's the kind who, if he marries at all, will find the perfect society lady who knows how to give hunt balls and run fetes and put a blue-blooded heir in the nursery. Rather full of himself is Lord Barbury. Peaches was, too. Imagine, she had her own man of business."

"Did she? What for?"

"I haven't the faintest idea. Like as not, she made it up, or the man handled her parents' will, or something."

"Did she mention his name?"

Marianne shook her head. "If she did, I do not remember. She probably invented him. She was prone to inventing things about herself, to make her seem better than she was. Poor thing, she did not have much."

"And so she decided to marry Chapman."

Marianne wrapped a strand of her long hair around her finger. "Yes. She began working for another acting company just before she met him, and after that I did not see much of her. But rumor had it that she'd met him by chance while walking in Hyde Park. Two months later, they'd married. She probably knew by then she would never be anything more to Lord Barbury than his mistress. Chapman at least made a living, even if he wasn't lofty."

"Yet, she went back to Lord Barbury after she married," I said.

Marianne snorted. "Of course. Once she had Chapman for security, why not run back to a handsome lord who showered her with gifts and was madly in love with her?"

"I've been wondering why she married Chapman at all," I mused. "Lord Barbury gave her money and gifts and loved her desperately. She seemed equally besotted with him. Surely she was happy, even without marriage."

Marianne gave me a dark look. "You are a man, Lacey. You cannot even begin to understand. A gentleman who is

not your husband can be wild about you one day, weary of you the next. And, once he is weary—" She opened her hand, as though dropping something to the carpet. "You are nothing. If you have saved no money, if he takes back everything he has given you, you are destitute, and your character ruined. Marriage is much safer by far for a woman, even if it is not the happiest state."

"I have not noticed you pursuing it," I observed.

She gave me a smile. "I prefer scraping a living for myself to being a man's slave, no matter that the law says he has to take care of me. I've seen far too many wives beaten regularly by their husbands to want that."

"Peaches was willing to risk it."

"Peaches was always starry eyed, and not very intelligent. She thought marriage would fulfill her dreams, even if she had to settle for much less than she'd hoped."

And marriage had not saved her from being brutally murdered. Neither Chapman nor Lord Barbury had been able to prevent it.

"What about Mr. Kensington?" I asked. "Did you know him?"

Marianne wrinkled her nose. "Nasty little chap. I still seem him at the theatre now and again. How and where she met him, I do not know. They were simply always together. He hung on Peaches, acted as though he'd cling to her skirts and be taken to riches with her. She despised him, but he looked after her, and he got her introduced to Lord Barbury. In return, she paid him."

I wondered what other hold he'd had over her. Not every odious connection is easy to break, especially if one person has some emotional tether to the other.

I also wondered about this man of business. I had found no letters to or from a man of business in Peaches' rooms. He might be a thing of the past, but the mere mention of him was worth pointing out to Sir Montague or Thompson.

Marianne smiled again. "You are always stirring up trouble, Lacey. It is a bad habit of yours, that."

"I agree," I said. "I would like nothing more than a holiday from it."

She cocked her head. "You would not know what to do with yourself if you did. But I will give you this advice for nothing. Have a care of Lady Breckenridge. She can be a viper."

"You are well informed for a lady being kept prisoner."

She shot me a deprecating look. "I hear things, Lacey. I also hear that she can be rather ruthless."

I tried to sound neutral. "I do not imagine she has any interest in me whatsoever."

"You would be wrong, Lacey. But have a care. You are lonely. When one is lonely, one does foolish things."

We looked at each other. I wondered how many foolish things she had done and how many more I would do.

I thanked her for her information and asked her to inform me if she thought of anything else. I took my leave, admonishing her once again to try to be kinder to Grenville.

As I departed the room, I heard her close the door behind me and the click of the key as she locked it. I sighed. She and Grenville would have a long battle ahead.

GRENVILLE was still furious when we retreated to the carriage, though he strove to mask it. He looked, if anything, embarrassed. Grenville, I had come to learn, was not a man who shared himself lightly. More than anything else, he valued his privacy.

Nonetheless, I decided to approach the matter head-on and tell him, rather bluntly, that if he did not let Marianne off the tether, she would snap it altogether. He grew offended, of course. His answers were decidedly chilly. At last, as we approached Haymarket, on the way to Covent Garden, he heaved an exasperated sigh. "Blast it, Lacey, look what she has reduced me to."

"It is your business," I said, "and I will stay out of it. But my warning is fair. If you do not trust her, she will never trust you."

He did not answer. He looked away for a time, studying the passersby as we bumped slowly toward Covent Garden. "Tell me what you learned from her, at least," he said eventually. "Unless you discussed only me."

"Not at all. She proved to be most helpful." To cover the awkwardness between us, I related to him everything Marianne had told me about Peaches. By the time I'd finished, Grenville had softened at bit.

"The poor woman," he said. "She probably would have done a great deal better remaining a strolling player in the country. Married some actor chap and had a passel of children who'd tread the boards as soon as they could walk."

Thus spoke a romantic—a man who would never know what it meant to be cold and hungry and not know if the next town would provide enough money for food or shelter for the night.

"What do you intend to do, by the by," Grenville went on, "for the rest of the winter, once this problem is cleared up?"

"Do?" I raised my brows. "What I always do."

Which was damn little. Thanks to Grenville, I had his library available to me, and reading through the winter months kept me occupied at least. Then I had the Derwents to visit once a fortnight until they tired of me. Grenville would likely invite me to dine or to his club or to Tattersall's every once in a while. Mostly I strove to keep myself occupied and my melancholia at bay.

Grenville studied me. "You know, Lacey, you do not need to live alone. I have an enormous house. I will give you rooms of your own, and you can pay me rent to soothe your pride. We can be two lonely bachelors together."

I raised my brows. "You enjoy taking in strays, do you? First Marianne, then me."

"Touché, Lacey."

"I could not pay you the worth of the lodgings, and that would ever weigh on me."

He gave me a critical look. "Your difficulty is that you spent most of your life with overwhelming tasks to under-

take. Push back the Tippu Sultan in Mysore, push back
Boney in Spain. Now, nothing so dire engages your attention." He fell silent a moment. "I have had this in mind for
several weeks, and in fact, it was the news I wished to tell
you at my soiree. I have an old school friend in Berkshire,
a widower and a gentleman of means, now head of the
Sudbury School there. He is in need of a secretary. He
asked me, when I saw him at Christmas, if I knew of any
gentleman he could take on. I thought at once of you. How
about it, Lacey? Live in Berkshire and write letters for a
dull headmaster? Hot meals by night and a servant to light
your fire in the mornings?"

I sat still for a moment. He was offering me what I
wanted, a way to earn a living. A way to leave London and
its smoke and grime and loneliness. Perhaps a way in
which I could leave behind my melancholia and uncer-
tainty, perhaps find again my own respect.

I wondered suddenly what Louisa would think of the
offer. She would doubtless encourage me to take it. If I
were out of London, she would no longer have to watch
me bait her husband.

"It was good of you to think of me," I said.

"Not at all. It seemed the perfect solution."

I gave him a nod. "I might well be interested. I will
think on it."

Grenville nodded and we ended the discussion.

His coach dropped Bartholomew and myself at home,
then clopped away into the night. I went to bed, sending
Bartholomew up to the attics to do the same. The next
morning, Bartholomew fetched a newspaper for me as well
as bread and coffee from Mrs. Beltan's shop.

I gnawed bread and leafed through the newspaper, and
then I suddenly stopped, my blood freezing. On the second
page, in the middle of the column was a notice that a member of the peerage, Lord Barbury, a baron, had been found
outside his house the night before, shot through the head,
a pistol clasped in his hand.

CHAPTER 14

I hastened back to Mayfair, taking Bartholomew with me. Lord Barbury's home was in Charles Street, in a large house typical of the neighborhood. Pomeroy was there, along with another Runner from the Queen's Square house, asking the neighbors what they'd heard. Nothing, Pomeroy told me in disgust.

Lord Barbury had been laid out on his bed, pale and cold. A dark, red hole marred the black locks of his hair just behind his right ear. As I looked at him, my anger soared.

The fact that the pistol had been in his hand might convince the Runners that it was suicide—over grief for his dead mistress, they'd say—but I was not convinced. His coachman's story was simple. Upon leaving Grenville's, Lord Barbury had asked his coachman to set him down in Berkeley Square, and from there he'd walk home. He'd wanted to think, he'd said. Why he could not have thought in the carriage, the coachman couldn't say, but that was not his business. He set his master down as requested and re-

turned home. Later, the footman had heard a noise outside, opened the door, and had found Lord Barbury lying dead on the front doorstep.

The servants were shocked and grieved. I was in a boiling fury. I had Bartholomew fetch another hackney, then rode to Middle Temple.

I ought to have consulted Sir Montague or Thompson or even Pomeroy first, but my temper got the better of me. I was tired of waiting for them to uncover evidence through slow investigation. Whatever my thoughts were, they were not clear; I only knew that I wanted to find the killer and drag him to justice. In the affair of Hanover Square, I'd sympathized with anyone wanting to murder the odious Horne, but Peaches and Lord Barbury, though a bit misguided, were hardly in the same category as Horne.

I turned first to the most obvious suspect, the jealous husband.

Chapman's chambers lay in the Brick Court of Middle Temple. The house bore the same formal architecture of gray brick with white windows and doors as the houses around it. The Middle Temple coat of arms, the Agnus Dei, reposed over the door.

Mr. Chapman first sent down his clerk, then his pupil, to try to put me off. Very busy, the clerk said. The red-haired Mr. Gower made a face and said, "He's been closeted by himself all morning pouring over mucky books. Why, I do not know. I'm only thankful he hasn't made me help him."

"It's important, like," Bartholomew said. "There's been a murder."

Mr. Gower looked somewhat more interested. "Really? And you want to prosecute? Mr. Chapman works through a chap called Sandringham, in Fetter Lane. I'll give you his direction."

"No, Mr. Gower," I snapped. "I want to talk to Mr. Chapman about the murder of his wife's lover."

Gower's freckles spread as he raised his brows. "Good Lord." He looked at Bartholomew as though he expected it

to be a joke, then back at me, startled. "Well, well. Did Chapman do him in?"

"Maybe," Bartholomew said.

"Good Lord," Gower repeated.

"May we go up?" I asked pointedly.

He blinked at me, then nodded. "Yes, yes, follow me."

He led us up a flight of polished mahogany stairs, his gait agitated. He rapped briefly at a door at the top of the stairs, then pushed it open and fled before Chapman could say a word.

Chapman looked up from behind a stack of books, his graying hair awry. "I told you I did not want—" He broke off when he saw me, his mouth remaining open. I walked inside. Bartholomew stayed in the hall, but closed the door, shutting me in alone with Chapman.

"What do you want?" Chapman bristled. "I am a busy man, sir. What did my clerk mean by admitting you?"

"I am afraid I rather insisted." I dragged a chair from the wall and sat, facing Chapman. The chair was hard, the upholstery frayed. "Your wife's lover is dead."

He flushed at my bluntness. "What of it?"

"You have heard the news, then?"

"I do read newspapers."

"Yes, you make much of your living from the sordid crime that is reported there. Where were you last night?"

He stared, puzzled. "Last night? At home, of course."

"You have witnesses to place you there?"

"Witnesses?" He rose. "See here, Captain Lacey. What are you on about?"

"Do you?" I asked angrily.

"My housekeeper made me supper. I ate it and retired."

"What time was this supper?"

"Eleven o'clock. I am certain of that, because I arrived home at half-past ten."

"Why so late? Were you out?"

"No, I was here. I have much practice, and much work to do. Not that my good-for-nothing pupil helps me. He

whined that he wanted to waste time at his club with his friends, so I told him to go."

"At what time?"

"Why are you obsessed with the hours of the day, Captain?"

"Tell me, please."

He came around the desk. I remained seated. "Leave at once, sir," he said. "I do not have time for this foolishness. I have a difficult case for which I must prepare."

"Involving murder?" I asked. "Perhaps you are researching how a man might get out of hanging for a crime of passion? How to prove it was not premeditated?"

His flush deepened. "Just what are you suggesting?"

"Did you leave these chambers last night, meet Lord Barbury, and shoot him dead?"

His brow clouded. "Lord who?"

"Barbury. You saw him yesterday at your wife's funeral."

"Did I?" He looked confused.

"The tall man with the dark hair. That was Lord Barbury. Your wife's lover."

Chapman's face suddenly drained of all color. He crossed slowly back to his desk and sat, his eyes fixed in frozen horror. "*He* was her lover?" he asked, voice hoarse.

"Yes." I paused. "He was mentioned at Mrs. Chapman's inquest." After Chapman had left the room, I now remembered.

I could swear his astonishment was genuine. Not just astonishment, shock. He had known his wife had had a lover, but had not realized it was Lord Barbury. I wondered just who he'd thought the lover was.

Then it struck me. "Oh my God," I said. "You thought it was Simon Inglethorpe."

He looked at me, his face blotched red, his lips white.

I went on, my voice quiet. "You must have heard she had been going to his house in Curzon Street, and so concluded he was her lover."

His breathing was ragged. "It was an accident. He ran at me, and the sword just went right through him."

I let him sit there while I pictured what happened. I imagined Mr. Chapman approaching number 21, Curzon Street, filled with indignation, ready to dress down Mr. Inglethorpe for his improper relations with Peaches. Chapman might have gone to threaten Inglethorpe with a lawsuit, or perhaps he'd merely wanted to vent his feelings. Inglethorpe might have laughed at him, provoked Chapman to anger. Inglethorpe had had my sword-stick . . .

I paused. How Inglethorpe had suddenly produced my sword-stick, I still could not fathom, nor did I yet understand why he'd removed half his clothing.

"Tell me what happened," I said.

"No, I should say nothing." He made a vague gesture, his hands shaking.

I rose, opened the door. Bartholomew was sitting on a wooden chair, resting his muscled shoulders against the wall. I assumed he'd heard every word. "Run to Bow Street," I told him when he looked up at me, startled, "and fetch Pomeroy if he is back from Lord Barbury's. Tell someone to send word to Sir Montague Harris in Whitechapel. Tell them both it is urgent that they come here."

Bartholomew nodded once, sprang to his feet, and dashed off.

I stayed with Chapman, who mostly sat listlessly, forgetting about his books and everything else around him. Gower came to offer coffee, looking puzzled and very interested.

Pomeroy arrived in a remarkably short time, followed soon after by Sir Montague Harris and Thompson.

Chapman, looking defeated, told his story. He had learned from one of his maids that Mrs. Chapman was in the habit of going to a certain house in Curzon Street. She would never allow the maid to follow her in, and in fact

Mrs. Chapman would dismiss the maid at the door, saying she would return home later.

After Peaches had died, Chapman had wanted to see for himself who this wealthy gentleman was who'd been his wife's lover. He'd assumed the man lived in the Curzon Street house Mrs. Chapman visited. He'd gotten the house number from the maid and set off. When he reached the house, he'd found the door wide open and Inglethorpe in the reception room, shirtless, for heaven's sake, and looking annoyed.

The man had not even had the decency to pick up his coat and put it on. Inglethorpe had demanded to know what Chapman wanted, very high and mighty. Chapman had accused him of being Mrs. Chapman's lover, and then Inglethorpe had laughed at him. He'd not denied that Peaches came there regularly; she always had a marvelous time, he said. A sword from a walking stick had been lying on a chair next to the door. Chapman had picked it up, uncertain why, he said. He did not really remember, but suddenly, the sword was in his hand. He'd looked down the blade at Inglethorpe, angrier than he had ever been. Inglethorpe, alarmed, had lunged for him. Chapman had held the sword steady, and the blade had pierced Inglethorpe's chest.

Inglethorpe had dropped to the floor, Chapman had simply let go of the sword and fled.

His voice was hollow when he finished. Thompson and Sir Montague exchanged glances. Pomeroy said, "A nice story. Now then, sir, what about your wife?"

Chapman looked puzzled. "What do you mean?"

"Your wife, who was cuckolding you with a Mayfair gent. Did you kill her first, telling her you would kill her lover as well?"

He stared. "No. I did not kill Amelia. I told you, I never saw her after the time she left my house to journey to Sussex."

"Well, the jury will decide whether that's true," Pomeroy said cheerfully. "Who knows? Perhaps the gent

what prosecutes you will be one of your acquaintance from Middle Temple." He chuckled.

Chapman went white. The man who had aspired to become a silk would now have one staring at him across the courtroom at the Old Bailey, questioning his stammered explanation of how Inglethorpe had run into the sword-stick. I rather believed Chapman had simply stabbed Inglethorpe in fury, and had come up with the story of Inglethorpe skewering himself while sitting in this room "researching" his case. As Pomeroy had said, the jury would decide what was true.

Before Pomeroy dragged Chapman off, I said to him, "What is the name of your wife's man of business? I wish to speak with him."

Chapman stared at me, bewildered. "My wife did not have a man of business. All of our affairs were handled by my own."

"Oh, but she did," Sir Montague Harris broke in, his broad face smiling. "He sent the coroner a letter on hearing of her death."

Chapman continued to look surprised.

I was surprised as well. "So the man of business does exist," I said.

"Indeed." Sir Montague's eyes twinkled. "I think we ought to pay him a visit."

"THIS is most irregular," the thin man on the other side of the table said to us. He had sandy, almost colorless hair, narrow dark eyes, and pale skin stretched tightly over his bones. He kept a tiny room in a court off Chancery Lane, not far from the Temples, had a clerk as thin as he, and an office of painful neatness.

His name was Ichabod Harper, and he had been Peaches' man of business for six years, ever since she'd inherited property in a trust.

"Murder is irregular," Sir Montague replied.

"Indeed," Mr. Harper said.

"Now then, tell us, sir," Sir Montague went on, "what

was this property, how did she come to inherit it, and to whom does it pass on occasion of her death?"

Mr. Harper cleared his throat, a dry sound. "To answer that, sir, I must go back some years. Mrs. Chapman's parents were a rather low form of actors, strolling players, I believe they are called. Mrs. Chapman's grandmother had married one of these players, running away and disgracing her family, who then disowned her. The grandmother's sister—Mrs. Chapman's great aunt—took it upon herself to see that, after her death, her foolish sister's offspring would not be completely destitute. Mrs. Chapman's parents died of a fever eight years ago, leaving Mrs. Chapman, then Miss Amelia Leary, alone, although she continued to live on her own with the strolling players."

He looked disapproving. I understood Peaches' reasoning, however. A young girl, full of life, would rather stay with the people and the freedom she'd known her entire life than return to family connections who did not approve of her.

"Two years after that," Mr. Harper went on, "the great aunt died. She had never married. She'd named her sister's children and grandchildren as inheritors of a trust, of which I am the trustee. Mrs. Chapman's mother was the only offspring of the original ill-advised marriage, and because she and her husband had already died, Miss Amelia Leary was the only one left to inherit the trust. And so, upon learning she had inherited the property, she decided to come to London."

"Did the property not go to Mrs. Chapman's husband when she married?" I asked. That was usual, unless the trust protected the property very tightly. Most men inherited what their wives had absolutely, and could sell any property and squander the money however they wished.

Mr. Harper shook his head. "Not with this trust. It is quite specific. The property belonged solely to Mrs. Chapman and the heirs she named, and the trust ensured that her husband could not touch it. The great aunt feared the property going to, as she called them, lowly actors. Now, as

Mrs. Chapman had no offspring before she died, the trust reverts to the original estate, and we trace the inheritance from there."

Which sounded tedious to me.

"What was this property?" Sir Montague asked him.

"A house in London," Mr. Harper replied in his thin voice. "Number twelve, St. Charles Row."

"WELL, this is a turn up," Thompson said.

The three of us had adjourned to a coffeehouse, where Sir Montague partook of beefsteak and Thompson and I sipped rather over-boiled coffee.

We were all a bit deflated by the news. But the fact that Peaches owned the house herself explained why she'd not needed Lord Barbury to supply her with one. It also explained why she'd kept a room there after her marriage. It was a place of her own, a retreat from her unhappy life with Chapman.

A trust meant that although Peaches had technically inherited number 12, St. Charles Row, she could not sell it. But she could certainly hire it out and enjoy the income from it. The house had indeed been hired, Mr. Harper had said, to—no surprise to any of us—Kensington.

The news made me greatly disappointed in Peaches. She'd known what kind of house Kensington had turned it into, and what went on there, and yet, she'd let Kensington and Lady Jane continue. No doubt the house made much money and Peaches had reaped some of the profit. The riches she'd looked for upon first journeying to London had come to her, although perhaps not as she'd anticipated.

"Well, her husband wouldn't have killed her for the house," Thompson said. He took a sip of coffee. "He doesn't get it. Think he's telling the truth about Inglethorpe?"

"Possibly," Sir Montague said. "Or at least what he's convinced himself is the truth."

"He still cannot explain why Inglethorpe had taken off

half his clothes," I mentioned. "Nor why he had mud on his shoes."

Both men looked at me without much enthusiasm. They had found and arrested a murderer; they did not much care about the victim's eccentricities.

"What about poor Lord Barbury?" I continued. "Have you any idea who might have killed him?"

"Himself," Sir Montague said. "You told me his health had deteriorated greatly after Mrs. Chapman's death. Due to either excessive grief or excessive remorse, perhaps."

I shook my head. "I do not think he did it himself. I saw the wound that killed him. It was too far to the back of his head." I lifted my hand and tapped myself behind the ear. "It is more usual for a man to shoot himself through the temple, or through the mouth."

I had seen more than one corpse of a suicide in the army; once, of a man in my own company. Some in the army were very stoic about the fact that every time we rode into battle, we would likely die. Many had decided that death fighting the pesky French was more honorable than death by the infections that regularly swept through the camps. Many men were alone in the world, with nothing much to lose.

But there were those for whom the horrors of war had come as a shock, those who could not face shooting other men, those who were terrified by the thought of death by bayonet or musket ball. In the quiet hours of dawn, these gentlemen would creep away by themselves and end their lives quickly with a bullet in their brain.

No one stopped them. A man had to find honor where he could. We simply buried them, sent their effects back to their families, and marched on.

I'd always thought it a waste of life that these good officers and men were not put to use elsewhere than the front. But the pigheaded fear of cowardice, drummed into us since birth, made men prefer death at their own hand to being made a headquarters aide because they could not face bullets.

The head wounds I had seen on these men were usually in the temple, above the ear, or through the mouth. None had been behind the ear, where the man would have to pull his arm back at a slightly uncomfortable angle.

"Perhaps," Sir Montague agreed. "What we need is a witness or more evidence. Pomeroy continues to tramp through the neighborhood, but so far, no one admits they saw him killed. On the other hand, no one saw him shoot himself, either."

"I do not think Chapman killed him," I continued. "He was astonished when I told him Lord Barbury had been his wife's lover. He was fixed on Inglethorpe."

"Why would someone other than Chapman kill Lord Barbury, in any case?" Thompson broke in. "Unless he knew something about Mrs. Chapman's death? He told you and Mr. Grenville he had no idea of Peaches' plans that day other than to visit Inglethorpe."

I turned my cup around on the table. "I have toyed with the idea that Lord Barbury might have been blackmailing the killer, and the killer grew fearful or tired of it. But I do not think so. I would swear Barbury knew nothing of how Mrs. Chapman died."

"Unless he did it himself, then remorse built up so much that he took a quick way out," Sir Montague suggested, returning to his suicide theme. "Or perhaps after speaking with you and Mr. Grenville, he realized that he could not hide his guilt forever."

"Lord Barbury was a man of volatile passion," I said. "I saw that in him, and in those letters he wrote to Mrs. Chapman. I agree that he could have quarreled with Mrs. Chapman and killed her, perhaps even accidentally. Both of the bedrooms I saw had heavy brass fenders at the fireplaces. If she'd fallen and hit her head, the blow could have killed her. I did check both fenders and found no evidence of blood on either, but they could easily have been cleaned. The one in the attic was certainly shiny."

"Well, I shall ask Mr. Kensington about those fenders, when I have him up before me," Sir Montague said. "I in-

tend to arrest him before the week is out. I will need your testimony and that of the little girl, Lacey, but I will get him."

"What of Lady Jane?" I asked. I had mentioned her to Thompson on our way to see Mr. Harper, and now I related the entirety of what Denis had told me.

"I've heard of her," Sir Montague said. "So far, no one has been able to fasten anything illegal to her, but that may be because she's slippery, not innocent." He thought a moment. "Can Mr. Denis set us an appointment with this Lady Jane?"

"He and Lady Jane are fierce rivals," I said. "I doubt she'd let him pin her down."

"Mr. Denis might find it in his best interest to keep a magistrate happy," Sir Montague said, smiling.

I was pleased to hear him say so. "Unfortunately, that may not sway him."

"No harm in asking," Sir Montague said pointedly. "Or we can get to her through her subordinate, although I have the feeling that when we arrest Kensington, she, the larger fish, will slip the net. I would like to do this the easy way, Captain. I do not have the manpower to scour the city for her."

I gave him a nod, promising to speak with Denis if I could.

"I will have Mr. Harper keep me informed of who will inherit the house," Sir Montague said. "I hope this person is horrified to learn it is being used as a bawdy house and closes it. And if he is of a mercenary disposition and wishes the income from it, I will have a little talk with him."

Sir Montague looked buoyed. He had realized today that Peaches' death meant that the Glass House would be even more short-lived than he'd hoped.

"Lady Jane can simply open another house," I pointed out.

"Not if I have anything to say about it." Sir Montague laid down his knife, mopped his face with a napkin, rose

and stuck out his hand. "You have been of great help, Captain."

I got to my feet as well, shook his hand. "I have done very little."

"Nonsense. You got yourself into the Glass House where my patrollers could not go, you found the connection between Mrs. Chapman, Lord Barbury, and the Glass House, you got Chapman to confess to the murder of Inglethorpe. Impressive work to this plodding magistrate."

"It comes only from poking my nose where it does not belong."

"Yes, indeed." Sir Montague clapped me on the shoulder. "Keep it up, there's a good fellow."

CHAPTER 15

MUCH happened that afternoon. When I returned home, I wrote to James Denis, telling him, in stiff terms, that Sir Montague wished to speak to Lady Jane, and it would please him if Denis would help us find and meet with her. I doubted Denis would be impressed.

I had two letters waiting for me, one from Lady Breckenridge, asking me to join her in her box at Covent Garden Theatre that night. The other was from Grenville who, predictably, had learned of Barbury's death and was anxious to discuss it with me. I wrote my acceptance to Lady Breckenridge, and then journeyed with Bartholomew back across the metropolis, to be greeted by the impatient Grenville and invited to partake of yet another meal.

I ate savory chicken pastries with succulent wine sauce while I told Grenville all that had happened. He was astonished with the news about the Glass House, and as angry as I at Lord Barbury's death. He expressed a wish to pin it on Kensington.

"I dislike Kensington," I said as I finished off the excel-

lent dish. "He is manipulative and a liar. But he also strikes me as a coward. I easily believe he could have killed Peaches, but Lord Barbury was large and strong. Kensington is a small man."

"Lord Barbury was shot," Grenville pointed out.

"The gun was pressed against his head. The powder burns around the wound attest to that. I cannot imagine Lord Barbury standing still and letting Kensington shoot him. If he'd have seen Kensington coming at him with a pistol, he would have tried to fight him."

"Then he didn't see the pistol," Grenville suggested.

"But Barbury knew Kensington. He wouldn't have trusted the man for a moment. I, too, want Kensington to be guilty, but I am not certain he is. At least not of killing Lord Barbury."

"And Thompson is still not certain how Peaches got to Middle Temple Gardens?"

I shook my head. "And who would have noticed anyone scuttling down the streets on that afternoon? At just after four that day, it was raining and dark and cold. Anyone walking would have been heavily bundled against the weather—everyone looks like everyone else in such a circumstance, especially in the dark. Most people were indoors seeking warmth. Did the killer count on that, or did circumstance simply work in his favor?"

"Begging your pardon, sir," Bartholomew said from where he stood against the wall. "But I've thought of something." He and Matthias had taken up stations on either side of the room, waiting to serve us. It was not a footman's place to speak to his master or a guest while they served— servants were supposed to be invisible. Grenville, however, simply looked interested in what Bartholomew had to say.

Bartholomew approached the table, while his brother topped off our glasses with hock. "Seems to me that we are all thinking that since poor Mrs. Chapman ended up in the river, that she was tossed from the banks. But what if she was in a boat already? Rowed up to the Temple and heaved over the side? Or, since she fetched up under Blackfriar's

Bridge, why not put her in the river right there? The murderer might figure she'd wash far away downstream before anyone found her. His bad luck she stuck under the bridge."

I thought about it. Boatmen and others did go up and down the river all the time, scavenging for articles that they could sell or keep. They could be paid to transport people, if you wanted to share a boat with a smelly, ragged man and his family.

I remembered standing on the Temple steps, reflecting how the river used to be the main artery of travel in days gone by. Two hundred years ago, men had rarely moved about the city on horseback or foot or in any kind of conveyance. They'd had no need to.

"A long way to row from the Glass House to the Temple Gardens," Grenville said. "Upstream."

"Perhaps," Bartholomew said, "he was afraid that if Mr. Thompson figured out she went in by London Bridge or below that, he'd connect her more easily with the Glass House. If she went in by Middle Temple, she'd be more connected to her husband. Maybe the Glass House would never be mentioned."

"And wouldn't have been," Matthias added, putting the stopper in the decanter and licking a bit of spilled hock from his thumb, "if the murderer had noticed her wearing Lord Barbury's ring and took it from her."

"That would not have hidden things for long," Grenville argued. "Lady Breckenridge, for example, knew that Mrs. Chapman was his mistress. Barbury would have been questioned eventually, and the connection to the Glass House revealed."

Bartholomew shrugged. "Maybe the murderer didn't think of that. He was panicked and hauled off her corpse, supposing everyone would think her husband had done her in. Husbands usually do. Or wives, husbands."

I ignored this optimistic view of marriage and drank deeply of hock. "It is an interesting theory," I said. "But how much time would it take to go upstream from London Bridge to Blackfriar's Bridge in a boat? Peaches died at

about half-past four, and was in the river for a few hours before she was found at eight o'clock. Does the time fit?"

"One way of finding out, I suppose," Bartholomew said.

Grenville looked at the faces of his two eager footmen, glanced back at his wine, and groaned. "Oh, no. Why do I think I know what you're going to say?"

I suppressed a smile. "It is a possibility," I said. "But I hate to send Thompson questioning all the boatmen up and down the river if it proves to be a false one."

Grenville looked pained, then he sighed. "Oh, very well. I will ask Gautier to prepare a suit appropriate for riding in a fisherman's boat."

I doubted the wisdom of Bartholomew's plan once we were out on the water. It was not raining, and the clouds had cleared a bit, but the wind was sharp. It was just a mile between Blackfriar's Bridge and London Bridge, but the current was strong and the boat full.

The boatman we hired seemed oblivious to the cold and the wind. He took one look at the gold guineas Grenville offered him and shuffled us into his boat in a trice. His wife stood on the bank, hands on hips, and watched while her husband and son pushed us off.

The boatman bent his back to the oars, while Grenville sat in the bow, watch in hand. The man's son, a spindly lad of twelve years, manned the tiller. The river was dense with traffic, boats scuttling this way and that, fishermen hauling nets in and out, the occasional large vessel moving silently upriver, carrying goods to the upper Thames or to the narrow barges that would traverse the canals.

The boatman and his son skittered around and out of the way of other craft with the ease of long experience, but still the going was slow. Matthias had professed an aversion to boats and had remained with Grenville's coach near London Bridge. Halfway along our journey, I, hunkering into my coat, envied him. No doubt he'd found a warm tavern or a corner out of the wind where he could play dice and swap gossip with the coachman.

The smell from the river was unpleasant. I could not help thinking of the wide open meadows of Spain and Portugal, warm and sweet under the summer sun. I thought of sleepy towns with brick plazas and people sauntering about their business in no hurry. Those places had been bright and warm and beautiful, and the gray of London depressed me.

After a time, the arches of Blackfriar's Bridge drew near. We passed the place where the waterman had fished Peaches' body from the river and so on under the shadow of the bridge. The smell grew intense. Refuse clung to the stones and pilings under the bridge, and rats swarmed everywhere.

"Take you in here?" the boatman asked, the first words he'd spoken.

Grenville closely studied his watch. "A little farther, to the Temple Stairs."

The boatman grunted. The boy swung the tiller, and we moved slowly toward the Temple Stairs, which lay not far west of the bridge.

In a few minutes, the boat bumped the slime-coated steps, and the boatman's boy sprang off, holding the boat in place with a line. Bartholomew stepped off first, then gave his hand to Grenville, then me. I slipped a little on the step, but Bartholomew's rock-solid arm kept me from falling.

Grenville had returned his watch to his pocket. "Forty-five minutes," he told me.

No one had been terribly precise about the times of Peaches' movements that day. Lady Breckenridge had her leaving Inglethorpe's a little past four. Jean thought she saw Peaches in the Glass House at half-past. Thompson put her death at half-past, but the doctor had said anywhere between four and five. There was enough discrepancy that she could well have reached the Temple Gardens before she died. Or she could have died at half-past and been brought here, as Bartholomew suggested.

"It could have been done," I mused. "Winding through town in a hackney would likely have taken even longer."

"Are you wanting to go back?" the boatman asked.

Grenville looked a question, and I shook my head. I was quite ready to be free of the chill river. "I can walk to my digs from here."

Grenville handed the boatman his payment. "Go back and tell my coachman I went home with Captain Lacey. He will give you another shilling."

The man took the guineas; they vanished quickly into his pocket. Before he departed, I asked him, "Did anyone else ask to be taken upriver to the Temple Stairs last Monday? Perhaps one or two people?"

The boatman shrugged. "Never heard of it."

The lad looked hopefully at me. "I can ask, sir." No doubt visions of more shiny coins danced in his head.

"No," I said. The last thing I wanted was someone silencing an innocent boy for asking the wrong questions. "But," I added, "if you happen to hear of anything, send word. Ask for Captain Lacey in the rooms above the bakeshop in Grimpen Lane, off Covent Garden."

"Right you are, sir," the boy said.

The boatman looked less interested, but he nodded a farewell and picked up his oars again.

Grenville, Bartholomew, and I trudged up the steps to the Temple Garden. If any of the pupils and barristers walking purposefully about were surprised to see us emerge from the river, they made no sign. The clouds had parted today, rendering the garden a refreshing bright green, with the bare trees making delicate patterns against the sky.

The only pupil who noticed us was the tall, gangly Mr. Gower, whose face brightened as he waved to us.

"Well met, Captain." He grinned, more cheerful than on any occasion I'd seen him previously. "So, you got old Chapman arrested for murder. Never thought he had it in him."

"What happens to you?" I asked. "You are out a mentor."

"Had a stroke of luck there. A gentleman of the Inner Temple, a silk no less, announced he would take a pupil, just today. I ran to him at once, and he said he'd take me on.

Not because he thinks I'll make a great barrister, but because I'm tall, and will look impressive in court." He grinned, freckles dancing. "Sir William Pankhurst's a fine orator and takes only the most interesting cases. Perhaps he'll even prosecute Chapman, wouldn't that be a lark? With me assisting?"

I found his callousness a bit distasteful, but he was young, and he'd had no love for Chapman.

"Congratulations are in order then," I said. I turned to Grenville and introduced him. Gower's eyes widened.

"You are Mr. Grenville?" He stuck out his hand. "I am honored, sir, truly honored. You won't forget the name of Gower, will you? In case you need assistance prosecuting in a court of law some day."

Grenville bowed courteously.

"Perhaps you could adjourn to that tavern you mentioned before?" I asked. "For a celebratory ale?"

Gower shook his head. "I cannot, Captain. Sir William has me on a close tether. No more nipping out to the tavern or onto the green for a cheroot." He grinned. "Everything has its price."

I chuckled, then a thought struck me. "You didn't happen to nip out to smoke a cheroot on Monday evening last, did you? When you were supposed to be dining in the hall?"

He stopped, then blushed. "Perhaps. I have been known to do so from time to time."

"While you were enjoying your smoke, did you notice anyone coming up the Temple Stairs, as we did just now? A man, perhaps?"

His eyes narrowed. "Can't be sure, you know. I think it was raining that night, pretty fierce. I remember giving up on the cheroot before long—too damp to enjoy properly. But now that you've called it to mind, I believe I did see someone. A bloke came up the steps, all bundled against the rain. A tall chap. I wondered, I remember, what he was doing down there in this wet. Then he hurried off and I went inside and didn't think any more about it."

"Tall?" I prompted.

"Well, best as I could judge. Didn't get a proper look at him, and didn't really notice, to tell the truth." He smiled. "Am I being helpful? If you arrest the bloke, would you put it in the papers that I assisted you?"

I grinned back. "Your name will be prominent, Mr. Gower."

"Excellent. Well, I'm chuffed to have met you, Mr. Grenville."

Grenville said something polite, and we took our leave.

"I suppose I was that young and cocky once," Grenville said as we strolled up Middle Temple Lane and back to Fleet Street. "But I must say that the suit he wears is first rate."

I came out of deep thought about tall men on the rainy Temple Stairs. "How did you notice his suit? His gown covered it."

"I noted his collar and his sleeves. His coat was made by a fine tailor in Bond Street. No doubt provided by a proud and ambitious papa."

I could only muse that Grenville was fixed on dress. I had never noticed Gower's coat.

As we trudged slowly back to Covent Garden, we discussed what we'd learned from the boat ride. I told him I'd inform Thompson of our discoveries; he, of the Thames River patrol, could easily order his watermen to run up and down the river questioning boatmen and fishermen.

"It would be pleasing if we could find someone who truly saw something," Grenville said crossly. "Mr. Gower sees a tall man in the rain—he thinks. Young Jean hears Kensington and Peaches argue, but does not see anyone with Peaches when she leaves the Glass House. None of the hackney drivers Thompson questioned remembered seeing Peaches at all. Lady Breckenridge does not observe Peaches speak to anyone but Inglethorpe last Monday at Inglethorpe's gathering. And Inglethorpe, of course, cannot tell us anything, because Chapman skewered him. It's dashed annoying."

"Perhaps," I said, deep in thought.

"You are having ideas, Lacey. Will you share them?"

I shook my head. "Not ideas. Threads of ideas. Which might lead nowhere."

"Well, I am completely baffled." We strolled in silence for a few minutes. "Tell me, Lacey, what have you decided about Berkshire? I've had another letter from my friend, Rutledge. He was most interested in you. An army officer of good family and quiet habits is just what he'd like. What shall I tell him?"

I hesitated a moment, then I answered. "I have been thinking that a sojourn in Berkshire would be most pleasant, to tell the truth."

"Excellent. I will warn you, however, that Bartholomew wishes to accompany you. And I will visit often, of course, to make certain you are not getting up to anything exciting without me. Can you bear it?"

I gave him a faint smile and a nod. "I would enjoy the company."

"I will write to Rutledge tonight." He pulled the collar of his greatcoat higher. "Let us move along. If anyone sees me strolling the Strand, on foot, my reputation will be at an end."

"Nonsense," I said, feeling slightly better now that I'd made a decision. "It will become the thing to do."

Grenville burst out laughing, something he did rarely. "True. That would be a most excellent joke."

Chuckling, he ambled on, and we at last turned north to Covent Garden and Grimpen Lane.

GRENVILLE invited me to dine with him again, but I told him I had an engagement for the evening. He nodded, looking curious, but he was not rude enough to ask me for the details. He left me, and Bartholomew went out to shop for our supper.

I had worried at first that keeping Bartholomew would be costly, especially since Bartholomew enjoyed stoking my fires high. But Bartholomew had assured me on that

point. He knew where to get the best goods the cheapest, he said, having connections all over Covent Garden and into the City. I only half-believed him, but did not argue. Grenville had rather relieved me when he indicated that Bartholomew wanted to accompany me to Berkshire. I had grown to appreciate him.

Not many minutes after both Grenville and Bartholomew had departed, someone tapped on my door. I opened it, expecting Mrs. Beltan with coffee, but I found Mr. Kensington on my doorstep.

We stared at each other for a good minute. His dark hair was thinning on top, which I could well see because I stood at least a foot taller than he.

"What do you want?"

He gave me his oily smile. "To speak with you, Captain. On a matter we will both find important."

I did not invite him in. Though he held his hat in both hands, and I saw no sign of a weapon, I certainly did not trust him.

"What matter?" I asked abruptly.

"Shall we speak privately?"

"We are private enough."

He looked up and down the stairs with a slightly worried expression, obviously unsure whether we were alone in the house. He took another step forward, lowered his voice. "You are acquainted with James Denis."

"Somewhat," I said coldly.

"I have a connection to him as well, which might surprise you." He lowered his voice still further. "I am his cousin."

He was correct. I was surprised. They were nothing alike, save in coloring. Kensington was small and stout, his eyes narrow, while Denis had an almost Spartan appearance, except for his costly clothes.

"He has never mentioned this," I said.

"Nor would he. We do not exactly see eye to eye. But times are changing, and we must decide who our allies are."

I had not yet made up my mind whether to believe him. "What of it?" I asked, my voice hard.

"My dear, sir, we can be of help to one another. I only ask that you put in a good word for me with Denis. Tell him I have seen the error of my ways."

I gave him a sharp look. "First, I have no reason to believe you. Second, I have no reason to help you."

Kensington's eyes took on a light of desperation. "But I have helped *you* at every turn. I let you see Peaches' rooms, I have answered your questions about her, I can help your magistrate friend make short work of Lady Jane."

I leaned against the doorframe, arms folded. Cold air seeped up the stairwell, but I was not ready to retreat into the warm rooms behind me. "Helped me?" I asked. "You have lied or evaded me at every turn. You did not mention that Peaches owned the Glass House. You only allowed me to search the real room she kept when I threatened you. You have not told me why you and she quarreled on her final day."

"Help me return to James Denis' good graces, and I will tell you all."

I caught his coat lapel, jerked him off his feet. "You will tell me now. Beginning with why you are so anxious to betray Lady Jane, who has no doubt helped you make a fine profit from the Glass House."

"How can you ask? She is a ruthless and wicked woman, and I rue the day I met her."

"I don't doubt that. Let me put to you why I think you are willing to sell her out. Now that Peaches is dead, the Glass House will revert to another owner, and your days are numbered. No doubt she is furious. If you killed Peaches, she will be more furious still."

His small eyes bulged. "I did not kill her. I swear it."

"You had better be able to prove that. What did you and Peaches quarrel about?"

"I don't remember."

I shook him once. "I believe you do."

He wet his lips. "Lady Jane is dangerous. She may be a

woman, but she has men at her beck and call who will do anything for her. Nasty types who would kill you as soon as turn a hair. I want to get away from her. You would, too, if you understood. If I go back to Denis, Lady Jane can't touch me."

That, I at least believed. I shook him again. "You have not answered my question."

He quivered. "Peaches found out that I wanted to leave the Glass House and return to Denis. She threatened to tell Lady Jane. When I remonstrated with her, she laughed at me."

"And you killed her to prevent it?"

"No! I never did. I swear it, Captain. I take a Bible oath on it. I did not kill Peaches. She was alive and well when she left me."

"To go where?"

"I do not know! She said she had an appointment."

I shook him again. "With whom?"

"I don't know, devil take you. She did not confide in me. She never confided in me."

I set him on his feet with a thump. He drew a breath, loosened the fabric at his throat with shaking hands.

"She did not like you," I said. "What did you do to her, I wonder, to make her despise you? To make her turn around and threaten to betray you?"

His face reddened. "I do not know. She was always ungrateful. I took her, poor and innocent, knowing nothing of the ways of London, and found her a position on the stage. I introduced her to wealthy gentlemen. I showed her how to make income off her house. Helped her when no one else would."

"For a price."

"Well, of course. I am a man of business."

"I am not speaking of a commission," I said clearly. "I am certain you demanded more than money from her."

His face grew still more red. "I deserved it," he said defiantly. "Everything, I deserved."

"Do not elaborate on what you took from her, or I might

have to throttle you right now. What about Lord Barbury? Did you kill him?"

"Of course not. I am not a killing man, Captain. I can't abide murder."

"Your protests do not convince me that you are a moral man. You have the best motive of all for murdering Peaches—she threatened to betray you to Lady Jane, whom you fear. Peaches had the power by then, not you. She was married to a barrister, had the protection of the wealthy and powerful Lord Barbury, who would do anything for her, had the rent from the Glass House—and profits, too, I imagine—and she was free of you. You were about to lose everything, and there she was, laughing at you."

He shook his head vehemently. "No."

"She would have told Lord Barbury all about it. At least, you would assume so. Lord Barbury shut himself at home, grieving for Peaches, until her funeral. He saw you there, threatened you. Grenville invited him for supper while you stood there listening. All you had to do was wait for him, follow him, shoot him somewhere in the dark, and drag him home."

"I never did!" His voice rang with defiance. "I was nowhere near Mayfair that evening, and I can prove it."

"You will certainly be hanged if you cannot," I said remorselessly. "But it does not matter, because you have done so many other things. Running a bawdy house, exploiting children; Peaches was still a girl when you exploited her, was she not? And I imagine that once you knew Peaches was dead, you forced the lock on her room and removed any evidence of your dealings with her, including any money that she might have kept there so that she could buy herself silver pen trays and pretty dresses."

"There was nothing left," Kensington said angrily. "She'd spent it all."

"I would be interested to learn how you know that."

Kensington breathed hard. "Very well. I did break into her room and search it when I learned she'd died. Why shouldn't I? I did find the box in which she kept her money.

But there weren't enough coins in it to buy a pig breakfast. She'd spent it all."

"Serves you right," I said.

"You cannot prove any of this, Lacey. You cannot take me to court."

"I am sickened by you, and beyond caring. I am happy to leave you to the mercy of Lady Jane."

His face whitened. "You cannot, Lacey. I will confess to anything, to your magistrate or whomever you like, as long as you help me. Take me to Denis. We will speak with him together."

"No," I answered.

For a moment he looked panicked. Then the angry light returned to his eye. "You are a bloody fool, Captain. I came to offer you a bargain. If you will not help me, then I cannot answer for what happens to you."

"Do not threaten me," I said coldly. "You tell me you are incapable of murder, but I do not claim to be so."

He paused, fear lighting his eye again, then the defiant look returned, and he clapped his hat to his head. "You will regret that you did not help me," he said. "Oh, yes, you will regret it." He glared at me one last time, then turned and marched down the stairs.

I did not answer. I slammed the door, and stood in the middle of my chamber, seething with anger. Needing release, I picked up the ebony walking stick that Grenville had lent me and hurled it across the room. It made a satisfying crash against the wall, but the strong shaft of it remained whole.

CHAPTER 16

❧

I was still seething when I walked to the Covent Garden
Theatre at the end of Bow Street not long later. I had
badly wanted Kensington to fall to his knees and confess
that he'd killed Peaches and Lord Barbury. I had wanted to
grab him by the neck and drag him off to Pomeroy and
punishment.

I was angry at him for what he'd done to Peaches. Marianne's story had portrayed Peaches as a starry-eyed girl,
certain that happiness and good fortune lay in London.
Luck seemed to be with her when an aged relative had died
and left her a place to live. And then she'd met Kensington. She must have trusted him at first, wanting the fame
and fortune he promised her. But he had drained innocence
from her. He had made her into a grasping woman who'd
think nothing of owning a bawdy house or of cuckolding
her respectable husband, a woman who wanted and needed
excitement and sensation to make her life livable. I hated
him, and I wanted to hurt him.

My emotions roiling thus, I was in no mood to be cut dead by Louisa Brandon.

I saw her just inside the theatre, after I'd strode past the grand columns and its usual collection of ladies in flimsy silks and rouged cheeks. I saw her in her long-sleeved matron's gown of dull maroon, its lighter pink trim matching the three feathers in her headdress. I thought her far more becoming and delightful than the professional women outside the doors. The only color Louisa ever wore on her face was her own, color that heightened when she saw me.

She'd just said something to her maid and had turned to make for the stairs to the boxes. Our gazes met for an instant. I saw, even around the substantial number of people between us, recognition—and dismay. Just as I was about to bow to her, she abruptly turned and walked away.

I lost my temper. I strode through the crowd, never minding the pain in my leg, easily reaching the doorway to the stairs before she did. I planted myself in her path, and waited for her to act.

She of course had to stop. I bowed to her, and in a low voice said, "I remember you promising that you would not cut me entirely."

The cold spark of anger in her eyes flared. "I do beg your pardon. I did not see you."

She lied. She had certainly seen me. "It is of no moment." My lips felt stiff. "Shall I escort you to your box?"

"There is no need."

"It would be rude not to."

She gazed at me frostily, and I gazed back. I remembered us in a similar situation, once upon a time, at a regimental colonel's dinner. Louisa had been furiously angry at me for some fault or other, but because we'd been in the colonel's tent with the other officers and their wives, she had not been able to shout at me, nor I to retaliate. We could only glare at one another and offer strained politeness. Later, of course, she had dressed me down, and I'd shouted back until we'd cleared the air and become friends again.

We now faced another restraining situation, her glare twice as angry as it had been at that regimental supper. At long last, she silently slid her gloved fingers under my arm, and we proceeded to the stairs, neither of us speaking.

I led her to her box and inside. She let me, both of us now determined to go through the charade. I settled her in a chair, draped her shawl over her shoulders, and sent for coffee, just as I would any other time, but my movements were deliberate, my questions cold.

I hoped, very much hoped, that she would at last burst out laughing and say, "This is nonsense, Gabriel, do sit down." But she remained stiff, her responses terse.

I handed her her coffee, asked her if she'd like anything else. She lifted the cup to her lips and said clearly, "No. Go away, Gabriel."

"Louisa."

Her eyes hardened. "I do not wish to speak to you. Go."

I looked down at her, my anger undimmed. "You have been my friend for twenty years," I said. "I will never be able to just go."

But I picked up my walking stick and departed. Several ladies who had spied Louisa entering slid into her box past me with cries of greeting. They barely noticed me.

I hardly felt my sore knee as I stamped around the perimeter of Covent Garden Theatre to Lady Breckenridge's box. Louisa and I had quarreled before, but this felt very different. She was tired of me. I did not blame her. And yet I did blame her for being cruel. She was cutting me off from the last thing that gave me joy—speaking to her. Later on, I would hurt. Now, I was simply angry.

In such a mood, I entered Lady Breckenridge's box on the upper tier.

A gilt-embellished door led to a tiny room of exceptional elegance that contained a dining table and chairs. An oriental carpet covered the floor and a crystal chandelier hung from the ceiling. A double door beyond this led to the box itself. The sounds of laughter and loud conversation drifted through it from the theatre proper.

The lackey tapped on the door, then opened it and ushered me through.

Six ebony chairs stood in a row overlooking the stage far below. Lady Breckenridge reposed on the chair in the middle, in a gown of lavender that left her shoulders bare. Her dark hair was threaded with diamonds.

Next to her sat a gentleman I did not know. On Lady Breckenridge's other side, with an empty chair between them, was Lady Aline Carrington. The gentleman wore a suit to rival any of Grenville's. He was somewhere between forty and fifty, with gray hair at his temples and a neutral face. He returned my nod when Lady Breckenridge introduced us, but without much interest.

I seated myself between the two ladies. A stout woman, Lady Aline had her gowns made cleverly, so that the dress neither pointed out her stoutness nor hid it. She rouged her cheeks bright red and outlined her eyes in kohl and had coiled her white hair around a feathered headdress.

"Lacey, my boy, I am pleased to see you," she said warmly.

"And I you, my lady."

"I will forgive the lie. I hear you have been haring about town again, solving crimes like a Bow Street Runner. Disgraceful."

I took her admonishment good-humoredly. Lady Aline liked me, and I her.

"Was that Louisa Brandon I saw you speaking to?" Lady Aline went on in a loud voice. She waved her lorgnette, indicating that she'd spied us through it. "I had not thought she was coming tonight."

I responded that she had indeed seen Louisa. I hoped my tense anger did not betray itself.

"I shall have to call on her tomorrow and have a good chat," Lady Aline said. She seemed in no hurry to rise and round the theatre to speak with her now.

I had no idea what the opera was below, and the players seemed not to have much idea either. The audience laughed at the tragedy and shouted at the comedy, and a

group of tall lads, who reminded me a bit of the lanky Mr. Gower, sang along at the tops of their voices.

Lady Breckenridge wore a thick perfume tonight, smelling of eastern spices. She made little movements with her fan that sent the smell into my nose.

I learned that the gentleman on her other side was called Lord Percy Saunders, and that his father was the Duke of Waverly. Lord Percy said little, and occasionally wiped his nose with a handkerchief. When he did speak, he confined his remarks to Lady Breckenridge and ignored me and Lady Aline.

When the opera wound to an interval, Lady Aline gathered her things and rose. "I've had enough of this nonsense. Good night, Donata. Give my love to your mother."

Lady Breckenridge smiled and gave her a pleasant "good night." Lord Percy rose and bowed, looking bored.

I escorted Lady Aline downstairs, since Lord Percy did not seem inclined to bestir himself. I walked with her all the way to her carriage in King Street, her footman and maid trailing us. She told me I had manners, unlike many gentlemen, a high compliment from her, as I shut her carriage door.

When I returned to Lady Breckenridge's box, I found that Lord Percy had gone.

Lady Breckenridge was just coming into the little dining room as I entered it from the other side. She paused a moment at the doors that led to the box, an odd look on her face. Then she shook her head and closed the double doors behind her. The noise from the second act of the opera faded somewhat.

"Your friend Lord Percy has no manners," I observed. "He should not have left you alone."

"He is ghastly," she agreed. The diamonds in her hair sparkled as she turned her head. "He believes I should give up being the dowager Viscountess Breckenridge to become his wife." She shuddered. "I could not bear to be called *Lady Percy*."

"But you might be called *duchess* later," I pointed out.

"He is a younger son," Lady Breckenridge said dismissively. "He is unlikely to ever become the duke." She gazed at me again, eyes narrowing. "Do you know, Lacey, that just for a moment, when you came in, you looked remarkably like Breckenridge."

I grimaced. Her late husband had been a brute of a man with little to redeem him. "I am sorry to hear you say that."

"I do not believe there has been a morning I have not awakened thanking heaven that he is dead." She punctuated the callous remark by removing a cigarillo from a silver case. She lit it with one of the candles on the table and put it to her mouth. "Do sit down, Lacey. Unless you would rather listen to that racket that is supposed to be opera."

I did not, so I took one of the Louis XV chairs, waiting for her to sit before I did.

She looked me up and down, her dark blue eyes assessing. Tendrils of acrid smoke wove about her head. "You seem in much better health this evening."

I half-bowed in my chair. "Your butler's cure worked wonders."

"He is marvelous," she said. "But I see you have not recovered your walking stick. Although that is a fine one."

"Grenville kindly lent it to me."

"It is a pity about the other. It must have been a wrench to lose something that close to you."

I was surprised she understood that. "It is, yes."

"And I read in the newspaper this evening that Mrs. Chapman's husband, of all people, had been arrested for Inglethorpe's murder. Do you think he did it?"

"He confessed," I said.

"Probably mistook Inglethorpe for having an affair with his wife," she said with uncanny perception. "Peaches was a silly young woman, and I am not surprised she brought everyone around her to a bad end. Quite common, as I told you."

"Yes, so you said." Her opinion coincided with Mari-

anne's. Peaches had been a woman other women had had little use for.

"Do not pity her too much," Lady Breckenridge said, observing my expression. "She brought many of her troubles upon herself."

"I cannot forget seeing her lying on the bank of the Thames," I said softly. "It was a brutal death."

"I daresay it was. But do not let it cloud your judgement to what she was."

"You are a bit brutal yourself," I said.

Her eyes took on an enigmatic light. "I am honest. And not always polite, I am afraid."

I smiled a little. "I am surprised you speak with me at all. I am hardly in your class."

She returned the smile. It was surprisingly warm, and her eyes twinkled. "Nonsense. You come from a fine lineage. I looked you up."

"A rather overly pruned family tree," I said dryly.

"And you have no sons?"

I shook my head.

"Pity. But you were married, weren't you?" she asked.

I raised my brows. My marriage was not common knowledge—not because I wanted to hide it, but because I simply did not wish to talk about it.

Her smile deepened. "You have the look of a man who's had a wife, who has experienced the hell that can be marriage. A widower, you know, looks a different man from a bachelor."

I only nodded, not correcting her that I was not a widower. My wife still lived, in France, possibly with the French officer for whom she had left me. She had changed her name, but I still knew her as Carlotta.

Lady Breckenridge smoked in silence for a few minutes, drawing on the cigarillo and letting smoke trail from her lips.

"My news is scarcely news any more," she said at last. "Now that you know who murdered Inglethorpe. But I thought you'd like to know just the same."

My interest quickened. Lady Breckenridge, though acerbic, was also observant. "Yes?" I prompted.

"I know who took your walking stick in the first place." She laid the cigarillo in a porcelain dish, where it continued to burn. "I have no idea how Chapman got hold of it, but I know how it left the house that day."

"Do you?" I stared. "Why the devil did you not say so at the inquest?"

She shrugged. "Because I am not as callous as people believe I am. I did not truly think that the person who took the walking stick killed Inglethorpe, but Bow Street would have pounced on her at once, would they not have? Dragged her off to the magistrate and then Newgate, most like. I did not wish that on poor Mrs. Danbury."

I stared at her. "Mrs. Danbury?" I clearly pictured Mrs. Danbury smiling at me in Inglethorpe's drawing room while we danced, and then later, looking at me with innocent gray eyes when I'd questioned her at Sir Gideon's, declaring she had not seen what had become of the walking stick that day. "You must be mistaken."

Candlelight danced in the diamonds in her dark hair as she shook her head. "Not a bit. I saw her."

"Saw her? When?"

"As my carriage pulled away from Inglethorpe's house. I looked out of the window and saw her walk out of Inglethorpe's front door with your walking stick in her hands. Not seeing you, she went to her own coach and got in."

"Bloody hell," I said, with feeling. "Why the devil didn't you say so at once?"

She shrugged. "I assumed she'd send it back to you. You are acquainted with her cousins, I believe. I happened to see Grenville yesterday afternoon, and he told me you were still very puzzled about the walking stick. So I wrote and invited you here."

I got to my feet. "Oh, good God. Much trouble might have been saved if you'd simply told me."

She rose as well. "Well, I had no idea the bloody thing would end up in Inglethorpe, did I?"

We faced each other, both angry, her eyes glittering.

Mrs. Danbury had lied to me. She'd sat before me and lied and lied. "Damn it to hell," I muttered.

"I am sorry if I have distressed you, Captain. I thought it only a peculiarity."

I balled my hands. My gloves, cheap, stretched over my fingers until the stitching split. "The next time you come across a peculiarity, for God's sake, tell me right away."

"You have a foul temper," she observed.

"I know that."

"I hardly thought it your way to swear at a lady."

I looked up at her, fire in my eyes. "You seem to want me to tell you my true thoughts."

"Yes, but you are rather straining the bonds of politeness."

"To hell with politeness," I growled. "No doubt baiting me amuses you, but I grow tired of it."

She breathed rapidly. "I want friendship. I told you."

"Your definition of friendship is decidedly odd."

"You mean because I lay in bed with you the other morning? You looked as though you needed comfort, to be in too much pain for anything else."

"That did not give you the leave to take such a liberty. You ought to have a care for your reputation."

She gave me a pitying look. "Let me worry about my reputation. I did not notice you sending me away, by the by."

I recalled her head on my shoulder, her warm arm flung across my chest. It had been comforting, without heat or fever.

"I did not wish to send you away," I said. "That does not mean I acted honorably."

"It was meant in friendship," she said stubbornly.

No doubt she thought so. She was maddening, one of the most unfathomable women I'd ever met.

"Why did you not tell me about the walking stick?" I re-

peated. "As you observed, it was not something I wanted to lose."

"Well, I do not quite know," she retorted. "I was not paying sufficient attention. I do apologize." Her voice dripped with sarcasm.

I raked my hand through my hair. I was frustrated, and angry, so angry at all the lies and deceit and cruelties. She had probably not thought the matter of any importance. She did not see what I saw, feel what I felt. I could not expect her to.

"I beg your pardon," I said, my lips tight. "I am out of sorts. I have had a terrible afternoon."

She shook her head. "Poor Captain Lacey."

The words were mocking, but I liked that she said them.

Perhaps because I was so angry at Mrs. Danbury and also at Louisa, that I realized that when I'd been ill and in pain, Lady Breckenridge had been the only one to soothe me. She had said *friendship*, but she meant companionship, something she had certainly never gotten from her husband.

Her black hair curled about her forehead, loose from her headdress. She had a pointed chin and fine laugh lines about her eyes. I touched one of those lines.

She looked at me, startled. I thought she would back away, fling more scorn at me, but she only lowered her lashes. I traced her cheekbone with my thumb. She stood still for a moment, then silently leaned into my touch.

She had brazenly thrown herself at me in Kent. Now, all fever gone, she gently lifted her hand and caressed mine. Emboldened, I leaned to her and lightly kissed her lips.

She laughed, just as I'd wanted Louisa Brandon to. "Oh, Lacey," she said.

For a time, I forgot about my frustrations, the tragedy of Peaches and her husband, my walking stick, Mrs. Danbury's lies, the opera. Lady Breckenridge soothed me again, and I let her.

*   *   *

IN the morning I awoke to the peal of church bells all over the city. St. Paul's, Covent Garden, chimed the loudest, with the church of St. Martin's, on the west end of the Strand, a close second. Those bells blended with that of St. Mary's on the east end of the Strand, and beyond that, in the distance, I could hear the booming bells of St. Paul's Cathedral.

They chimed and rang in the winter sunlight, and Bartholomew whistled a tune in the front room as he stoked my fire to overflowing.

I lay in bed, listening to the sounds of Sunday, thinking about Saturday, and all that had happened: Barbury's death, Chapman's arrest, our boat ride up the Thames, Kensington's revelations, the opera. I needed to write Sir Montague Harris of our findings and about Kensington. If Peaches had been ready to betray him, how much easier for Kensington if she were dead. He'd had the opportunity, been on the spot. The circumstances were damning. I simply needed the tiniest piece of evidence, or a witness.

A witness. I turned that thought over in my mind. I would ask Sir Montague to accompany me to speak to the potential witness I had in mind.

I also thought about kissing Lady Breckenridge. After a heartbreak last year, I was not in the mood to fall in love with another lady, but Lady Breckenridge had demanded nothing of me. She was intriguing and interesting, and, I admitted, refreshingly candid. She took me for what I was and did not ask me to be anything else. Her kisses had been unhurried, without heat. She'd kissed me because she enjoyed kissing me. It was a heady feeling.

I wish that the cheerful Sunday morning had prepared me for what was to come. But at the time, I simply enjoyed the first sunshine in a long while, and listened to the music of the church bells.

When I rose, I began to prepare myself for moving to Berkshire. Mrs. Beltan was unhappy to learn she'd lose me as a tenant, and promised to hold the rooms for me in case I changed my mind. I wrote of it to the few acquaintances,

like Lady Aline Carrington, who would care, and even to
Colonel Brandon. I had Bartholomew hand-deliver these
as well as a missive to Sir Montague Harris with my information and outlining my ideas of finding a witness.

I informed Bartholomew I would be dining at the Derwents' that evening, and he brightened at the chance to
brush my regimentals again. Dining with the Derwents
would give me the opportunity to question Mrs. Danbury
about the walking stick, questions that would pain me, but
I would ask them. I needed to know the truth.

Sir Montague sent a message in return that he'd made
an appointment to speak to Lady Jane at a Mayfair hotel,
courtesy of James Denis. He invited me to join him there
at two o'clock that afternoon.

I spent the morning putting my affairs together, then
journeyed to Davies Street to arrive at two, my curiosity
high, hoping we'd see an end to the Glass House this very
day.

The hotel on the corner of Davies and Brook streets was
fairly new, lived in by those staying in London for the Season but not wanting the bother of opening a house. Lady
Jane was not staying there, Sir Montague informed me;
rather, we were using the hotel as neutral ground.

We were taken to a private sitting room, which was el-
egantly furnished, and there, we met Lady Jane.

She was a stout matron, and so unlike what I had been
expecting that I could only stare at her at first. She wore a
widow's cap over her black hair, and her face was round
and red and lined, a provincial woman's face. Her mauve
pelisse of fine fabric was tastefully trimmed with a gray
fringe, and her gray broadcloth skirt shone dully in the
candlelight. The suit spoke of care and expense, but her
eyes held a light as hard and shrewd as a horsetrader's.

She held out her hand to me, and I bowed over it as expected, then she withdrew, scarcely looking at me, and sat
down in a chair. The hotel's footman set a footstool at her
feet, fetched another for Sir Montague, then faded away.

"Sir Montague," she said. Her accent was only slight, barely betraying her origins. "What may I do for you?"

"I would like you to tell me about a gentleman named Kensington," Sir Montague began, settling himself. "I believe you employ him."

"Possibly." Lady Jane smoothed her skirt, looking from Sir Montague to me. "I employ many gentlemen."

"He is not quite a gentleman," Sir Montague said. "In fact, I would like to arrest him."

CHAPTER 17

⚜

L ADY Jane looked appropriately distressed. "Indeed?"
"Yes," Sir Montague said cheerfully. "I will arrest
him for running a bawdy house, but I want to be careful.
Witnesses are all very well, but magistrates in the past
have been persuaded to drop the case against the Glass
House, and I fear the same will happen again."

"Will it?" Lady Jane's eyes flickered, although I could
tell she knew bloody well that it would be. "I sympathize
with your frustration, Sir Montague."

"So, I probably will not be bringing charges against the
Glass House itself, since my aim was simply to close it.
But I would like to not let Kensington get away. He would
simply find another house to manage."

"You are no doubt correct."

"So it would be very helpful if I could find more to arrest him for. And witnesses. I would appreciate any light
you can shine on this gentleman and his activities."

Lady Jane sat in silence. The quiet in the room belied
the tension there. The fine silk furnishings, the paneled

walls, and high ceiling, all fine and tasteful, seemed to cringe at the rather sordid business taking place there.

Lady Jane remained still, but I sensed the thoughts behind her eyes. If she betrayed Kensington, she would not be trusted in her world again. But if she did not betray him, Sir Montague would simply turn around and have Kensington betray her. No doubt Denis had thought of this, which is why he'd arranged for the meeting. I wondered what Denis had threatened Lady Jane with to coerce her to attend.

Lady Jane wet her lips. "I believe I have heard," she said, "that Mr. Kensington banks at Barclay's. And he has a man of business in High Holborn. If Kensington does make money from this Glass House, no doubt you will find the evidence there. And perhaps, just perhaps, you will find servants at the Glass House who might help you against Mr. Kensington in return for being spared prosecution."

Sir Montague smiled and nodded. "Perhaps. I had thought of that. Your suggestions are apt." He shifted his bulk on the chair, and the legs creaked. "The Glass House is now closed. The owner has died, the property has passed on. A reformer has spread the word about it, and some members of Parliament have taken notice, enough to make magistrates in the pay of the Glass House nervous."

He beamed, happy. Lady Jane simply sat, quiet in defeat.

Sir Montague turned to me. "Captain? Was there anything you wished to ask?"

A small smile flickered at the corner of Lady Jane's mouth. "Ah, yes, Captain Lacey. Mr. Denis speaks highly of you."

I ignored her. "Last Monday," I began, "The woman who owned the Glass House was killed. Peaches—her real name was Mrs. Chapman—left the house just after four o'clock. She told Mr. Kensington, with whom she'd quarreled, that she was on her way to keep an appointment. I

would very much like to know what appointment, and with whom."

Lady Jane stared at me for a long time. Her eyes were shrewd and cold. She reminded me of James Denis—careful and unemotional—though she did not share his elegance or smoothness of character.

Lady Jane at last spoke. "I am afraid I cannot help you, Captain. I did not know Mrs. Chapman very well."

My irritation rose. "I know she told Kensington she wanted to see you, to tell you a few things about him. Right after that, she departed to keep an appointment. Was that appointment with you?"

"No," Lady Jane said coldly.

"And you have no idea with whom she was meeting?"

"No, Captain."

"Question the servants, you said. I wonder, if we arrested your coachman and beat him until he confessed, would he tell us that he was instructed to have the coach ready for Mrs. Chapman's use any time she wanted it? Including on the last day of her life?"

The room grew silent again. Sir Montague was watching me, a faint smile on his face, brows raised.

Lady Jane's long hesitation betrayed her. Of course, I thought. Thompson had found no hackney drivers that had taken Peaches anywhere. A private conveyance, he'd concluded, but whose? Not Lord Barbury's. His coachman had been questioned. Chapman did not keep his own carriage, and Peaches would hardly use it to visit to the Glass House anyway. But what if Lady Jane's coach were available to Peaches as part of Lady Jane's payment for the use of the house? Peaches could easily start for Sussex then arrange for Lady Jane's carriage to retrieve her from a coaching inn and bring her back to London. Lady Jane's coachman would not run to the magistrate to report such an irregularity.

"I believe," Lady Jane ventured, "that Mrs. Chapman enjoyed the use of my carriage now and again."

"I am pleased to hear it," I said. I glanced about the el-

egant room again, which seemed to have brightened. The maroon and blue hues stood out more, the gold glistened. "Now I know where we stand."

Sir Montague beamed at me. All was well in his world.

I had a second appointment that afternoon, which I'd nearly forgotten in the week's events, but which I remembered just in time. I made my way to Hyde Park after Sir Montague and I left the hotel and reached the stables at my appointed hour of three o'clock. Every second Sunday, I met a young man called Philip Preston and gave him a riding lesson. I had met him during the affair of Hanover Square, in which he had been much help, and it pleased me to be able to assist the lad in return. His mother's doctor still insisted he was weak and sickly, but Philip was stronger and more robust each time I saw him.

I would have to tell him today of my plan to move to Berkshire, and this saddened me. I would miss him, though he had told me that his father would send him back to school sometime this term, so our lessons would have been short-lived in any case.

Philip's father allowed me to ride a gelding from his stables when I gave the lesson, a fine beast with good gaits. When we finished an hour later, and Philip went off home, I asked leave to ride the gelding a bit longer for the exercise. The groom saw no objection, and I trotted away, lost in thought.

On horseback, my injury did not hinder me as much as it did on foot. I could manage to sit a sedate walk, trot, and canter, though I could ride nowhere near as well or as long as I had in the cavalry, nor could I perform the acrobatics I had in the past. But mounted, I felt more in league with the world, and I had missed the time in the saddle. I hoped Grenville's friend would not object to his secretary borrowing a horse every now and then and riding off into the Berkshire countryside.

Lost in thought, I did not see Louisa Brandon and her pony phaeton until I was nearly upon her. She drove alone,

the reins held in her competent hands, her high, mannish hat set at a jaunty angle. A Brandon groom clung to the back of the phaeton, his face set against Louisa's swift pace. She often drove out in the afternoons, and I realized, ruefully, that I had probably lingered in order to see her. I had finished with my fit of temper of the night before, and hoped she would allow me to apologize.

In my turbulent life, Louisa had been a constant. I had met her when I'd been twenty, and from then until now, we had spent little time apart. She had married Brandon, but her friendship had carried me through fire and storm. Even now, after she'd told me to keep my distance, the most difficult part about leaving London would be leaving her.

Louisa turned her head, saw me. I feared for a moment that she would pass me by without a word, try to cut me dead as she had last night. As she neared, I saw the indecision in her face, then she drew beside me and pulled the pony to a walk.

"Gabriel," she said in her clear voice. "Good afternoon."

I let out a pent-up breath, which I hid by tipping my hat; then I turned my horse and fell into step with her.

"I am always pleased to see you on horseback," she said neutrally. "You look almost like your old self."

"A little grayer," I answered, matching her tone.

"We all are, are we not?"

"Not you."

She smiled. "Only because gray is more difficult to see in blonde hair. But it is there, I assure you."

The groom, who was about nineteen years old, stared stiffly ahead, uninterested in our conversation.

"I was abominably rude last evening," I began. "I wish to beg your pardon."

"As was I." Her voice was cool. "May we forget it?"

"If you wish," I said, my heart hammering.

We rode for a time without speaking. When she took up the conversation again, her voice was deliberately light.

"Aloysius read out the letter you sent him explaining your decision to go to Berkshire."

"Yes." I imagined he'd read it with glee.

"When would you leave?" she asked.

"Soon."

Her reins went slack, and the pony, bored, slowed and stopped. "Such a thing will be fine for you. Do you believe you have the temperament to become a secretary?"

I shrugged. "It can be no worse than writing reports for a regimental colonel."

She tried to smile. "We will—" She broke off. "I will miss you."

We studied one another. Aware of the groom looking on so close, I could not say, *Please, ask me not to go*.

She drew a breath, and the moment passed. "You must write, of course." Another smile curved her mouth, but did not enter her voice. "It will be your profession now."

"Indeed, I will write lengthy and tedious reports of life in the country. How many flowers wilted at dinner and whether the vicar's wife has a new hat."

Her smile faded. "We will miss you." I noted the firm *we* that time.

She seemed to remember that her cart sat unmoving. She flicked the whip and the pony woke up and trotted on.

We spoke of other things, then, light things of little consequence, but the air between us was strained.

THAT evening, I turned up at the Derwent mansion in Grosvenor Square in my regimentals at the precise hour of seven. Mrs. Danbury was there, her color high. I tried to behave as usual to her, but I was still angry and puzzled, and I had difficulty remaining polite. I felt my manners straining to the breaking point.

We had supper in the grand dining room amid the sparkle of crystal glasses and the gleam of silver. A row of French windows between mirrors gave out into a garden, which had been lit with festive paper lanterns. I had learned, on my first visit with the Derwents the previous

summer, that they turned out their finest plate and cutlery and lit the house as though for a ball for these suppers, although I was the only guest.

They flattered me, but they had genuine liking for me. I at first had been bewildered by them, then I'd decided simply to enjoy them without protest. I grew to like the Derwents and their innocent enthusiasm. They loved more than anything to hear tales of my adventures in the army, and would sit for hours listening to me speak.

Sir Gideon was bluff and genial, very much the country squire. Fair-haired Leland seemed to have survived public school and university without scars, an amazing feat. His sister, Melissa, looked much like him. Both had a frailty that worried me. I hoped that when the time came for Melissa to marry, she would find a gentleman who would understand her naïveté and not break her. Tonight, she watched me shyly as usual. In the last six months, I believe she had said all of five words to me.

Lady Derwent did not cough much during the meal, and seemed better. She talked with a bright animation that matched her son's and husband's. The butler served champagne.

Mrs. Danbury behaved as though she had nothing on her conscience. She ate the fine food readily and chatted with me and her family with ease. I began to wonder if Lady Breckenridge had invented the tale of Mrs. Danbury leaving Inglethorpe's with my walking stick, but I could not for the life of me think of any reason for her to do so.

We finished supper and adjourned for cards. I had a lively game of whist with Leland and his father and mother, while Mrs. Danbury and Melissa played upon the pianoforte and the harp.

As the light music filled the room, I was reminded anew why I never turned down an invitation to dine with the Derwents. True, I could partake of one of the finest meals in London and spend a warm night playing whist, but those were not the only reasons I came. I came because whenever

I was with these people, something marvelous happened. *I forgot.*

I forgot that I was poor and lonely and that my career was behind me. I forgot that my former closest friend had turned into my bitterest rival, and that his wife had told me she'd had enough of me. I forgot about murder and deceit and the ugliness of the world, forgot everything but the pleasant music, the sincere laughter, the soft slap of cards, and the clink of pennies as we settled up—we never played for more than a farthing a point. The Derwents drew a curtain between themselves and the world, and I enjoyed retreating behind the curtain with them.

I breathed the peace of this place, happy I'd found a refuge. I knew in my heart that the peace would not last. Lady Derwent was dying. It was only a matter of time before this bright house became one of mourning. Perhaps that was why they were so cheerfully determined to enjoy themselves now; they knew the darkness was coming.

After cards, the Derwents proposed a walk in their garden. The fair weather had lasted all day, and the moon was bright. I joined them, breathing the clean air, which, though cold, was refreshing. The paper lanterns danced, spreading blue and pink and red lights, rendering the garden colorful even in the bare winter night.

But I had come here for another purpose. Mrs. Danbury had not joined us in the garden, and I excused myself, declaring I'd forgotten my gloves. I quickly walked back to the drawing room where Mrs. Danbury lingered to put away the harp.

She was just covering the instrument when I entered the warm room. The smell of beeswax and the ladies' mixed perfumes lingered in the air, and the laughter and music seemed to as well.

Mrs. Danbury looked at me in surprise. She settled the dust cover, flapping it like a drapery over a bed. "Will you not walk?"

I moved to her, and she watched me, puzzled. My expression must have startled her, because she looked at me

in consternation. "Is everything all right? Has Lady Derwent taken ill?"

"No," I said. "She is well."

Tonight Mrs. Danbury wore a dress of blue and lighter
blue stripes, bound by a wide sash. Her bodice held a row
of false black buttons down the front. She looked quite becoming, and I'd always thought her pretty.

"Mrs. Danbury," I began quietly. "I discovered yesterday that you lied to me about my walking stick. You took it
away with you when you left Inglethorpe's on Wednesday
afternoon, did you not?"

She froze. The cloth fell from her hands. "Why do you
say so?"

"I am trying to understand what you did and why. I
admit I am most puzzled."

Her color rose. Mrs. Danbury was different from the
Derwents in that the she did not share their innocence. She
had been married twice, and from what Lady Aline had
gossiped to me, neither marriage had been very happy.
Mickey Danbury had enjoyed the beds of many women
across London, while sparing little time for his wife. He
had been a robust young man and had died breaking his
neck while racing his horse from London to Brighton. *A
mercy he did*, Lady Aline had said.

I could only wonder what the humiliating marriage had
done to Catherine Danbury. It must have made her more
world-wise than her uncle and aunt and cousins. Perhaps it
had hardened her, but she had learned to dissemble. I
wanted to think of her as a gentle and pretty widow that I
longed to know better, but I could not make her into something she was not.

"Captain Lacey, I am uncertain what to say to you." She
gave me a cool look, reminding me of the time I had first
met her. She had been among the guests invited to view an
artist's work; she had looked me over indifferently when
I'd been introduced, then ignored me completely. "Of what
precisely are you accusing me?"

"I want you to tell me exactly what happened with In-

glethorpe. I know you took the walking stick. And I cannot help but remember how he was found. He had been in the act of removing his clothing when Mr. Chapman burst in and killed him. For an assignation, we assume. But Inglethorpe was not in a hurry. He removed his clothing and folded it. He would not have done that unless he'd been well acquainted with the woman with whom he was about to carry out the affair. A woman who would wait for him in the next room, or who hid there when Chapman came rushing in. Lovers of long standing, who no longer need to undress in a frenzy of passion."

Her cool look turned to a glare. "Are you implying that you believe that woman was me? How dare you? Shall I call my uncle, Captain, and tell him what you have said? He will be shocked. And most disappointed in you, I think."

"Mrs. Danbury," I said in a hard voice, "a man was murdered. The weapon was the sword in my walking stick, and you were seen taking it away with you the day before. For God's sake, tell me what you did, and please tell me that you had nothing to do with his death."

Her breath caught. She looked at me a long moment, lips parted, her eyes moist. "I had nothing to do with it," she said, her voice losing its defiance. "Nothing at all, I swear to you. When I left Mr. Inglethorpe, he was alive. I never knew he was murdered until I heard of it later that day."

So she had been there. My heart sank. I had hoped she would tell me that the walking stick had been stolen from her and that she had no idea how it had ended up at Inglethorpe's.

My throat tightening, I said, "Begin from the beginning, and tell me. You discovered my walking stick left behind on Wednesday, and took it away with you. Did you realize it was mine?"

She rested her hand on top of the harp, half-shielding herself with the instrument. "Yes. I realized you'd left it. I caught it up, ready to take it down to you. But when I reached the street, you'd already gone."

I nodded. I had leapt into Lady Breckenridge's coach, eager to hear what she had to tell me about Lord Barbury.

Mrs. Danbury went on, "So I simply brought it home with me."

"And then the next day, you took it back to Inglethorpe's."

Color rose in her face. "Yes."

"I must wonder why you did so."

"Because—" Her flush deepened. "Oh, dear heavens, Captain. I was a fool. He told me he would have another gathering at his house that Thursday, and that I could return and partake of more of his magic gas. I did not want to; it made me rather sick, as I told you. But he said he had invited you as well. So I thought, the next day, I'd simply bring your walking stick and give it back to you."

"But when you reached Inglethorpe's," I said, "you realized that you had been deceived."

Her gray eyes sparkled in anger. "Yes. The odious man tricked me. He had me wait in his reception room; I did not realize at first that I was the only person to arrive."

"When did you discover your mistake?"

"When he returned to the reception room to see me. I wanted to leave right away, but he bade me stay."

I frowned. "The servants swore that they saw no one. But the butler or footman must have let you in."

"He answered the door himself. He must have been waiting for me. My footman had knocked on the door, then nipped down the scullery stairs to the kitchens. When Inglethorpe appeared, I grew nervous. I meant to call my footman back, but Inglethorpe came outside and drew me in."

Thus explaining the mud on his indoor shoes.

"I am beginning to be happy you had a weapon with you," I said. "What happened then?"

"Mr. Inglethorpe asked, rather rudely, why I was carrying a gentleman's walking stick. I explained that you had left it and that I had brought it to give to you. He looked annoyed and snatched it away from me."

My voice became a growl. "Blackguard."

"That was not the worst of it. He pulled the sword partway out, and he—" Her face turned scarlet. "He made lewd gestures with it."

"He needed calling out," I said, calm with anger.

"I was mortified. I tried to leave, but he blocked the way. Then he began talking about my late husband, Mickey, and how he'd always admired him. He said—oh, dear Lord, I can hardly repeat it."

"Do not, if it distresses you so."

"No, I want to tell you. I cannot bear to keep it in any longer. He said that he'd always wanted to take Mickey to bed, but that as Mickey was gone, I would do. It was horrible." Tears of mortification stood in her eyes.

My rage grew. "I can only say that Mr. Inglethorpe is lucky he is dead."

"I could not think what to say or do. I had gone there out of my own foolishness. He began taking off his coat and waistcoat. He was between me and the door. He was very careful and deliberate about it, almost taunting me. I had never been so disgusted and afraid in my life."

My hands curled to fists. "Please tell me you got away."

She nodded. The tears spilled from her eyes to her cheeks. "When he turned to lay his clothing on a chair, I ran. He grabbed for me and nearly had me, but mercifully, I was too quick. I ran out of the house. I climbed into my carriage and told the coachman to go, quickly." She laughed suddenly, tears choking her voice. "I left my poor footman behind. He ran up the scullery stairs as we pulled away, swearing like a sailor. But I was afraid to stop, and the poor fellow had to walk home."

She twisted her hands, her laughter dying. "Later when I heard Mr. Inglethorpe had been killed with the swordstick, I did not know what to think. I was afraid to mention my part in the matter; I was afraid the magistrates would believe I killed him. I swore my servants to silence and I lied to you and to the coroner. I have been so afraid."

"It no longer matters," I said. I studied her, watching her

cry. She'd been foolish, I thought, relieved, but not guilty of evil. "Mr. Chapman confessed to murdering him, and you no longer need to worry."

She sniffled, drew a handkerchief from her sleeve. "It has been horrible. I kept expecting the magistrates to arrive and arrest me. And at the inquest, I dreaded the moment when one of the others would announce that they'd seen me take the walking stick. I can only thank heaven that none of them did."

"Lady Breckenridge saw you."

Mrs. Danbury stared in surprise. "Did she? Why did she not say so?"

"Her own sense of honor, I suppose," I said. "She thought it would be unfair to you."

Mrs. Danbury looked puzzled, but merely wiped her nose again.

"I wish you would have told me," I said. "I might have been able to help."

She shook her head. "I did not want to. I was so humiliated; I did not want you to know I was anywhere near the man, and I did not want you to think I'd killed him. I could only imagine that you'd share the story with Mr. Grenville, and then it would be all over London."

"You mistake me," I said stiffly. "I would never have done so."

"I know." She gave a rueful laugh. "Uncle and Leland say over and over that you are the most honorable gentleman alive. But I can scarcely believe you are as fine as they paint you."

"And they are apt to believe the very best of everyone."

"Yes." She smiled faintly. "But I do believe they are correct about you."

A warmth began in my breastbone. "They are far kinder than I deserve. I put you into the situation in the first place. Inglethorpe ought to have been flogged, but so should I for leaving my walking stick behind."

"Do not blame yourself, Captain. I was terribly foolish

for believing Mr. Inglethorpe. I ought to have left well enough alone."

"You had no need to bother with it at all, you know. You could simply have left it with Sir Gideon, knowing I would come here to dine soon. Or had him send it on to me."

"Yes, I know. I thought of that."

"Did the laughing gas hold such appeal for you, then?"

She reddened. "Goodness no. I simply thought—" She stopped. "I thought it would be much more pleasant to return it to you myself."

I stared at her in surprise. She sounded shy. Shy, when I knew this woman was popular in society and courted by the most eligible bachelors in London. "That is very kind of you," I said. "I do not deserve such attention."

Her shyness fell away, and her look was almost flirtatious. "But I so enjoyed waltzing with you, Captain."

Heat suffused my face. "I made quite a fool of myself leaping about like a caper merchant. I apologize for that liberty. I was not myself."

"I seem to recall I did not mind in the least." She flashed me a smile. It was a nice smile, one that deepened the corners of her mouth. While Mrs. Danbury was much more aware of the world than her ingenuous cousins, she still possessed the sweetness that they had, the gentle compassion for others.

She took my arm. "Shall we walk?"

I acquiesced. We strolled together to the garden. The January night was colder now, far too cold for traversing garden paths, but the Derwents seemed to create a warmth of their own. Soon we were laughing and talking together, never minding the weather. Mrs. Danbury's story relieved me, and her flattery was appealing, but I remained wary. Her hand was warm on my arm, but my heart still carried a slight chill.

THE chill only increased later. When I returned to my rooms later that night, Kensington was there waiting for me.

CHAPTER 18

KENSINGTON was sitting before my fire, and had lit all my candles. The light fell on his round face, which looked a bit strained and haggard. "Good evening, Captain," he said. "I am a bit put out with you."

I closed the door. I had allowed Bartholomew to return to Grenville's to visit his brother tonight, knowing that I'd soon be taking him off with me to Berkshire. I now regretted doing so.

I had seen no evidence of lackeys or brawny footmen downstairs such as James Denis kept. Kensington had come to face me alone.

"For Sir Montague's visit with Lady Jane?" I asked. "I cannot apologize for that."

He smiled. "I recall telling you on my last visit that you would pay for what you have done. Your nose may not be as long as your friend Grenville's, but you continue to push it where it does not belong."

I remained by the door, Grenville's walking stick in my hand. "Why hasn't Sir Montague arrested you yet?"

"Because I have not been at home. When one of my informers heard he'd gone to see Lady Jane this afternoon, I made myself scarce. I am not naïve enough to believe that the bitch would not betray me. So I have set plans in motion. But before I disappear for good, I wanted to visit you and let you know what I think of you and your deeds."

"I already know what you think of them. And I know what I think of yours."

"I did not kill Peaches and Lord Barbury, Captain, much as you wish I had."

"I have concluded that," I said. "That does not mean you are guilty of nothing. You kept a young girl in that house against her will for your filthy customers. I found only her, but I am willing to hazard that there are and have been more. I am only happy that Peaches found a way to make you squirm."

He shook his head. "She was never a sweet innocent, Captain. Always hard as nails, was Peaches."

"Because you made her so," I said, the walking stick warm under my gasp. "I know she was not angelic; her life must have been harsh—her family wanted nothing to do with her, she was orphaned at a young age, she must have spent many years being pawed at by lecherous men wanting a pretty young actress. But I still cannot help wishing she were alive, and you were dead."

His smile became strained. "You will not kill me, Captain. You are a man of honor."

"But you are not, and so I have no reason to spare you. What I will likely do is haul you around the corner to Bow Street and give you over to my old sergeant, Pomeroy. He is not terribly scrupulous about how he obtains a confession."

He gave me an unreadable look. "No, you will not, Captain. I am leaving England, and you will keep your bullying Runner and magistrate friends from following me."

"Will I?" I slapped the walking stick into my hand. Ebony was a strong wood, good and solid.

"Indeed, you will."

We shared a wordless moment. Then his small, smug smile returned. "I realize that you present a danger to me, Captain Lacey. I also very much want my revenge. And I have it. I will leave unmolested for the Continent, or a lady you care for very much will not return home this night."

I went still, my blood turning to ice. Then I was across the room, my hands at his throat.

Kensington yelped. "Strangle me and you'll not know what becomes of her!" he cried.

I barely heard him. A berserk fury had come upon me. We struggled in the dark corner, he trying to get away from me, me doing my best to throttle him. I was stronger, but he used his weight to counter me. We grappled, he punched me with heavy fists.

I had never mentioned Louisa in his presence, but it would not have been difficult for him to discern my friendship with her; it was common knowledge that I and the Brandons were close, and Kensington or his lackeys could have seen me speaking to her at the theatre last night, riding with her in the park today.

I would have killed him I think, and what would have happened to Louisa I scarce dare imagine. As it was, he kicked me hard in the left knee, a lucky shot but effective.

I loosed him in a flare of pain, and he ducked from my hold and raced for the door.

I shot after him. I could run on my leg when I was afraid or enraged, and I was both. Despite his kick, I was only five steps behind him on the stairs and closer still while he fumbled with the door.

Outside, the stones were slick, but plenty of people milled about, despite the dark and cold. Kensington wove through the crowd and I pounded behind. "Stop him!" I shouted.

The good citizens of Grimpen Lane and Russel Street hastened to oblige. Unfortunately, too many of them did, and they got in my way trying to seize the elusive Kensington.

My leg gave out with an abruptness that paralyzed me.

One moment I was running, the next, and I was on the pavement. I caught my knee, moaning and cursing. More concerned citizens stood over me, offering advice and sympathy.

"Did anyone catch him?" I ground out.

Heads were shaken. No one had. I sank back, my head pounding, my knee throbbing in pain.

I had only one comfort. I did not need to catch him.

I dug in my pocket for a penny and thrust it at one of the street boys. "Get me a hackney. Tell the driver I want to go to St. Charles Row, near Whitechapel."

The boy caught the coin and bounced away. I spent the intervening time crawling to my feet and leaning against the wall, waiting for the arrival of the hackney.

I knew where Kensington had put Louisa—the only place he could have. The Glass House might effectively be closed, but Kensington must still have a key.

When the hackney arrived, the boy helped me climb into it. Before the door closed, I gave him another coin and bade him go to Bow Street and tell Pomeroy where I'd gone.

WHEN I reached St. Charles Row, all was quiet. The moon had moved behind a bank of rising clouds, rendering the street nearly black. A candle or two shone in windows, but the citizens of this neighborhood would not have the money to waste on too many lights. Many of the hardworking ones had gone to bed long ago.

The Glass House was silent, the scarred door locked, possibly bolted. The windows, too, were heavily muffled, and high from the street.

I recalled how the girl, Jean, had described Peaches leaving the house through the kitchen. No scullery steps descended from the street to a door below, so the kitchen must lead out to the spaces behind the houses. In Mayfair, back gardens led to mews, where horses and carriages were kept. In this area, where the inhabitants likely could not afford their own horses, the passage behind the houses

was likely only wide enough for the night-soil removers who crept in and out in their noisome task.

I left St. Charles Row for Aldegate High Street, searching for the narrow passage that backed onto the Glass House and its neighbors. I stumbled upon it almost by accident; a darker space between dark walls. The passage when I entered it was so black that I could find my way only by running my hand along the wall and counting the gates. My boots sloshed through refuse the likes of which I did not want to contemplate. The smell told me well enough.

The gate of number 12 opened easily. In the dark, I nearly fell down the short flight of stairs that led to the kitchen door, catching myself with Grenville's walking stick at the last minute. The door was locked, but the lock proved to be flimsy. I was angry enough that bringing the walking stick down on the latch several times made it give way. If the neighbors heard me and called in the watch, so much the better.

The kitchen was cold and black. I tapped my way across it like a blind man. My leg still hurt like fire, but I was beyond caring. As soon as I got Louisa safe, I would let it hurt, but not until then.

After a long time, too long for my patience, I reached the far wall of the kitchen, then groped along it until I found a door. Hoping it led into the house and not a cupboard or scullery, I pushed through.

My stick struck a stair. I climbed. My leg hurt, and I had to pull myself up holding onto the walls. I emerged at last into the entrance hall. Faint light entered through the fanlight above the door, glistening on candlesticks on a half-round table, candlesticks useless to me because I had no way to light the candles.

I found the main stairs easily after that and groped my way to the first floor above the ground floor. I wondered where Kensington had put Louisa. Would he have found it amusing to lock her into one of the windowed rooms? I had only to break the window to get her out in that case.

Or was she lying unconscious behind the glass, where the shards could cut her? I did not like the thought of that, but my greatest worry was simply getting her *out*.

I went into the main room. I could just make out the outlines of the card tables and chairs in the darkness. The gleam of glass led me to a window. I could see nothing inside.

I cupped my hands and shouted. "Louisa!"

The sound reverberated from the glass window, the dark ceiling, the empty tables and chairs.

All the windows were dark. The house was silent, and it had the feel and smell of desertion. I left the main room and made my way, slowly in the near pitch black, to the stairs up which Kensington had led me to the attics. I climbed these painfully and emerged once more in the tiny hall where I'd found the room in which Peaches had kept her most precious things.

"Louisa!" I called.

I heard a faint cry, not from Peaches' room, but from the one opposite, the attic room I'd not seen. I swung around, groping for the door.

I heard footsteps on the stairs, a heavy tread that shook the stairwell. I wanted to shout out, *Pomeroy, she's here,* but I knew that it was not Pomeroy.

I tried to turn and duck when I felt the whistle of the cudgel. It struck my knee, and I started to go down. Then pain exploded in my head. I fell, sick and dizzy. I heard the faint cry again, the voice behind the door asking what was wrong. I tried to climb to my feet.

I was struck again while on the floor, pain washing me. Someone grabbed me beneath the arms. I tried to twist away, but I could not get my weak leg under me to rise, to fight. A sack was thrust over my head, cutting off my words and my air, and I was plunged into darkness.

A long time later, I heard a voice, low, sweet, and urgent.

"Lacey. Wake up, for God's sake."

I opened my eyes. All was black and close, and I could not breathe. I struggled.

After a time I realized that I lay face down on the floor, a canvas bag firmly in place over my head and my hands tied behind me. I tried to draw a breath, coughed.

The bag reeked of human sweat and other odors that did not bear close examination. Its drawstring encircled my throat, not tight enough to choke me entirely, but enough so that I could not dislodge it. My hands were bound firmly behind my back with chafing twine. They had not needed to bind my legs. Any attempt to rise brought excruciating pain.

"Lacey?"

The voice was not Louisa's. She sounded far from me, and I wondered why she did not hurry to my side and help me.

I answered, but my words were muffled through the bag.

"Thank God," she said. "Are you all right?"

"Not really," I mumbled. I do not think she heard me.

"I do not understand what happened." Her voice was thick. "I was leaving the theatre in Drury Lane. On a sudden, a large man was beside me, and he had hold of my arm. My servants were nowhere in sight. I believe I fainted, which is odd, because I never faint. Then I woke up here, bound hand and foot. I do not even know why."

I could not tell her, muffled as I was.

I found that if I used my chest and shoulders, aided by my right leg, I could move across the board floor about an inch at a time. The exercise was tiring and the bag stifled me, so I only progressed about half a foot at a time before having to rest.

She ceased talking, but I heard her hoarse breathing. Sick and dizzy from the beating, I could only make for her at a snail's crawl.

A few feet along, I came, surprisingly, to the edge of a carpet. I smelled dust and wool through the cloying bag. The raised lip of the carpet was about an inch high.

I began my arduous climb to the rug, then stopped, frustrated, when the carpet caught on the bag and pulled it tight against my head. I fumed for a few moments, until my buzzing brain made me realize that if the carpet could pull the bag one way, it could pull it another.

I leaned my cheek on the carpet and inched backward. The carpet held the bag in place, and my chin came hard against the cord. I continued to wriggle and work at the edge of the bag with my jaw, until all at once, the cord came loose and the bag rose halfway up my face.

Luckily, my assailant had not tied the cord, only pulled the drawstring tight. I wriggled some more. The bag caught on the corner of the carpet, and at last I was able to withdraw my head.

I lay for a moment, simply breathing. The air seemed as sweet as that of a spring morning. A spicy perfume laced the air, very different from the lemony scents Louisa Brandon wore.

I could see little. The room was nearly pitch black, but for the faint glimmer of starlight through a window high in the wall. I rolled myself into a sitting position on the carpet. "Where are you?"

"Here."

Her voice was weak. I managed to move my right leg under me, but I could not stand. "Talk to me. I will find you."

"Lacey." She sounded tired. "Why the devil am I here?"

"It has to do with me and my meddling. I am sorry."

She gave a faint laugh. "I ought to have known. Where am I, by the by?"

"The Glass House."

"Truly? I had thought it would be a bit more lurid."

"We are in the attics. The lurid rooms are downstairs."

"I see." I was happy to hear the acid in her tone. Any other woman, Mrs. Danbury, say, might have been in hysterics, too frightened for coherence or rational thought. Lady Breckenridge's tone was sardonic. She was frightened, but not defeated.

"The house is closed, out of business."

"I take it that somebody is displeased about that."

"Mrs. Chapman owned it," I said, my breath short as I struggled to crawl across the carpet. "But the man and woman who ran it are not happy with me, no. Kensington threatened me with revenge. He did not say he would drag you into it as well."

"Oh, dear."

"He will not have it. Once I get myself free, we will go."

"Will they kill us?" She asked in a matter-of-fact voice, a lady requesting information, just as she would turn to me at the theatre and ask if I thought there'd be an acrobatics act between plays. "Perhaps dispose of our bodies in the Thames, like Peaches?"

"Such optimism," I said. But I could not argue with her. I had no idea what Kensington planned.

At long last, I reached her. Lady Breckenridge lay on her side, facing away from me, her hands and feet bound. Her long hair, loose, spilled over the carpet.

The cords about my wrists had loosened a bit from all my crawling about. I knelt and continued working my hands and wrists. The twine cut my skin, but little by little, the bonds slackened.

My position, half-raised on my knees, my hands frantically working, was not stable by any means. My left leg gave way in a sudden wash of pain, and I fell over, unfortunately, on top of Lady Breckenridge. It was a fine, soft landing place, but I feared hurting her.

She gave a soft grunt, and her eyes gleamed in the darkness.

"Are you all right?" I asked.

"Not quite. You must weight twenty stone."

"Untrue. It only feels that way having it fall on you all in a heap."

She did not laugh. "I would be happier if I had use of my hands."

"So would I. I am almost free, I think."

I worked madly at the thin rope. My wrists were raw.

"I suppose after this, I cannot expect you to speak to me again." I kept my tone light.

"We shall see. If you manage to free us, I would be most grateful to you."

"For a time."

My bonds came loose. My hands, wooden, fell forward. I pushed myself away from Lady Breckenridge, landing heavily beside her. I lay like a drowning man who has just found shore, breathing hard, willing the circulation back into my hands.

"It would be rude of me to cut you after you saw me home safely." Her tone was light, but her voice was slightly hoarse, as though she'd wept. She was trying to put a brave face on it, the English upper-class bravado that remained calm in the face of danger. Panic was for lesser beings. I had known a lieutenant in Spain, who, when unhorsed and faced with four French cavalrymen, with nothing but a single-shot pistol with which to defend himself, had said to the lead horseman, "Move to the right a bit, there's a good fellow. I want to at least get one of you." He'd shot, and then they'd cut him down where he stood.

I wanted to hurry, to get her far from this place, but my body was tired. The pain in my head had not subsided, my leg still hurt, and I could barely feel my hands. But we had to leave quickly. I had believed Kensington when he said he was not a killer, but that did not mean he would not hire someone to kill for him.

I had realized, when speaking with Lady Jane, that Kensington had not murdered Peaches himself. He might have wanted to, but he had not. I had decided the truth after rowing up the Thames with Grenville, after I'd heard what Mr. Gower had observed while having his secret smoke, after learning that Peaches had had no money in her attic room and the fact that Lady Jane sometimes lent Peaches her private coachman.

Most of it had come to me as I'd lain in bed that morning, listening to the church bells and enjoying a clarity of

mind I'd not had in a while. I had told Sir Montague about
my last witness, and could only hope he would pursue it if
I did not survive.

But I wanted to survive. I was angry, and determined to
see this out. Nor did I want Lady Breckenridge to come to
harm because of my slow stupidity.

"I will try to untie your hands, now," I told her.

She merely nodded, her hair rustling on the carpet. An
investigation of my pockets showed me that Kensington's
man had relieved me of the small, sheathed knife I usually
carried. I groped for her hands, my own aching and
clumsy, and found the cords at her wrists.

For a long time I tugged and picked at the bonds. *Hurry,*
my mind urged. But my body was fumbling and slow. Beneath my touch, her fingers were like ice. "I could wish for
your butler just now," I said, trying to keep our light conversation going. "My leg hurts like fury."

"He would certainly be useful. I imagine he and my servants are searching for me by now. Not that they'd think to
look here." She closed her mouth over those depressing
words.

I worked for a while longer, striving for something to
say, something witty and funny that would put her at ease.
But Lady Breckenridge was an intelligent woman. She
knew that being trussed up in an attic of an empty house
would lead only to no good. Kensington was a fool to have
taken her; kidnapping a high-born lady could take him
straight to the gallows. But no doubt he'd been panicked,
wanting to hurt me and run at the same time. He'd far more
feared Lady Jane and Denis than the law.

What he intended to do to Lady Breckenridge and me,
I could not say. I only knew I did not want to be here when
he or his brute returned. Lady Breckenridge was no fool;
she was afraid. I could hear it in her breathing, in the glis-
ten of her eye as she turned her head to watch me.

"How was your leg hurt, Lacey?" she asked. She, too,
was groping for something innocuous to say. "Was it in the
army?"

I picked at the knots. "French soldiers amusing themselves." Led by a grinning, leering ensign, in fact, delighted to have captured a lone English soldier. He'd decided to take out his frustration over the recent French defeats by torturing me. I remembered his rather fanatical laughter, the worried look on his sergeant's face, the glee in the voices of the men who'd decided to follow their officer's example. I remembered gritting my teeth against the pain, not wanting to give them the satisfaction of hearing me scream. "They shattered the leg," I said. "Then, they hung me up by the ankles for safekeeping."

"Good God," she said in shock.

I said nothing, and the memories faded. The French soldiers had gotten their comeuppance when an English patrol had blundered by. The tiny ensuing battle had killed the French ensign. The English had not found me and had ridden away, leaving me with the dead. I had stolen the ensign's pistol and his water bag and crawled.

"You are making me feel rather sorry for you," Lady Breckenridge said.

"It could have been worse. The surgeon did not have to amputate." When I had heard this verdict, I had nearly wept with relief.

Her bonds at last gave way. Quickly I slipped her wrists from the ropes and began rubbing them, trying to restore the blood to them. Once she began to weakly move her fingers, I moved to untie her ankles.

A quarter of an hour passed before I at last got the bonds around her ankles loose. Then I had a devil of a time climbing to my own feet. I sought the wall behind me, leaned there, catching my breath.

Lady Breckenridge sat up, brushing the hair from her face. She wore only a thin silk gown, made for attending the opera. Whatever shawl or wrap she'd had, they must have taken it. I removed the coat of my regimentals; I had a devil of a time unfastening the cords with my clumsy hands. I draped the coat over her shoulders, and she gathered it to her gratefully.

"I will try to get the door open," I said, my voice dry as dust.

"That would certainly be to our advantage," she replied.

I had to use the wall to support me while I made my way to the door. Except for the starlight in the high window, I could see little.

I had not heard anyone in the house below during our sojourn. No one had mounted the stairs, rattled the door handle, shouted to us. That did not mean we were alone. I must have made plenty of noise when I'd wormed my way across the floor, and anyone in the rooms below could no doubt hear my fumbling tread now. I wondered whether the lad I'd paid had actually gone to fetch Pomeroy. In any case, he'd not come. I'd struggled with our bonds for the better part of an hour, and I did not know how long I'd lain unconscious.

I found the door when my groping hand bashed painfully into the doorframe. The door was locked. I bent to the keyhole, felt a faint draft on my face. That meant that that no key had been left on the other side. I remembered that I'd been able to force open the door of Peaches' room rather easily; I hoped that would be the case here.

They'd taken the walking stick, of course, the fine, strong cane that had helped me make short work of the kitchen door. My bad leg hurt too much for me to stand on it while I kicked with my right boot heel. The left leg was too weak to make much of an impression if I kicked with it instead. This door also seemed much more stout than the one to Peaches' room.

I felt for the hinges and found them, cold and metal. If I could remove them, I could easily pry the door loose. I would need a tool. I fumbled my way across the room, hoping to find something to aid me. My boot crunched glass, then I tripped over the remains of a mirror frame. I crouched to discover if anything in the debris would be of use.

I cut myself on the shards as I sifted through them. I grunted and cursed under my breath. Lady Breckenridge

asked if I was all right. I said no. While I picked through the glass, I explained to her what I planned to do. "I might need your help," I finished.

She was silent for a moment, then I heard her struggle to her feet.

I found, by cutting myself on it, a fairly large piece of mirror. It might help, but only if the glass was strong. Lady Breckenridge's outstretched hand touched me. I grasped her under the arm, before she could cut herself on the glass, and pulled her with me back to the door.

The mirror did not work. The door's hinges were old, but frozen with rust. I could not pry a gap large enough to lever out the hinge-pin on either hinge. The mirror slipped, cut my hand open. I swore without apology.

"They did not even leave me a handkerchief," I muttered, popping the pad of my hand into my mouth.

"They left mine." Lady Breckenridge slid a warm piece of silk from her bosom and pressed it into my hand. I promptly ruined the fine handkerchief sopping up blood.

I kicked the door, out of temper. It remained solidly closed.

"We could try to climb out of the window," Lady Breckenridge suggested. "If we can reach it."

The window in question sat high on the wall, a dormer that would look out over the street. "It is a long way down," I said. "We could not climb it without breaking our necks."

"We might at least shout out of it," Lady Breckenridge persisted. "Someone may hear us and help."

"We can try," I agreed. I thought her optimistic; if anyone had heard me break in through the back door, not to mention the men who'd brought Lady Breckenridge here and tied me up, no one had sent for help. Perhaps they'd put their heads under the bedclothes and gone back to sleep, having learned to ignore what went on at number 12, St. Charles Row.

The only way to reach the window was for me to lift her

to it. She proved light and agile, and climbed to my shoulders without much difficulty.

"I climbed many trees as a girl," she said. "To my governesses' despair. They might be happy to know it's proved to be useful."

Standing on my shoulders, she could just reach the window. Happily, the catch moved, but she was still not high enough to open it.

We decided to try what we'd seen acrobats do; she would stand on my hands while I lifted my arms above my head. She agreed shakily, and I promised to catch her if she fell, and hoped that I could. She leaned her weight on the wall and braced herself on the sill as I lifted her, and was at last able to open the window and look out.

"There is a man below," she said excitedly, and then she began shouting, her voice strong.

When she stopped, I heard the unmistakable, smooth tones of James Denis asking, "Is Lacey with you?"

"Yes," Lady Breckenridge called down.

Why he was there, what the devil had happened to Pomeroy, I could not imagine. Denis and Lady Breckenridge exchanged more words, which I could not hear, then Lady Breckenridge was admonishing me to let her down.

"He is coming," she said, her voice shaking, but with her sangfroid in place. "But there is a bit of a problem. Someone has set the house on fire."

CHAPTER 19

WE smelled the smoke soon after that. We stood against the wall under the window, waiting for rescue and trying not to think of the fire rising beneath us. It had started in the kitchen, Lady Breckenridge reported, and had reached the ground floor. Both of us knew how quickly fires could spread, consuming all within their reach in no time at all. We could hear more commotion in the street now, as the neighbors in St. Charles Row and the street behind poured out of their houses and rushed about to stop the blaze from spreading.

Lady Breckenridge huddled into my regimental coat, the cording hanging loose. We stood side by side, shoulders touching, taking comfort in each other's presence.

"Donata," I said in a low voice. I took a great liberty using her Christian name; a gentleman did not call a lady, especially not one of her class, by her name until invited. My father had always referred to my mother as "Mrs. Lacey," both before and after her death. "You are here because of me, and for that I can only beg your pardon. But

I vow to you that the men who did this, who dishonored you, will pay for that dishonor. I swear it to you."

She looked up at me, her hands resting on the lapels of my coat. "I've heard you were a man of great honor," she said, her voice light. "I would expect no less of you."

"You are an infuriating woman," I said, "but a fine lady. You do not deserve to be here."

She laughed at my bluntness, then she said, "You did not expect to find me here at all. You called out for some-one else."

Her eyes glittered in the darkness. I paused. "Louisa Brandon," I confessed. "She is a dear friend to me. Anyone who wishes to hurt me can do so by hurting her. I assumed Kensington would have known that."

"This Mr. Kensington made a foolish mistake, then," she observed, without rancor.

"He has made many mistakes. And I will not forgive him for putting you in danger."

"We are still in danger," she pointed out. We could smell the smoke intensely now, and the acrid, charring smell of burning wood and cloth.

"I know that. You do not deserve to be." I put my hand over hers. She twined her fingers through mine, and held on tight.

Not many moments later, the door splintered open. I stepped instinctively in front of Lady Breckenridge, trying to shield her from smoke and flying wood. Blinding light silhouetted a large man on the threshold, the coachman turned pugilist from Denis' house. Without preliminary, he grabbed us both and dragged us out behind him.

JAMES Denis served us brandy in his elegant coach, and told us how he'd come to find us.

"The boy you'd sent running off for the hackney was one of mine," he said. "He came at once to me and told me where you'd gone."

"One of yours?" My anger rose. "Keeping an eye on me, were you?"

"You have the habit of trifling with quite dangerous people, Lacey. But you will not see him again. In any case, I believe you are leaving London soon."

Lady Breckenridge, who had not heard this, looked surprised.

"To Berkshire," I said in a hard voice. "Which you no doubt already know."

"Indeed. The countryside is quite lovely there. It will no doubt be pleasant for you to leave the city for a time."

I did not answer.

What he'd said chilled me. Denis often made me angry, and once before he'd had his thugs beat me in order to teach me a lesson. But he'd made me realize that he was much too powerful for my anger to reach. He saw everything, knew everything, and did anything he wished. I'd toyed with the idea once that I could stop him. And so he'd begun to draw me into his net. He was right; I trifled with dangerous people and did not realize my own folly.

"What of Kensington?" I asked, my throat dry.

"Mr. Kensington has been delivered to your magistrate friend," he answered easily. "He was a fool; he ought to simply to have run. It will not be easy to get him free."

I raised my brow. "You intend to help him?"

Denis permitted himself a faint smile. "He is family. Even if he is not much of a family."

He finished talking after that, and gazed out of the window at the rainswept night.

We returned to Mayfair first and South Audley Street, where Lady Breckenridge was assisted from the carriage by a very worried Barnstable and two hovering, crying maids. They got her into the house in short order and slammed the elegant door. Then Denis, very courteously, took me home.

AT eleven o'clock the next morning, a hackney drew up in Middle Temple Lane. I, Sir Montague Harris, and Mr. Thompson of the Thames River patrol emerged from it. We traversed the lane, walking past the gray buildings,

barristers in robes, pupils hurrying after them carrying thick books or striding freely, alone.

We made our way from the Middle to the Inner Temple and looked up Sir William Pankhurst and his pupil, Mr. Gower.

Mr. Gower, as always, seemed happy to see me. He had smudges under his eyes and ink stains on his fingers, evidence that his new mentor liked him to work. I asked if he could stroll with us to the Temple Gardens. Because Sir William was out conferring with colleagues in King's Bench Walk, Gower smiled and agreed.

Our pace was slow, in deference to Sir Montague's labored stride and my still-aching knee. Bartholomew had arrived this morning quite upset that he'd missed my adventures, and he'd made up for it by fixing me a scalding bath, massaging my leg, bringing me beefsteak and ale for breakfast, and generally fussing over me until I ordered him to stop.

Sir Montague and Thompson had come for me soon after I'd eaten and dressed, and Thompson had informed me of his results in querying Lady Jane's coachman.

The Thames was as gray and faceless today as it had been one week ago, when I'd first seen Peaches. Clouds were rolling in, blotting out the blue sky of Sunday, closing the city in a gray haze once more. We stopped at the top of the Temple Stairs, watching the river roll by below us.

"You saw him emerge here?" I asked Gower.

"Eh?" The lad jerked his gaze from the river, his ingenuous blue eyes fixing on me. "Oh, the bloke last Monday. Yes. Popped up pretty much here. It was getting dark, of course, so I couldn't tell you what he looked like."

"It probably doesn't matter."

I looked across the Thames again, watching the mist slowly consume the buildings on the other side. "A coachman this morning told Mr. Thompson that he brought Mrs. Chapman to Middle Temple last Monday afternoon, just as dark was gathering. Let her off in Middle Temple Lane.

Which was mostly deserted, I imagine, with everyone at dinner."

Gower nodded. "Would have been, yes."

"It was an excellent hour," I said slowly, "in which to meet her."

The lanky youth simply looked at me.

"That's the truth," Thompson agreed. "It was just dark. Everyone would be eating or diligently finishing his work. Or smoking cheroots," he added, with a grin at Gower.

"I found it interesting," I said. "That you never mentioned you were anywhere near the Temple Stairs last Monday evening until I suggested that someone had climbed them into the Gardens. Then suddenly, you remembered seeing a chap."

Gower blinked. "You made me call it to mind."

"You also mentioned that you'd come to Middle Temple to apprentice, because, you said, someone in the family needed to make money. Yet, Mr. Grenville identified your suit as being made by a fine tailor in Bond Street. He was much impressed. Very few men can afford a suit that would impress Lucius Grenville."

He shrugged. "I had a windfall. Had a flutter and made a packet. Spent it all on fine living."

I watched him a moment. So did Thompson. Sir Montague kept staring at the water.

"You would make a fine barrister, Mr. Gower," I observed. "You have a smooth answer for every question. What if I ask you one point blank—did you meet Mrs. Chapman here last Monday afternoon? And ask her for money?"

He met my eyes easily, his blue gaze warm and friendly. "Why do you ask, Captain Lacey?"

"Because I believe you did. And I believe that you killed her."

He at last lost his smile. The freckles stood out on his face in dark patches. "Why should you?"

"Because Mrs. Chapman kept her share of the profits from the Glass House in her attic room. Yet, when a man

broke in and stole her money box after her death, he found it disappointingly empty. He assumed that she'd spent it all. But I do not think so. While I found a few trinkets and fripperies in her rooms, there were no jewels or anything very expensive—nothing a middle-class woman living on a barrister's income could not buy. She wore no jewelry when she died, just a keepsake ring given to her by her lover. But the Glass House was one of the most popular houses in town; the wealthy upper classes went there. She must have made a substantial sum from it. So I wondered, where had all that money gone?"

"Perhaps this bloke that broke into her room stole it," Gower said. "Killed her, too."

I touched the collar of his fine coat. "I think, instead, that much of it went to a Bond Street tailor."

"What did you blackmail her for?" Thompson asked easily.

Gower looked back and forth between us. "You have no evidence that I did."

"Life with Chapman was dull, you told us," I continued. "I imagine the tedium in his rooms made you look for ways in which to entertain yourself. I am not certain how you discovered Mrs. Chapman's secrets, but you did. Did you threaten to tell her husband that she had a lover, or about the Glass House? Either would suffice. Chapman could have her arrested for adultery, or if he did not want that humiliation, he could at least restrict her movements, make certain she never saw Lord Barbury again. He also could have demanded the money she made from the Glass House, kept it from her. In short, make her life with him even more miserable than it already was."

"What was between Chapman and his wife has nothing to do with me," Gower said evenly.

"Perhaps not at first. I am not sure how you found out about Mrs. Chapman's life. From your Oxford friends who might have known Lord Barbury? From research into such dull subjects as trusts for Chapman? Or, was it another rea-

son? She was a pretty young woman. Perhaps you fancied her, and she snubbed you."

"She had a lover, didn't she?" Gower said, belligerent. "A lofty lord. Yes, she was pretty. So I followed her about. Then I saw her with him one night, her dressed like a high-flyer, his arm around her waist. Wasn't that interesting, I thought?"

"So you blackmailed her."

"Not right away. I followed her for nigh on a sixmonth, until I knew every single one of Mrs. Chapman's dirty little secrets."

"Blackmailers always come to bad ends, you know," Thompson remarked.

"Why did you kill her?" I asked, holding my temper with effort, "if she was keeping you in fine suits?"

Gower looked stricken. "I didn't. She only gave me money once. It's not like I bled her dry."

"She came here to see you last Monday evening, just after dark," I said. "You met her in the Gardens—here—and she gave you the money. Perhaps you quarreled, perhaps she threatened to tell Lord Barbury, perhaps she told you she'd already informed him. Perhaps you panicked, and killed her to keep her quiet."

Gower shook his head. "You're wrong. I never killed her. She was angry with me, right enough. She told me it was for the last time."

"What did you do then? Did you strike her? Or perhaps you asked her for more than money, and killed her when she refused you?"

"She slapped me." His eyes sparkled in outrage. "Acted like she was better than me, her an actress and a tart. So I slapped her back. Then she flew at me, ready to claw my eyes out. It was raining hard. She slipped and fell and came crashing down on the steps. She gasped once, and then she just lay there."

He stared down at the steps, looked bewildered, as though he still watched her lying there.

"Why the devil didn't you run for help?" I demanded.

"She was dead already. Besides, if I'd gone for help, I'd have had to explain what I was doing out on the Temple Stairs with Chapman's wife. I didn't want Chapman to sack me, dull as he is. I must become a barrister; I told you, my family needs the money. But no one had seen. So I rolled her off into the Thames. The rain took care of the blood. Simple as that."

I walked down a few stairs, then turned and looked up at him. The dome of St. Paul's Cathedral, ghostly in the rain and mists, rose above the high houses of the Temples behind him.

"She died here," I said. "While you stood and watched. Then you took the money, and bought yourself a new suit."

"What would you have done?" Gower said defiantly. "I did not kill her, Captain. It was an accident."

I moved back toward him, anger suffusing my every move. "You did kill her. You brought her here because of your greed and your meanness. She would not have been here to die, if not for you."

"She was the one cuckolding her husband and running a bawdy house," he snapped.

I took step toward him. Gower backed away in some alarm. Thompson moved between us. "Now, Captain," he said, eyes quiet. "Let us not have another body in the Thames."

The jovial admonition made Gower look still more worried, but I subsided. "Accident or no, you are responsible."

Sir Montague at last turned from watching the river, as though he'd done no more in the last twenty minutes than enjoy the view. "On the other hand, Lord Barbury's death was no accident," he said in his cheerful tones. "Unless you accidentally put a gun to his head and shot him?"

Gower went dead white.

"I am a magistrate, Mr. Gower," Sir Montague went on. "Why don't you tell me what happened?"

Gower looked at him for a long while, then at Thompson, who stood quietly beside him, then at me. He drew himself up. "You must have proof to arrest me. Or a wit-

ness. You cannot prosecute on Captain Lacey's specula-
tions. You must have evidence. I know the law."

Sir Montague chuckled. "That you do. But so do I, Mr.
Gower. And I have a witness."

Gower stared. I did as well. I had not heard of this.

"There is a Bow Street Runner called Mr. Pomeroy. A
friend of the Captain's here. He much enjoys his duties. He
pounded Charles Street up and down for two days, questioning everyone he could get his hands on. And he found
a witness, a footman, who was awake very late on Friday.
A footman who looked out the window in time to see you
walk past Lord Barbury, then suddenly turn around and
shoot him in the head. You dragged him to his own front
doorstep, then ran off fast as you could. You put the pistol
in his hand to make it seem as though he'd shot himself."

"I do not believe you," Gower said, though his bravado
was flagging. "If he had seen someone shoot Lord Barbury, he would have run at once for the watch."

"But this particular footman, though he'd been a
respectable servant for fifteen years, once had been transported for the crime of theft. A transported man returning
to England usually means his death. He'd come back to
take care of his family, reformed his ways, and took honest employment. Didn't much want the magistrates to
recognize him, so he kept quiet, until our diligent Mr.
Pomeroy got the story out of him. I've promised to help
him, if he stands up as a witness."

"A convicted thief?" Gower asked incredulously. "Who
escaped his punishment? What sort of a witness is that?"

"Oh, I agree that the jury might take his character
against him when they listen to his evidence. But he saw
you. And it is on that evidence that I am arresting you, Mr.
Gower, for the murder of Lord Barbury. A peer of the
realm, no less." He clucked his tongue. "What the devil
were you thinking?"

Predictably, Gower tried to run. Mr. Thompson caught
him at once. Thompson might be thin, but he was wiry and
strong. Sir Montague praised his effort, then they walked

Mr. Gower back between them to the hackney, and took him to Bow Street.

MR. Gower had likely believed Peaches had told Lord Barbury that Gower had tried to blackmail her. That is what Grenville and I speculated that afternoon in a tavern in Pall Mall, over ale and beef. If Gower's schemes had come out, especially in light of her death, he would have lost his position as Chapman's pupil, and no other barrister would have taken him on. He'd have lost his chance to become the great orator he'd wanted to be. He'd never become a barrister, a silk, a high court judge.

Gower confirmed this at his trial the next week, at the Old Bailey, him on the wrong side of the dock. He was convicted of the murder of Lord Barbury, and sentenced to hang.

I left the courtroom, my melancholia stirring. Gower had tried to brave it out until the last, but he had been no match for the prosecutor, a prominent man from Lincoln's Inn. Lord Barbury's family had paid for the best. Gower's family, likewise, was there, respectable, middle-class people, stunned at this aberration in their lives.

Such a needless one. If Gower had not panicked and shot Lord Barbury, he would have been convicted of nothing. Peaches had died by accident, and there was nothing to prove a case of blackmail.

In this mood, I returned home to Grimpen Lane to finish my packing. I would leave on the morrow for Berkshire.

I met Bartholomew coming down the stairs. "Just nipping to the Gull, sir," he said, naming the tavern from which he usually fetched supper. "Was he convicted?"

I nodded, told him what happened. Bartholomew looked interested, but also in a hurry. He barely waited for me to finish before he hastened past me and into the darkened street.

I made my way upstairs, my feelings mixed. I had found my villain, and he would hang. Peaches was

avenged. But I also still blamed Peaches' husband and her lover for her death. Each of them could have paid more attention, could have cherished her and protected her, kept her safe. Instead, they'd simply gone on with their lives, assuming that she would be there when they wanted her, just as, God help me, I had done with my own wife. They did not understand—they could not know what a hole it left when you turned around, and the one you'd thought would always be there was gone.

With these dismal thoughts in my head, I opened the door to my rooms. I heard the rustle of silk, smelled faintly lemony perfume, and suddenly, my melancholia eased.

Louisa crossed the room to me, stretched out her hands. I took them, and she squeezed mine, smiling at me like Louisa of old. We stood thus for a few minutes, looking at one another, hands clasped, tight, until I leaned down, gave her a dutiful kiss on the cheek, and released her.

"Gabriel," she said. "You look dreadful."

"It's pouring rain and all-over mud and I've been to a dreary trial," I answered. "Was it you who sent Bartholomew racing away for dinner?"

"I told him to hurry, so it might be hot for you when you returned."

"I would be pleased to share it with you. Although it will be barely edible."

Our words were light, unimportant, but I felt the strain of them. I wanted to seize her hands again, ask her why she'd come, ask her what she really wanted to say. I remained across the carpet from her, my hands at my sides, my restraint remarkable.

"I will not stay," she said. "I am dining with Lady Aline this evening." Her eyes went quiet. "You are leaving to-morrow."

"Yes."

She had known that. I'd written her and Brandon this week, telling them when I was to leave and how to write me at Sudbury. I knew neither would, but I'd gone through the motions anyway.

"I am quite angry with you," she continued.

She looked angry. Her eyes sparkled, and her color was high.

"I know. You have told me."

"This is for an entirely new reason. I spoke to Mr. Grenville yesterday evening. He seemed quite astonished that I had not heard of your adventures of last Sunday week. And I was astonished also. Why the devil did you not tell me?"

I had wanted to. I had wanted to rush to her after Sir Montague had arrested Gower and lay the entire tale at her feet. I had always told her of my triumphs, and my sorrows, and she had always praised or comforted me. This time, I'd made myself stay home.

"There was little to tell. I survived, as you can see."

"Do not be flippant, Gabriel." Her tone softened. "I could have lost you, my friend. And the last thing we had done was quarrel."

"I did not hold that against you."

"Stop." She held up her hands. "Stop being noble. You are dear to me, you know that. Why do you insist on making me so angry?"

I let myself relax, let my heartbeat return to normal. "That is what dear friends do, Louisa. Quarrel and forgive over very stupid things. If we were strangers, we would not care."

"You have turned philosopher," she said, giving me a deprecating look. "I will put things simply. If, while you are in Berkshire, you find you need help, you will ask me. Your pride aside."

"Of course," I said. Relief was singing through me. She was still angry at me, but she had realized she did not want me out of her life entirely.

"And if you escape from death by a hair's breadth again, you will at least have the courtesy to tell me."

"You will be the first to hear the tale."

She gave me a severe look, then she shook her head, saddened. "We have been friends too long for this, Gabriel.

Please know that I still think you are too stubborn for words, and I will not stand tamely by while you needle my husband, but I am not ready to lose you, yet."

"And I will never be ready to lose you."

We studied each other, her gray eyes clear in the candlelight.

"Do not think I have forgiven you," she said. "I still believe you are in the wrong."

"I know."

I would capitulate to Brandon if she wanted me to, as bitter as the words would taste. I could at least cease hurting her.

We returned to watching each other in silence. We did not always have to speak; we had said plenty over the years. She could cut me with a single word. I doubted I had such power over her.

I heard Bartholomew bang back inside downstairs, and then the odor of overcooked beef and the clink of pewter plates on a tray wafted up the stairwell. He entered the room without looking at either of us, deposited a tray on the writing table, and bustled around for the cutlery.

I smiled at Louisa, and she smiled at me.

"I might forgive you not telling me of your adventures," Louisa said, in her usual, bantering tone, "if you sit down and tell me everything, right through from beginning to end. Leaving out no detail, however small."

I accepted her terms. I seated her in the wing chair, sat down to my afternoon repast, and began my tale.

THE next afternoon, I departed London. Grenville had offered his chaise and four to take me to Berkshire, and I had accepted. Much as I disliked taking his favors, I could not argue that his private conveyance would be much more comfortable than the mail coach crammed with passengers. Grenville declined to accompany me himself, and I knew why. Lucius Grenville, the world traveler, easily succumbed to motion sickness and ever did his best to avoid it.

Bartholomew was going with me to Sudbury in his capacity as my personal servant. He eagerly anticipated the sojourn, looking forward to more adventure. I privately hoped I would find none.

Before we left London proper, I had one more call to make. I bade Bartholomew wait for me in the chaise in South Audley Street, while I approached and knocked on Lady Breckenridge's door.

To my good luck, Lady Breckenridge was at home. Barnstable led me upstairs to her private chambers, and announced me, after inquiring about the state of my leg. I assured him his cure had done me well.

I had not seen or spoken to Lady Breckenridge since our adventure, although she had responded to my written inquiry as to whether she were well, stating that she was resilient and in good health. She even thanked me for giving her an evening free of ennui.

Today she reclined on a chaise longue in a lacy peignoir, her dark hair covered with a white cap. She held a slim, black cigarillo in her fingers, and acrid, woody-smelling smoke hung in the room.

"You have come to say good-bye?" she asked me, without rising. "You are always the gentleman, Lacey."

"I try to be."

"Berkshire," she said. She took a long pull on the cigarillo. "The country is hopelessly dull, you know."

"I am looking forward to it," I said.

We regarded each other in silence a moment. Our silences were not like the silences between me and Louisa Brandon; I did not know Lady Breckenridge well enough to discern what she was thinking.

At last I said, "I came to tell you that any letter addressed to me at the Sudbury School, near Hungerford, will reach me."

"Ah." She set the cigarillo carefully aside on her dressing table. "You wish me to include you in my correspondence."

"I would honor any correspondence from you."

Her brows arched. "A lady writing to a gentleman. How scandalous."

"I believe you enjoy scandal."

She looked at me a long time, a glint of humor in her eyes. "Yes. I believe I do."

I gave her a military bow. "I will say good-bye, then. Thank you."

I was uncertain what I thanked her for—perhaps for simply existing.

"A moment." She rose gracefully and glided across the room to the armoire. "I meant to send this on to you. But I may as well give it to you now." She withdrew a long bundle from the armoire, unwrapped it. She brought it to me, put it into my hands.

It was a walking stick. It had a polished mahogany cane, which was burnished a rich red-brown, and a gold handle in the shape of a goose's head.

She closed her hand over mine, gently slid the handle outward. "It has a sword, like your old one. And the handle is engraved." She turned it over in my palm, indicating the inscription, "Captain G. Lacey, 1817."

I slid the blade back into the sheath. "It is a thing of beauty. Thank you."

"Grenville had said he would buy one for you. But I told him I was already having one made and not to spoil my surprise."

I smiled. "It is a fine gift."

She looked pleased, then strove to hide it.

Friendship, I had learned, was a gift not to be scorned.

I leaned down and kissed her lips, then departed for Berkshire.

ABOUT THE AUTHOR

Ashley Gardner has lived and traveled all over the world and is currently settled in the southwestern United States. Learn more about the Regency mystery series through its Web site, www.gardnermysteries.com, or contact Ashley Gardner directly at ashleygardner@gardnermysteries.com.

Meet Captain Gabriel Lacey in

The
Hanover Square
Affair

by

Ashley Gardner

IN WAR OR AT PEACE,
CAPTAIN LACEY KNOWS HIS DUTY.

His military career may have ended with an
injustice, but former cavalry officer Gabriel Lacey
refuses to allow others to share his fate.
The disappearance of a beautiful young woman
sets Lacey on the trail of an enigmatic
crime lord—and into a murder investigation.

0-425-19330-6

Also in the Regency England Mystery series:
A Regimental Murder
0-425-19612-7

Available wherever books are sold or at
www.penguin.com

B927

THE BERKLEY PUBLISHING GROUP
Published by the Penguin Group
Penguin Group (USA) Inc.
375 Hudson Street, New York, New York 10014, USA
Penguin Group (Canada), 10 Alcorn Avenue, Toronto, Ontario M4V 3B2, Canada
(a division of Pearson Penguin Canada Inc.)
Penguin Books Ltd., 80 Strand, London WC2R 0RL, England
Penguin Group Ireland, 25 St. Stephen's Green, Dublin 2, Ireland (a division of Penguin Books Ltd.)
Penguin Group (Australia), 250 Camberwell Road, Camberwell, Victoria 3124, Australia
(a division of Pearson Australia Group Pty. Ltd.)
Penguin Books India Pvt. Ltd., 11 Community Centre, Panchsheel Park, New Delhi—110 017, India
Penguin Group (NZ), Cnr. Airborne and Rosedale Roads, Albany, Auckland 1310, New Zealand
(a division of Pearson New Zealand Ltd.)
Penguin Books (South Africa) (Pty.) Ltd., 24 Sturdee Avenue, Rosebank, Johannesburg 2196,
South Africa

Penguin Books Ltd., Registered Offices: 80 Strand, London WC2R 0RL, England

This is a work of fiction. Names, characters, places, and incidents either are the product of the
author's imagination or are used fictitiously, and any resemblance to actual persons, living or dead,
business establishments, events, or locales is entirely coincidental.

THE GLASS HOUSE

A Berkley Prime Crime Book / published by arrangement with the author

PRINTING HISTORY
Berkley Prime Crime mass-market edition / December 2004

Copyright © 2004 by Jennifer Ashley.

ISBN: 0-425-19943-6

Berkley Prime Crime Books are published by The Berkley Publishing Group,
a division of Penguin Group (USA) Inc.,
375 Hudson Street, New York, New York 10014.
BERKLEY PRIME CRIME is a registered trademark of Penguin Group (USA) Inc.
The Berkley Prime Crime design is a trademark belonging to Penguin Group (USA) Inc.

PRINTED IN THE UNITED STATES OF AMERICA

10   9   8   7   6   5   4   3   2   1

THE
Glass
House

ASHLEY GARDNER

BERKLEY PRIME CRIME, NEW YORK

Out from the Thames . . .

I stepped past the waterman who smelled of mud and un-washed clothes into the circle of light. They had laid the woman out on a strip of canvas. Her gown, a light pink muslin, was pasted to her limbs, the sodden cloth outlining her thighs and curve of waist, her round breasts. Her face was gray, bloated with water. A wet fall of golden hair, coated with mud, covered the stones beside her . . .

I went down on one knee, supporting my weight on my walking stick. "She had no reticule, or other bag?"

"Not a thing, Captain," Thompson replied . . .

I lifted the hem of her skirt and examined the fabric.

"Fine work. This is a lady's dress . . ."

More praise for *The Hanover Square Affair*

D0724822